A Rochfield Mystery

A DEADLY ACCOUNT

by

RIC THOMPSON

A DEADLY ACCOUNT
by
RIC THOMPSON
A Rochfield Mystery

The fourth in a series of murder mysteries featuring Detective Chief Inspector Andrew Sutherland, Dean Simpson and the team at Rochfield CID.

All people and events in these books are fictional and bear no relation to real people, living or dead.

These books are dedicated to my wife Elizabeth, for her encouragement. To Adam who was the inspiration for Sutherland, and to my son John for the cover design. To DC for her ongoing support and encouragement. To Dr CM for her medical/technical help.

The right of Ric Thompson to be identified as the author of these works has been asserted in accordance with the Copyright Designs and Patents Act 1988.

All rights reserved. Without limiting the rights under copyright reserved above, no part of this manuscript may be reproduced, stored in or introduced into a retrieval system, or transmitted, in any form or by any means (electronic, mechanical, photocopying, recording or otherwise), without the prior written permission of the copyright owner of this manuscript, other than by way of legitimate purchase.

Each book, while part of a series stands alone, though I hope you will enjoy all of them.
Other titles in the Rochfield Mystery series, available on Amazon Kindle® and in paperback.

Episode 1: Killing the Witch
Episode 2: Spin a Web of Death
Episode 3: Stone Dead
Episode 4: A Deadly Account
Episode 5: Dead Man Walking
Episode 6: Final Tally
Episode 7: Acted to Death
Episode 8: Death in a High Place
Episode 9: Millennium Bug
Episode 10: Final Refuge
Episode 11: Hydinge Seek
Episode 12: Death in a Low Place
Episode 13: Unfinished Business

DCS Sutherland Mysteries
An Analytical Death

Political Thrillers by the same author:
Target North
Target Portugal

Email: ric.thompson@tms-email.co.uk.
Also on Facebook, and Twitter.
www.facebook.com/rochfieldmysteries
www.twitter.com/ricsfiction

Copyright © 2019 Ric Thompson
All rights reserved.

Chapter 1

The Mutual Capital Life Assurance Company of Rochfield building was as Victorian as its name suggested. A magnificent four storey neo-Georgian building built from local carboniferous sandstone, its only concession to modernity being the double glazing on all the windows that still failed to prevent the building from being sufficiently warm in winter, or cool in summer.

The ground floor had long since been re-developed as retail outlets, two of which had been unoccupied for over a year. The next two floors of the property were let out to a variety of small businesses that required limited office space. The property wasn't close enough to the catchment area of the town's main shopping centre and its adjacent multi-storey carpark. On-street parking in the one way system was prohibited by the double yellow lines on their side.

Risking a dash across that busy thoroughfare where the nearest pedestrian crossings were the best part of a hundred yards to either side was seldom undertaken.

On street parking on the same side was a two minute walk away. Altogether the site was not a profitable location.

The top floor was occupied by The Mutual Capital Life Assurance Company of Rochfield and had offices with commanding views over the town.

When it had been built in the third quarter of the nineteenth century everything had been very different. Large sums of money were being invested in the business of The Mutual Cap as it was colloquially known. The company provided a range of pensions, life cover, and investments for the local population, and through the careful investment of that money in Railway Stocks, mining companies and in prospering local industry, the people of Rochfield, the rich and the less well off, were more than pleased to entrust their spare income to the business, or to set aside money for their eventual retirement or for their dependants.

For most of the first eighty-five years of its existence the head office of The Mutual Cap had been full of employees. There had been several branch offices throughout the north of England. Employees ranged in status from the directors and the trustees of the company down through the actuaries, the sales people, insurance advisers as they were known, the sales support staff, to the collectors who walked their districts collecting the weekly or monthly contributions.

In the mid-fifties the company had been absorbed by a much bigger rival. It had maintained its name, but now the head office was merely a branch office of the parent company.

A DEADLY ACCOUNT

Now, in the words of Bob Dillon, the times they were a changing. Indeed they had already changed.

With the reduction in the level of industry and in the general level of employment that had yet to be turned round with new business investment, the fortunes of The Mutual Cap were precarious.

Their sales force numbered six including the sales manager, Richard Tillsworth. The actuarial business was centralised at the parent company headquarters. The sales support staff for The Mutual Cap consisted of two girls fresh out of college, who would probably stay until something better came along, and a spinster lady, Miss Hackett, who had been with The Mutual Cap for all of her forty years of working life and from before it had been absorbed.

She did all of the book keeping and office management, and regarded the rest of the employees as her children.

Like all of the employees, Miss Hackett had money tied up in the fortunes of The Mutual Cap.

Nobody could remember a working day when Miss Hackett had been absent before. The only holidays that she had taken since her mother had died twenty years earlier were Bank Holidays when the offices of The Mutual Cap were closed for business, and before that, a week by the seaside at Bridlington with her mother had been her only time off. Never a day's ill health.

She had phoned Mr Tillsworth on the Sunday evening with the news that she was unwell, and that her doctor was arranging for her to go into the private clinic paid for by her company private health insurance scheme for a week of tests and bed rest, followed by a further week of convalescence.

She had advised Mr Tillsworth how sorry she was for the inconvenience and that he should perhaps secure the services of a temporary book keeper from an agency. She even recommended one that he might speak to.

To Richard Tillsworth it sounded as though Miss Hackett might be more than unwell to be taking that much time off, and to be suggesting that he employ anybody temporary to take charge of her books.

He thanked her for phoning, hung up and phoned his boss, Jeremy Harmsbury.

Rachael Tillsworth, his wife, looked up from the television as he re-entered the living room.

"Who was that, dear?" she asked.

"Miss Hackett," Richard said before going on to explain the seriousness of the phone call.

"It must be serious if she's suggesting that, Richard!" His wife knew all about Miss Hackett. Rachael Tillsworth had worked for The Mutual Cap for some years as a sales agent before they were married. It was a couple of years before his promotion to Sales Manager. He had been her up-line manager and as such had got a percentage of her sales commission, as he did from the other three agents in his team.

He had been responsible for recruiting, training and supplying their early leads. If they brought somebody on, they got a portion of that person's

A DEADLY ACCOUNT

commission and picked up all the clients from those who subsequently left, as many did.

Insurance selling was a bit of a revolving door for sales people. The natural sales people kept bringing in the business and the new sales people, and gradually rose up the ranks and their earnings rose accordingly. Technically, only the Directors, office staff and managers were employed by the company. Everybody else was self employed, relying solely upon commission.

It was a cut-throat, dog eat dog existence and the market was saturated with similar companies, some small, some very large in the same business.

Richard Tillsworth was one of the business survivors. He could charm the birds out of the tree; well, certainly he could charm sales out of the most reluctant of prospects.

As well as being Sales Manager he kept bringing in new business and new recruits.

Every sales person and recruit wanted to be like him. If he could do it, they felt, why shouldn't they? And that was the belief that he gave them.

Every Monday morning he would have them all in the conference room for the weekly sales meeting or for a bit more training. The more training he could give them, sometimes on new products, sometimes of a new sales technique that he had mastered, the more they would go out fired with enthusiasm and sell more policies or better, more profitable ones and he would earn more, lots more.

The Monday morning meetings tended to separate the sheep from the goats. Each sales agent would give their figures for the previous week. Calls, appointments, presentations and – most important – sales. CAPS it was known as. It was the yardstick by which performance was measured.

There would be applause for success, commiseration for the ones that got away, and pep talks for those who were seen to be underperforming. Some mornings there were empty chairs. Some mornings there were new faces. That was the nature of the business.

Rachael Tillsworth had joined The Mutual Cap after six years working in the local Social Services office in Rochfield. She got on well with people, and was attractive to men while not seeming to be a threat to their wives or girlfriends. She had a wide circle of friends, relatives and former work colleagues and was an ideal recruit to the insurance business.

Richard had recruited her one evening after they met at the Rochfield Golf and Country Club. He had been celebrating with fellow agents and a couple of the Directors of The Mutual Cap after he had won the coveted Agent of the Year Award for the second year running.

Rachael had been celebrating with friends from the Rochfield Hockey First XI after winning the County Cup. She was the team captain and the centre of attention. Richard had been aware of her presence at the next table from the start of the evening.

He knew a good prospect when he saw one. From where he sat he was able to watch her for most of the evening every time he happened to look up from the table, or from talking with his fellow agents. Two things Richard had learnt from the beginning in the sales agency business: first, always drink less than anybody else at the table, keep a clear head at all times; and second, if you wanted to succeed you never stopped working. The second piece of information he always passed on to new recruits. The first he kept to himself.

When his party started to go the way of most Mutual Cap social events he quietly moved from his table round to hers. A number of her co-hockey players had already left, one or two with partners sat on, drinking and chatting, but Rachael seemed to be alone. As the captain she saw her role as that of last man standing, the dutiful host who stayed until everybody had left.

He had introduced himself, explained that he wasn't much of a drinker and that his colleagues wouldn't miss him.

They talked. He told her about himself, what he did for a living, didn't boast or try to impress her, and listened intently while she talked about herself and her work, the Hockey Club, other sports that she played, and a little about her home life. She lived with her parents.

He had his own house.

"Oh, lucky you. Where abouts?" Rachael asked.

"Parkmount," he answered. Parkmount was one of the new housing developments that had sprung up on the outskirts north of Rochfield in the early eighties, and had been very desirable at the time.

"Gosh! You must be doing alright!" Rachael said.

"You could too, you know," he had replied, and that was how it started.

He had recruited her, trained her, mentored her and finally married her. Now, nearly ten years later, they had two children, but now lived in Meadowland, in a bigger house, one of the first to be completed, and were struggling. Rachael had given up working at The Cap after Lucy, their first child was born. Now, with both children in primary school full time, she had a part time job back in Social Services. It suited their lifestyle and the additional income was useful.

Business was no longer booming. The gravy train had hit the buffers for The Mutual Cap.

Richard Tillsworth should have taken his talent elsewhere some years before when he had the opportunity, but he had always hankered after a directorship. It had been promised to him on one occasion when he had talked about moving, but, as yet, nothing had come of it.

The person standing in Richard Tillsworth's way was the man who had brought him into the business. Managing Director Jeremy Harmsbury had worked his way up The Mutual Cap from the bottom. He had been recruited in 1957 after finishing his National Service, which had included involvement in the Suez Crisis the previous year.

He had hoped to escape National Service but was only able to defer call up for a year while he sat his A-Levels, hoping to get sufficient passes to be admitted to university. He wasn't successful in that. Not wanting to be just another squaddie, he put his name down for The Parachute Regiment, and having successfully passed through basic training and parachute training he was posted to Cypress and from there to The Canal Zone.

It was thanks to his brief time in the army that he was able to talk the language of many of the military and ex-military personnel that he came across in his work as a sales agent, and they were able to provide him with an endless stream of referrals, the backbone of any good agent's prospecting.

He had finally reached the top of the greasy pole. The coveted directorship that gave him a salary as well as bonuses and his commission earnings. Most of the good fortune that had secured his place at the boardroom table of the parent company had been through the efforts of people like Richard Tillsworth. The top flight sales agents who had made their way up to the level of branch manager and were looking to rise higher.

It was only when a high-flier like Tillsworth threatened to leave that the carrot of a directorship was held out. Perhaps, if Tillsworth had moved to work at the company headquarters, or for one of their own branches, this might have been a realistic expectation.

Some realised that the carrot was at the end of a very long pole, and that, no matter how hard they ran they could not reach it. They left for fresh pastures. Tillsworth had stayed, and now, like Harmsbury was trapped in a sinking ship. The difference being that Harmsbury knew at first hand how bad things were.

The parent company was in secret negotiations with a bigger, national life assurance group to divest itself of The Mutual Cap and the success of those negotiations depended on two things. The state of The Mutual Cap's books, and the quality of their personnel to carry the business forward under new management.

When Harmsbury learned that Miss Hackett had been taken ill and that temporary cover would be required, he was concerned who they might get as her replacement, and what exactly their role might be and what, if they dug deep enough they might uncover. Harmsbury was under no illusion about Miss Hackett's abilities. She was a very conscientious book keeper, but her duties tended to be minimalist, confined to processing the staff payrolls and the payments of commissions and any purchase ledger items like stationery and printing, payments to the photographers who provided all of the classy photographs for the company brochures and the graphic designers who put the brochures together using script supplied by Harmsbury and his fellow directors on the parent company board.

The parent company's auditors did all the rest of the work to produce the end of year accounts, which were several months away.

Chapter 2

Tommy Adams looked at his watch. Friday afternoon, half past four, time to be heading home. Home to an empty house and another weekend alone. Being an agency book-keeper, working a couple of weeks here, or a month or two there, sometimes longer if the person he was filling in for was on maternity leave, meant never staying in one place long enough to form meaningful friendships.

His wife had left him the previous summer for her ballroom-dancing teacher.

Their divorce had gone through two months ago but Tommy hadn't felt ready to play the dating game yet. He would be forty next birthday, and it didn't matter how many times he heard people say that forty was the new thirty, to him forty was forty. The onset of middle age, if he expected to live to eighty, and why shouldn't he? He hadn't smoked for over fifteen years. He seldom drank much. He even exercised – occasionally. Maybe that was something he could take up again.

He put his few personal possessions into his briefcase. That was another job finished, and as yet the agency hadn't given him an assignment for the coming week. Occasionally there wouldn't be jobs available and he would be forced to take some unpaid leave. It suited him. There were always jobs to be done in the garden or to the house.

He said his farewells to the office manager and the nice lady in personnel and crossed the road to where his car was parked. The drive back to Rochfield would take the best part of an hour at this time on a Friday. He didn't mind the drive. Classic FM, would keep him company.

When he arrived home he picked up the mail from the doormat, mostly circulars and junk mail or communications from the taxman. It would be nice, he reflected, just once in a while to get a post card from somewhere, or a letter from a past friend. Since most of *his* friends had been swept aside after he and Margaret had started going together, to be replaced with *her* friends, friends that never became *their* friends, and these had left along with Margaret, he had lost touch with any friends from his youth.

Another good reason to take up exercise again. He'd start by joining a gym. He'd get fit and then he'd see if there were any Saturday or Sunday league amateur teams that would accept a thirty nine year old who hadn't played any sort of sport since his mid-twenties.

Buoyed by that decision, he opened the fridge to see what he would have for his evening meal.

"Bugger!" He had meant to call in at a Tesco's on the way home and do his weekend's shop.

Well, here's to the start of healthy eating. There were eggs and the milk hadn't gone off, and vegetables in the freezer compartment. It would have to be an omelette. And a glass of cheap white wine. Hell, let's celebrate getting fit!

The shopping could wait until the morning.

His shopping was carefully thought out, lots of fruit and veg. Lean cuts of meat. Nothing for the frying pan. After he had stored it away he went back out and drove across Rochfield to the new gym and health spa that had opened on the York Road to see what they had to offer.

Since his earnings only had to keep him, and he didn't have to pay alimony or anything towards his ex-wife's upkeep and there were no children to provide for, he considered himself quite well off. Even so, he thought that the fees at the gym were extravagant. He decided to try the Municipal Leisure Centre.

After being shown round by one of the fitness instructors, and seeing that the equipment that his council tax paid for while not as modern as the new gym, was more than adequate for his needs, he signed up and paid the modest supplementary charge. The instructor advised him what the most suitable clothing and footwear would be and suggested a couple of stores that could provide it.

Satisfied, he went into the town centre and bought the suggested items, and a sports bag to carry them in.

That afternoon, after a light, healthy lunch he returned to the leisure centre to spend a couple of hours being put through a very basic pre-training course which he finished off by having a swim in the pool.

Tommy Adams felt better that evening than he had done in a long time, and wondered why he hadn't joined months earlier.

He spent Sunday afternoon back at the leisure centre, and, as no news of a new assignment had been forthcoming, he was looking forward to spending a few mornings or afternoons there in the coming week. His hopes were dashed on Monday morning shortly after nine when the phone rang. It was the agency.

Tommy Adams was to report to the head office of The Mutual Capital Life Assurance of Rochfield straight away. An initial two week engagement that might be longer if the regular book keeper didn't make a full recovery. That was the brief instruction. Tommy made up a quick lunch which he placed in his briefcase along with his working equipment of calculator, ruler, pens and pencils before locking the house behind him and driving to his new job.

On the Tuesday morning he would probably walk to work. As much a part of his new fitness regime as the probability that it would be easier than trying to negotiate the one way system and finding somewhere to park.

He decided to park in the multi-storey car park and walk through the shopping centre and up the one way system against the flow of the road traffic. Seeing a break in the traffic, he made the crossing without incurring the wrath of drivers and entered the magnificent portico of The Mutual

Cap.

He had been instructed to report to the Managing Director, Jeremy Harmsbury, and was shown to Mr Harmsbury's office by a young receptionist.

"Ah, good, you must be the feller from the agency!" Harmsbury said with that archetypal 'Hail fellow, well met' greeting that so may sales people seemed to adopt, or maybe they were born with, as he came round the desk and shook Tommy firmly by the hand. "Thank you Miss Lewis." He dismissed the receptionist, and pointed Tommy Adams to a chair, "Take a seat."

Harmsbury retreated round to his side of the desk and pulled some papers towards him.

"I'll need your name and address, if that's alright. It's to do with fire drills. We have to have a record of everybody on this floor in case we have to evacuate the building. Bloody stupid really. Never had to in earnest in all the time I've been here, but Head Office insist on it."

Tommy Adams suspected it had more to do with sizing him up as a possible future client but gave his details without comment.

Jeremy Harmsbury went on to explain why his services were required and what he would be expected to cover before showing him down the corridor to Miss Hackett's empty office, and explaining where all the office facilities were, and who worked where, if he needed to speak to any of the staff.

The room smelt faintly of lavender furniture polish but was bright and airy with a westerly view across Rochfield. Tommy could easily make out Crozier's mill, its factory chimney spouting a faint curl of smoke, and steam rising from some process plant in the mill yard. Adams wondered as he looked at the distant mill for how much longer the smoke and steam would rise. Already there had been significant lay-offs in the Yorkshire textile industries. The two remaining mills, Croziers and Featherstones seemed to be riding out the recession better than most, but could it last?

He turned and thanked Mr Harmsbury for the guided tour.

"I'll leave you to it, Tommy. You know where I am if you need anything," Harmsbury said and breezed out.

Tommy settled into Miss Hackett's chair, adjusting it for his height. Miss Hackett, he rightly assumed was a lot shorter than he.

Harmsbury had provided him with Miss Hackett's computer password and the keys to her desk and the various cupboards in the office. He set about familiarising himself with her books and the way she worked, being surprised how little actual book keeping she appeared to be doing.

He wondered if Harmsbury was aware of this.

* * *

Over the next couple of days while doing all the work that Miss Hackett had been doing with ease, and being left with time on his hands, Tommy Adams delved a bit deeper into the workings of

The Mutual Cap. What he managed to put together from the books and computerised ledgers that he had access to did not make good reading. He wondered how much the parent company knew about this.

The relationship between The Mutual Cap and its parent company was a bit of a mystery to Adams. The Mutual Cap seemed to have a considerable degree of autonomy, more like a wholly owned subsidiary, and appeared to be a separate profit centre.

It seemed a strange arrangement.

Unlike many book keepers of his acquaintance, Tommy had practised accountancy for the first few years of his working life. He had worked for one of the top accountancy firms in the country, been well trained, and had spent time as an audit clerk. He knew his way round accounts. It was not something he talked about. The agency that he worked for had not been told by him, or, as far as he was aware, by anyone else of his background.

He had spent a few years running his own business, trying a complete change of career in retail after he had inherited a furniture shop from an uncle that he barely knew. It had been quite successful during his early years but the rise of furniture superstores in out of town retail parks had made it less and less competitive.

He managed to get out of it without losing his shirt, and had made a small profit on selling the stock and the property, and had joined the agency a few days later after seeing their staff advertisement in the local evening paper, the

Rochfield Echo. The company was based in Leeds, but worked all across the north of England.

His first week at The Cap was as much an exercise in getting acquainted with the people as with the books.

On the evening of the Monday of his second week he decided to go to the leisure centre before going home. He explained to the fitness instructor that he'd just started a new job and things had been a bit hectic, but now that he was settled in, he would hope to get to the centre most evenings and at the weekends.

After a good workout and a swim Tommy arrived home feeling refreshed. He changed into running shorts and a singlet and pulled his tracksuit on over them and went running for an hour, more of a fast jog than a run, but he enjoyed it.

He showered again before cooking and eating his evening meal.

He followed the same routine on the Tuesday evening, arriving home shortly after eight.

The phone was ringing as he pushed the door open. He grabbed it before whoever was calling could hang up.

"Tommy Adams?"

"Yes? That's me," he answered. The voice sounded vaguely familiar.

"You probably don't remember me. It was quite a few years ago," the man at the other said, "Mark Parfitt," he gave the name of the major league accountancy firm that Tommy had trained with.

"Good God! Mark! Long time no talk,"

Tommy said, intrigued as to why his old mentor was phoning, and how he had got Tommy's number.

"Can you talk?"

"If by that, do you mean is anybody here with me, the answer's no. She's very much ex. I have the house to myself these days." Tommy didn't feel entirely comfortable having to admit that.

"These things happen, Tommy. I'm in the same boat, but that's not why I'm calling,"

"Well, in all honesty, I didn't think it was. What can I do for you?" Tommy rightly assumed that he was being phoned for a purpose.

"I believe you are working at The Mutual Cap as it's called locally," Parfitt said.

"You are well informed. I've been there since Monday of last week, doing a bit of book keeping. Their regular lady is on sick leave."

"Yes, I know. I take it you haven't forgotten all you learned from us?"

Tommy laughed.

"Mark, I think we ought to meet – face to face so that you can explain the purpose of the surprise phone call."

"I was hoping you would say that. I'm staying at the Lion," Parfitt said. Tommy knew it. Everybody in Rochfield knew the Lion; it was the only decent hotel in the centre of the town. "How soon can you get here? I'll treat you to dinner unless you've already eaten, save you having to cook!"

"I won't say no to that. I'll be with you in twenty minutes if that's okay. It'll give me a chance to get cleaned up and changed into more suitable clothes."

"Make it half an hour. I'll see you in the bar," Parfitt said and hung up.

Tommy put the receiver back on the cradle and stood looking at it. What was all this leading to? There were ethics involved here. He wasn't at liberty to discuss a client's business with an outsider. Parfitt would know that. It was the same set of rules that accountancy firms followed.

He went upstairs, showered and changed into a sports jacket and casual trousers. A pair of casual shoes finished his attire.

On the way to the hotel he stopped at an ATM and took out fifty pounds so that he could buy a round if it seemed appropriate. He was uncertain as to what was going on, and whether this was a business meeting, a recruitment-drive; a piece of industrial espionage or, least likely a meeting for old time's sake. It wasn't as though he and Mark Parfitt had ever been particularly close. The other man was ten years older than Tommy.

Parfitt was sitting at one of the small tables in one of the window bays of the bar. He clearly recognised his old protégé as Tommy entered, because he raised an arm in salute, beckoning Tommy from across the room and stood up as the younger man approached.

"Hey, you've not changed much over the years. I'd have recognised you anywhere!" Parfitt said and pointed to the empty chair. Tommy sat and returned the compliment. His former mentor must have put on at least four stone since Tommy had last seen him.

"Running to fat, old son. Too many expense account lunches and hours behind a desk, I'm afraid. What about you, are you still playing football?" Parfitt asked jovially.

"Haven't played any football in ages, but I use the leisure centre whenever I can find the time," Tommy said modestly.

"Can I get you a drink?"

A waitress was hovering nearby. Parfitt called her over.

"Just a half of bitter. I'm driving," Tommy said.

They waited for the drinks to arrive before continuing their conversation; a second scotch and soda for Parfitt and Tommy's beer.

"Have you guessed why I asked you to meet me?" Parfitt asked.

"Should I?" Adams responded cagily.

"Ah yes. Client confidentiality."

Tommy nodded.

"You must have wondered, if only for a brief moment, how I came to have your home phone number. After all, we haven't been in touch for years."

"Yes, it crossed my mind, Mark. I assumed that the tentacles of your firm spread far and wide."

"Not quite, Tommy. Not quite. Slightly more mundane. We already have a mole in The Mutual Cap, but our mole isn't a trained accountant and would neither have access to the information, nor be able to make sense of it. I was quite serious when I asked if you still recalled enough of what we taught you."

Parfitt looked questioningly at the man opposite. He remembered Tommy has having a quick brain and a good grasp of figures and how they fitted together, and a good nose for dodgy book keeping; something they came across occasionally in the process of auditing a clients books.

Tommy laughed, "Mark, when you taught, it stuck, believe me."

"Hungry?" Parfitt asked.

"Yes," Tommy replied without hesitation.

"Right, let's head to the restaurant. I've already reserved a table in a quiet corner where we can talk in confidence." Parfitt stood up. Tommy followed him to the restaurant. They were shown to a corner table by the maitre d'hôtel and presented with the à la carte menu and a wine list.

"My treat," Parfitt said, "Order something extravagant, that way I won't feel as though I'm eating alone!"

Tommy scanned the menu carefully. He knew that the hotel's restaurant which was open to the public, served excellent food; better than the resident's dining room where the food was considered to be very good but not exceptional. He knew from having worked at the hotel for some weeks a couple of year's earlier that their public rooms, the bar, the restaurant and the function rooms provided most of the profit for the business and attracted customers from a wide catchment area, not just confined to Rochfield.

He had never had occasion to eat in the restaurant before, and was going to take full advantage of Parfitt's hospitality, or rather that of his accountancy firm.

They waited until the first course was served. Mark had chosen the chicken liver parfait with toasted brioche which he washed down with Sauvignon Blanc. Tommy preferred the sea bass Caesar salad and drank mineral water.

Mark Parfitt looked across the table at Tommy Adams, "How much do you know of the background to The Cap?"

Adams explained what he thought the situation was and the relationship between the business in Rochfield and its parent company.

"Yes, that's more or less it. And now, and this must remain between us, here's the problem. The parent company wants rid of The Mutual Cap."

"Oh!" This came as a surprise to Adams. He wondered who else knew about it.

"Our company has been asked by a large insurance, and by large, I mean global company, to look into the affairs of The Mutual Cap."

"I sense a potential hostile takeover," Tommy replied.

"Spot on. Our client wants the business, but they don't want to have to pay over the odds for a lame duck. I've managed to place somebody on the inside, but like I said, no access to the books, just enough contact with everybody to know whether the business is busy or merely limping along. That's why I need your help."

Tommy raised an eyebrow. This was totally irregular. "Surely, if your client is in negotiations with The Mutual Cap they would have every right to inspect the books."

"That's just it. They aren't at that stage yet. However, a rival company is already speaking to the board of the parent company. We don't know what stage those negotiations are at."

Tommy shook his head slowly from side to side in amazement.

"Mark, you don't seriously expect me to get involved in this, do you? Surely it amounts to industrial espionage, or some form of insider dealing," he said as he finished his first course and took a sip of mineral water.

"I admit that it's not quite above board, but it may prove to be in the best interest of The Mutual Cap. I think, armed with the relevant information, that our client's offer might prove a better deal for them."

"And they don't want to get into a bidding war, is that it?"

"Something like that," Parfitt nodded.

A waiter arrived and cleared their first course away and was followed by another waiter who served the main course. Parfitt had chosen the Aberdeen Angus flat iron steak. Tommy stuck with fish and had grilled trout with almonds, chipped potatoes, petit pois and a side salad. While Mark drank burgundy, Tommy took a glass of the Sauvignon Blanc.

When the waiter had left they continued their conversation as they ate.

"There's more to it though. We have reason to believe that the board of the parent company aren't being totally honest with their potential buyer."

"What makes you think that?"

"Sources within sources, Tommy. I can't go into specifics, but what we've heard doesn't seem to add up with our analysis of the state of Mutual Cap's business."

Tommy Adams didn't respond to this as he took another mouthful of the succulent trout, the petit pois and a chip. What Parfitt had said, added to what he already knew about the state of The Mutual Cap's books made him wonder exactly what was going on within the business. He personally didn't have any of their products, but he was aware of several of his former acquaintances, the pre-marriage friends who did. People who had all been lured by the exaggerated earnings claims based on the unsustainable performance percentages of the time.

One or two had sought him out at the time and asked for his opinion on their products. His usual reply had been that while he wasn't qualified to give an opinion, and that they should speak to an independent financial advisor, they would have to decide for themselves, but he doubted that such growth was sustainable over the full length of the policies. Some had taken his advice, most had not.

The monthly payments hadn't been excessive at the time, but as the economic climate changed over the years and his caveat had been revealed as sound, sales persons from the company had returned regularly to suggest that increased premiums would be needed to keep place with inflation.

Tommy's parents had quite a lot of their disposable income tied up in the company over the years, but they had been lucky, they were now living off that income and had used their personal pension capital to buy annuities with other providers.

He wondered as he took a drink of the wine whether others would be so fortunate.

He realised he would have to decide where his loyalty, or duty lay.

It seemed to him that the two were at opposite ends of the ethical spectrum. He looked across the table at Mark Parfitt.

Parfitt was looking straight back at him. It was as though Parfitt had engineered this dilemma, knowing what thoughts would be going through Tommy's head.

"Well?" Parfitt asked after a moment of silence.

"What do you need?" Tommy hoped that he hadn't sold his soul for a gourmet meal. A bit of a step up from a mess of pottage maybe; and the thirty pieces of silver hadn't even been mentioned.

Chapter 3

Detective Chief Inspector Andrew Sutherland stared out of his office window at the relentless October rain that swept over Rochfield borne on a chilly north east wind. If this was a foretaste of the coming winter, he wasn't looking forward to it. He turned back to his desk and picked up the next case file.

It was Wednesday afternoon, the light outside was fading, not that there had been much of it all day, but it served to make Sutherland's mood even darker. One thing was inescapable; crime figures for the Rochfield Police Division were on the rise.

Mostly, the increase was in crimes against property.

Maybe it was a reflection of the vagaries of the economic climate in the country. Widespread job losses in mining, steel-working and heavy industry generally weren't offset by a falling interest rate to make people's lives less uncertain.

Locally there had been a minor upturn in the fortunes of the woollen trade, but that tended to favour the female working population over the male.

Crimes against people, including murder

seemed to have taken a back seat which allowed Sutherland to concentrate his resources on the less glamorous tasks of clearing up some of the minor crimes. Minor as far as crime statistics were concerned, but quite major to the victim. He knew that in a world where there were finite resources, it would never be possible to please all of the people all of the time, but if his teams could clear up some of the crimes that the average tax-payer bore the brunt of, policing would be seen to be benefiting the community.

He read over the notes that he had been making on his yellow legal pad before picking up the bunch of the files that he had already worked his way through and carried them down to the next floor to the CID room.

That late in the afternoon, most of the detectives were back in the office and at their desks.

Detective Inspector Dean Simpson looked up as his boss entered and approached his desk.

"Ah, the files!"

"Indeed, laddie," Sutherland said quietly as he placed them on Simpson's desk. "Time to rally the troops, I think." As a former Military Policeman, Sutherland tended to think of his detectives in those terms. He looked around the room before walking slowly across to the desk from where the morning briefings were given.

The quiet susurration that had been obvious when he had entered the CID room had died away. Sutherland waited until DS 'Jimmy' Grieves had finished his phone call before addressing them.

"Mr Henderson, our ever watchful Chief Constable, has been reading the local papers. It would seem that we are in the middle of an unprecedented crime wave, and that the worthy burghers of Rochfield and surrounding districts are unhappy with our performance," he began. "I have spent the afternoon reviewing all of the open cases, and I would have to say that they have a point."

There were a few muted gasps of surprise from the assembled teams. They were used to Sutherland supporting them to the hilt.

"I am aware that you are putting great effort into each of the crimes you are investigating, but, on reading through a lot of the files, I think I have spotted a weakness."

He had got their attention. Nobody likes to be criticised, and on this occasion he wasn't about to criticise them.

"The problem doesn't lie with you; it lies with me and the system under which we presently operate," Sutherland said.

There was an almost audible sigh of relief.

"Cast your minds back to Easter, in particular those of you who were involved in tracking down Michael Hydinge." Those who had been involved sat up straighter.

Sutherland looked down at his notes before he continued, "We used technology to crack that case as much as foot slogging detective work. I am going to have a wee chat with Mr Henderson and see if we can't apply the same process to the more mundane crimes that we deal with on a day to day basis. I'm going to ask that Young Eric's expertise and his box of tricks be used here in CID along with a civilian to do the grunt work of deciphering your form filling into a form that Young Eric can feed to his toy and hopefully get some meaningful answers out of. If that works, we'll load the forms into your work stations and see how it goes with everyone filling in their own forms on their computers."

Sutherland looked around the room.

"This may require a bit of a re-think on all our parts to make this work, but I'm convinced that this is the way policing, especially detection of crime is going," he referred to his notes again, "If we work together and as a team, with each one of you contributing to the building of the systems that will be required to make this work, I think we can do it. Any ideas or suggestions as to ways of doing it will be more than welcome. And it doesn't matter how simple or daft the ideas are. You all know Young Eric, and you know that he is a good listener. Do I have your support with this?"

There were murmurs of assent from around the room. Several of them looked round at the constable.

Sutherland left them to it and took the stairs up to the top floor to see if Henderson was available.

Lynn Parker, his secretary, raised an eyebrow as Sutherland approached.

"Is he free?" Sutherland asked.

Lynn looked at the office phone. Henderson's

light was not on so he wasn't on the phone. She pressed the button to call him on the office intercom.

"DCI Sutherland would like to have a word sir," she said.

"Show him in, Lynn," Henderson's voice was tinny over the speaker.

Lynn nodded to the door, knowing that Sutherland was the last person who would expect the red carpet treatment.

He gave her a smile of thanks and crossed to Henderson's door and knocked.

"Come!"

Sutherland entered, closed the door behind him and walked to the Chief Constable's desk.

"Sutherland?" Henderson looked up.

Sutherland pulled up a vacant chair and sat, legal pad in hand.

"Crime figures, sir."

"They're up. We discussed this yesterday."

"Yes sir. I think I may have found a way to make better use of our resources and help get the figures down."

That got Henderson's full attention.

Referring occasionally to his notes, Sutherland went on to outline what he had in mind. He went into considerable detail about how he felt it should be set up and how he thought it could help. He cited the use that they had made of Young Eric and computer technology earlier in the year.

Henderson was impressed.

"You've obviously given this a lot of thought, Sutherland." Henderson sat back in his chair and looked across the desk at his senior detective. "Don't know much about computers myself," he said almost wistfully, "But I think you're right about them being the way towards modern detection. Right, go ahead, nothing beats giving it a try, and we'll be no worse off if nothing comes of it, will we?"

"No sir. I can assure you of that. I think it will also help the troops to look more critically at the crimes they are investigating," Sutherland said.

"Oh, in what way?" Henderson wasn't sure where this was leading.

"I think they'll start to see patterns. The trick will be getting them to avoid trying to make what they are looking at fit a pattern. Let the computer see if it can find a pattern. I want them to feed in exactly what they find, but to look closely to make sure they have found everything."

"Sounds interesting. Let's give it a six month trial, Sutherland, but I'll want regular reports on its progress."

"Understood, sir." Sutherland stood up, put the chair back from where he had taken it and left the room.

He gave a cheery wave to Lynn as he passed her desk.

"Do I detect that a Scots cat has just got the cream, or am I barking up the wrong tree?"

"Love the mixed metaphors, Lynn. Got to rush."

It was nearly the end of shift time when he got to his office. He quickly phoned the front desk and asked if anyone knew where Young Eric might be.

On being told that he was probably in the locker room, Sutherland asked that somebody go and find him and send him up to his office before going home.

Five minutes later a slightly breathless PC Eric Young knocked on Sutherland's door.

"Come in Eric. Grab a seat. You're not in a tearing hurry to get away laddie?"

"No sir," Eric sat opposite the Chief Inspector.

For the next twenty minutes Sutherland outlined what he had in mind. He had given Eric a note pad and had his legal pad in front of him.

"Which of the civilians are the best with computers?" Sutherland asked.

"I'd have to think about that, sir," Eric replied, "Probably one of the girls who helped with the data processing on the Hydinge case."

"Rather what I was thinking. That way they would know how you work, and how things in CID work. Better than that, we know they've had the confidentiality lecture!" Sutherland said.

"Yes sir."

"Give me a name in the morning and I'll make the arrangements. I'll make sure that you have a desk ready for the civilian. Hang on to the note pad. You may have a few ideas overnight."

Young Eric was already processing a number of ideas. This was something that he had always hoped would happen, but hadn't expected to see it for a few years.

He stood up, thanked Sutherland for the opportunity and moved towards the door.

"Henderson has given us six months. Will that be enough?"

Eric broke into a smile, "Oh yes sir. I think we can make a difference well before that."

"Ay, I thought you might say that. But I'd rather make haste slowly and get it right first time than rush into it and end up with a load of teething troubles and false starts. Remember, it's not me you have to convince; it's the rest of CID. You know how conservative old fashioned coppers can be."

"Point taken sir. I'll bear that in mind."

"See you in the morning," Sutherland said.

He could almost picture Young Eric skipping down the corridor like a new puppy anxious to please his master.

* * *

The following morning when Eric Young arrived in the CID Sutherland was already there organising desk space.

"Have you chosen a civilian clerk?" he asked.

"Vikki Gibson if you can get her. She's very clued in to computers, and she was one of the people we used at Easter," Eric told him.

"Leave that with me. You get everything set up. I take it you'll need a computer for her too?"

"Yes sir. I don't think the office would be too keen to lose her and her computer," Eric said.

"Probably not. Give procurement a ring, tell them what you need. Any problems, tell them I'm the one looking for it," Sutherland said. "I'll be down in Admin if they need to speak to me."

He left Eric to get on with it and went down stairs to the Administration office on the next floor. Procurement was located on the same floor, so they could find him there if Eric's word wasn't good enough.

While he was arranging for Vikki Gibson to be transferred to CID on a permanent basis, one of the pen pushers from Procurement approached with a clip board.

"Need you to sign this off sir," the clerk said pushing the clipboard under Sutherland's nose.

Sutherland quickly read over the order for the computer equipment without understanding one word of it, other than the obvious things like keyboard, mouse and monitor, if the rest was needed by Young Eric; that was good enough for him. He signed it. "How long to get it installed?"

"It'll be here in an hour, sir. Two at the most," the clerk said.

"Good man. Thanks."

The clerk departed happy to have been thanked for doing his job.

Vikki Graham, a casually dressed brunette that Sutherland remembered from the Hydinge affair, introduced herself to him.

They walked together back up to the CID room.

"Young Eric will be your boss for this. You've worked together before," he said.

"Yes sir."

"Same rules as last time, Vikki. Anything you hear or see in CID stays in CID."

"I know sir. It'll be nice to be working with Eric again," she replied.

"Any suggestions you have as to how we can put this together and make it work don't be afraid to speak up, either to Eric, or me. This is all going to be a bit new for all of us, and as I said to PC Young yesterday, selling it to me isn't going to be the problem. It's got to be easy for the rest of CID to work with. It's their information that's crucial to the success. We're going to need simple, efficient ways of transferring their input to the computer. That's where you come in. Make yourself known to them, work with them," he said as they entered the CID room.

For the next hour and a half, until the new computer equipment arrived, Eric and Vikki put their heads together to put together something that could act as a template for what they wanted to achieve. Several of the ideas that Eric had been toying with for the past number of months were examined. Eric had made the right choice with Vikki Gibson. She was quick to spot weaknesses and to offer alternatives and new ideas.

Along with all the computer equipment, Eric had put in a request for two printers, one a dot-matrix for generating listings on cheap continuous stationery, and the other an ink-jet printer for putting together reports for circulation or possibly for court use.

She watched as Eric set the equipment up, installed the supplied software and tested it all. He installed the printers and tested them before he was satisfied that they could start work.

A DEADLY ACCOUNT

Detective Inspector Dean Simpson wandered across from his desk to see how things were going. Sutherland had already had a long talk with his DI about what he hoped to achieve with this exercise. Simpson hadn't needed persuading. Being some years younger than his co-Inspector, DI Peter Lawson, Dean was adaptable to change, and welcomed anything that might help make their job easier, even if it prompted a tightening up of procedures. No policeman of his acquaintance liked paperwork, but as they had to file reports on every case anyway, it made sense to use that information on a shared basis.

If the computer could sift through all the detail and spit out a connection or two that hadn't been spotted before, that was useful. At the end of the day, it would be the boots on the ground that was doing the work, catching the villains, doing the interviews and taking the credit.

"So, where are you going to start, Eric?" Simpson asked.

"We thought we'd read through the open case files and start noting things down as though we were detectives working the cases. Now that you have a terminal at each desk, the guys are putting their reports from their hand written notes directly onto the computer anyway instead of using the old type-writers, and then printing them out. It would be just as simple to put your blank forms onto the computer and fill them in there. Then the computer could do the analysis in real time."

"Sounds as though he's trying to work you out of a job Vikki!" Simpson said.

"I think she'll have a job here for quite some time to come. There's all the old stuff to put on first, and stuff from closed cases. The computer works best with more information rather than less," Eric said.

"That makes sense. I think I'll have a word with Mr Sutherland. See if we can't move this on a bit faster. The sooner we get used to using computers to fill in forms in a standardised fashion, the sooner we'll get to see results."

Eric nodded and watched as Simpson headed towards the door.

"Well, well!" he said. "I hadn't expected that."

Vikki Gibson laughed, "One-Nil to the teckis!"

"Well, it's a step in the right direction. All depends on whether Henderson will go along with this way of doing it."

"Surely, if it speeds things up, and you get more accurate results, it's got to be a good thing?"

"You'd think so, Vikki, but we're up against a lot of tradition here."

Eric and Vikki spent the rest of the day working their way through file after file. Every two hours they would stop, get a tea or coffee and let the computer work on the information using the programmes that Eric had written to analyse the data.

It was just after four, Eric and Vikki returned from the canteen to find that the computer had finished its latest analysis and was prepared to divulge some information.

A little gnome was running backwards and forwards across Eric's screen. A little square of pixels on its helmet was blinking on and off.

"Was that your idea?" Vikki asked.

"Always say, if you can't have a bit of fun doing your job, find a different job!"

"A gnome?"

"In a police uniform!"

"And what does it signify?"

"Our program has found something significant. Hence the flashing light on his helmet. At least the computer thinks it's significant. Let's have a look and then we'll ask DI Simpson what he thinks."

Eric pressed a few keys and the computer spat words onto the listing paper. When it stopped he flicked his fore-finger off the tip of his thumb at the tear point and separated the sheets of printout paper from the printer.

Together he and Vikki went across to Simpson's desk.

Dean looked up.

"Eric?"

"Something of possible interest, sir."

"That sounds suspiciously like bullshit for 'Our toy has spoken', Eric."

"We'd rather you took a look at it to see if it's significant, sir."

Eric handed over the paper. Dean took it, spread it on his desk and started reading. He didn't speak until he had read all of the information.

It was a case concerning a break-in at an off license in Rochleigh. DC Fowler had been the investigating officer. There had been a break-in at a warehouse in the small industrial estate on the eastern outskirts of Rochfield. DS Cranfield had been the investigating officer. Simpson remembered reading her report. DI Lawson would have read Fowler's report. Only Sutherland would have read both reports.

The events had taken place several weeks apart and it was possible that the similarities hadn't been noticeable enough even for Sutherland to spot.

The computer had spotted them, and given them a sixty percent probability that the same people were involved.

"Pity we don't know who these people are, Eric."

"Not yet, sir. But I think that by the end of the week we might have a better idea. We've a lot more files to process yet. Something may come out of the closed case files."

"Well, it's a start. Can I keep this?"

"Of course. If we get more information we'll update you sir."

"Thanks. Is it too early to tell Mr Sutherland?"

"Maybe. Can we give it to the end of the week?"

"Unless he asks, yes. Keep at it guys."

Eric and Vikki returned to their computers and continued to feed report data into their computers until the shift ended.

Chapter 4

Tommy Adams turned up to work the morning after his meal with Mark Parfitt with a sense of apprehension. He already knew that the books of The Mutual Cap would not survive close scrutiny from even an average accountant.

He was at a loss to understand why the parent company hadn't already put their auditors in. It was the logical thing to do. Make sure the books would stand up to a critical scrutiny.

If, as Parfitt had said, they were in talks with a possible take over company, Adams wondered how soon it would be before the potential buyer's accountants would be knocking on the door asking to carry out an audit.

If what he suspected was being carried out by a director, and that could only be Harmsbury, then he must know that he was living on borrowed time. Either he had a plan to sort the problem out or he planned to do a disappearing act before he was caught. Doing that would point the finger straight at him, which suggested that it probably wasn't the intended strategy.

On the other hand if the irregularities were being engineered by a clever sales agent, they came and went like ducks in a shooting gallery and the perpetrator could have already left The Mutual Cap.

Between sorting out the mundane issue of agents' commissions, checking them against the receipts from clients, allocating the up-stream percentages and verifying that funds were available, most of which was monitored by the computer system, he was able to delve deeper into the financial workings of the business.

There was a serious shortfall between the actual funds and the recorded funds. He did not have access to the share dealing and trading accounts of the investment arm of the company but he was beginning to suspect that the answer lay there. That would require access to the parent company's systems.

As soon as he got home he phoned Mark Parfitt and suggested the Parfitt should come over and hear what he had to say rather than rely on the telephone.

Parfitt arrived at a few minutes after six. For the next hour Tommy Adams, with a short break while Parfitt went to the bathroom, laid out what he had found and what he hadn't found, and put forward his suggestions as to what he suspected was the scenario behind the discrepancies in the figures.

Parfitt asked a few questions to see if there was anything that Adams might have missed.

At the end he said that he would run it past some of his own people and see if they could some up with a way for Adams to access the trading accounts. He agreed that the answer probably lay there.

"That would suggest that somebody in the parent company is responsible for this," Parfitt said.

"Do you think this is likely to be at director level?" Adams asked.

Parfitt could see where this was leading.

"If it is, they're playing a dangerous game of brinkmanship. They have no way of knowing when the prospective buyer will demand an audit. It could explain why an internal audit hasn't been carried out."

"That's what I was thinking," Adams said as he showed Parfitt out.

"I'll make a few phone calls and get back to you, Tommy," Parfitt said as he got into his car, "Will you be in for the rest of the evening?"

"I was planning on going for a run before making my evening meal, why?"

"Oh, just in case I need to ask some more questions. Don't worry. Go ahead with your run. I can catch you later if needs be."

Tommy went back inside and locked his door behind him.

* * *

Across town, on the Meadowland estate, Richard Tillsworth and Rachael settled down to watch television. The children were upstairs in their rooms finishing their homework before going to bed.

"How's Miss Hackett's replacement getting on?" Rachael asked.

"Oh, I forgot to tell you, it's a man. Chap called Tommy Adams. Seems very competent. Quiet sort of bloke really," Richard said.

"Have you sold him anything yet?" she asked. The question was almost serious. Rachael knew that her husband rarely wasted an opportunity to make a sale.

"I think Harmsbury has his eye on him!"

"Odd to get a male book keeper, isn't it?"

"Oh, very equal opportunity these days! I think he might have been an accountant or worked for one at some time or other," Richard Tillsworth said.

"What makes you think that?" Rachael asked.

"He just seems the type. Very methodical; insists that we get our reports in first thing in the morning."

"Gosh! He's only been there a week and already he's laying down the law!"

"Not a bad thing really; some of the agents have got a bit slack over the years," he replied.

With that they lapsed into silence to watch the drama unfolding on the television.

Mike Blandford, a sales agent for the past eight years, was also glad that Adams was doing the book keeping. He had no problem with putting his reports in on time. He knew that it would mean that there would be no delays in getting paid his commission. There had been occasions when Miss Hackett's ways had led to delays.

He was out following up on some of his calls

A DEADLY ACCOUNT

with appointments. The idea was that an appointment would lead to a presentation at the same visit. Sometimes the best an agent could hope for was to stir an interest, leave some literature and a brief outline of the company's products and arrange for a follow up appointment to make the full presentation. A nicer term than sales pitch, but that was what it was.

If a good presentation led to a sale that was a job well done; if the sale led to referrals, that was the icing on the cake. Sometimes the referrals led to better business than the original sale. His first appointment was a referral from a couple he had sold policies to in the past. It had started with a term policy for the husband and a savings plan for the wife. These had been improved to a full life policy with built in savings for the husband and a personal pension. Both products were showing good returns and they had been glad to recommend him to their friends.

The couple he was visiting were a husband and wife with three school age children. The husband had his own business, the wife was a teacher.

By the end of his visit he had signed them up for life plans, personal pensions and a savings plan to provide for the children's university education. He had also persuaded the self employed business man to let him come to the little print-works that he ran to speak to the staff about a company pension scheme.

His second visit of the evening began confidently, but a disturbance upstairs from one of their children had brought the visit to a halt, but not without a promised rescheduling, so maybe all was not lost. He left a folder of brochures.

He headed home content that provided the first couple didn't change their mind; he would earn a good commission and look really good at Monday morning's sales meeting.

Sally Pickton had only been working as a sales agent for The Mutual Cap for six weeks. She had done the full week's sales training course at a hotel in Harrogate and done well in the role play exercises. She had spent two weeks with Richard Tillsworth as he mentored her and helped her secure her first sales. Now she was on her own.

She was finding it tougher than she had expected and wondered whether she was going to be good enough to hold onto her job as a sales agent. So far she had managed to make a couple of small sales each week, but it was only just enough to keep her from the bottom of the league at the Monday meetings. Like all sales people she needed the big sale that would give her the confidence to improve her performance and reduce the pressure on her.

She was driving home when her car stalled at the traffic lights at the bottom of the one way system leading up through Rochfield past the shopping centre and try as she could; she was unable to re-start it. She got out and lifted the bonnet, not sure what she hoped to find. Car engines were a mystery to her.

She was aware that another car had stopped behind her and was expecting to hear an angry honking of the horn. Instead, the other driver got out.

"Oh thank God, a friendly face!" Sally said in relief.

Mike Blandford approached, "What seems to be the problem, Sally?"

"It stalled, Mike. I can't seem to get it going again."

"Has it done this before?" he asked as he peered in at the engine. There was a faint whiff of petrol fumes and he suspected that she may have flooded the carburettor of the elderly Ford Escort,

"Not recently," she answered.

"Mind if I try it?" Mike offered.

"I wish you luck!" She watched as he got in, pushed the seat back a couple of notches and turned the key, checking all the dials before trying to start it. The petrol gauge registered about quarter full, so it wasn't running on fumes.

He made sure that it was out of gear before turning the key further, the starter motor laboured to turn the engine over. Giving a quick jab to the accelerator and to the clutch, a trick that sometimes helped his car to start in cold weather, the engine caught, spluttered a bit and then settled down. Smoke from unburnt fuel wafted towards him. He left the engine running and climbed out.

"Don't forget to adjust the seat," he advised.

"What do you think is the matter with it?" she asked.

"When did it last have a proper service, Sally?"

"Ages ago, I'm afraid," Sally admitted.

"Look, I'll tell you what, if you're not busy on Saturday bring it round to my place and I'll do what I can. It'll only cost you a few quid for basic parts, spark plugs, oil and air filters, that sort of thing and you can do all the hard work. How does that sound?"

"Didn't know you were a mechanic, Mike!"

"We all did something before getting into this business. I was a motor mechanic for three years. Look, I'll see you on Saturday. You know where I live?"

"No, sorry, haven't had the privilege!"

He scribbled down his address on the back of one of his business cards and handed it to her. It turned out to be only a couple of streets from where she lived in Rochleigh.

"We're almost neighbours!"

"Yeah, well it's a small town," he said as he got back into his car and watched as she drove away. He followed her to the top of her road in case she stalled again.

* * *

Miss Hilda Hackett sat in the easy chair beside her bed in the private clinic that her employers' insurance plan was paying for trying to read the romantic novel that one of her few visitors had brought her.

After a week of tests and re-tests she was feeling no better, but decidedly bored.

There was a knock on the door.

"Come in," she said, intrigued as to who might be visiting at this hour. All of the medical people had been and gone during the day. Her tray had been cleared away some minutes earlier, and the ward round for drugs wasn't due for at least two hours.

"You have a visitor, Hilda," the floor orderly said as she opened the door. Miss Hackett wasn't sure that she liked the familiarity of being called Hilda, but it seemed to be the modern way in hospitals, private or National Health.

"Mr Harmsbury! I hadn't expected to see you here," she exclaimed. She was genuinely surprised. Mr Harmsbury wasn't noted for expressing much concern where the office staff was concerned.

"Miss Hackett, how are you?" he said as he entered carrying a very acceptable bunch of flowers and a basket of fruit. Uncharitably, Miss Hackett assumed that his wife had chosen the gifts. "I remembered that you were partial to fruit."

She was.

"How thoughtful of you, Mr Harmsbury," she replied, taking the basket and placing it on her bedside table. "Can you put the flowers in the hand basin and run a little water for them. I'll arrange them later. It will give me something to do!"

"Are they taking good care of you?"

"Hard to say. They're running tests. Endless tests. You know how it is."

Harmsbury didn't. He couldn't remember when he had last been sick, let alone been a patient in hospital. Tonsillitis as a child was the last time that he could think of.

"Have they given you any idea of what's wrong?" Harmsbury ventured to ask, not being sure how Miss Hackett would react to the question. After this length of time, Harmsbury had expected that his book-keeper's problem would have been diagnosed and treated. He studied her as he looked down at her. She seemed to have lost a little weight, not that she had much to lose, and looked older than he had expected.

"Not yet. I don't know whether that's good news or bad. Well, never mind me, how are things at The Cap?"

"Plodding along. Good days and bad. You know how it is these days!" He pulled up the spare easy chair and sat down.

"And did you get a suitable replacement?" she asked, genuinely interested.

"He seems alright. Certainly knows his way round the book keeping side of things," Harmsbury said.

"He?"

"Yes, came from that place you recommended. Chap called Adams. Tommy Adams."

Miss Hackett twitched.

Jeremy Harmsbury noticed.

"You know him?"

"I know of him, yes. He used to have a furniture business, but I believe he inherited it from an uncle. He worked as an accountant before that," she said in her precise way, watching Harmsbury all the time.

This was news to Harmsbury. Unwelcome news.

"Miss Hackett, that is most interesting. An accountant. Well, that explains why he has got to grips with our systems so easily. He does seem very capable," he was trying to appear calm. "I'm afraid that I can't stay long. I have a client to see at eight thirty, so I'd better be getting along. Let me know if you need anything, Miss Hackett, and enjoy the fruit."

Miss Hackett watched him depart and wondered what Harmsbury was up to. The information about Adams had certainly put him on edge.

She carefully removed the cellophane outer wrapping from the basket of fruit, selected a pear, washing it under the tap before bighting into it.

Standing at the French windows of her bedroom she looked out over the gently sloping lawn, bathed in the artificial glow of Rochfield's light pollution, down towards the hedge that ran along the clinic's boundary with the river path. To the far right she could see a car, possibly Harmsbury's, but could not tell from where she stood in what direction it had turned at the foot of the clinic's driveway.

So, Tommy Hackett was doing her books at The Cap! She had no doubt that he would have already worked out what she had suspected for some time past, that all was not right with the accounts of The Mutual Capital Life Assurance Company of Rochfield. She wondered too, as she pulled the curtains closed, who, if anybody he might have expressed his concerns to, and decided that she was glad that she had kept her knowledge to herself and was now safely, if unwillingly incarcerated in the private clinic.

Chapter 5

Wednesday's relentless rain had given way to a bright clear October morning. A beautiful autumn day, Sutherland thought as he drove from his suburban home to the modern glass and concrete block that was Rochfield Central Police Headquarters, or the Factory as the people who worked in it called it. In a past life the site had been a textile mill.

He sometimes wondered about that. Factories made things. What did a police station make? Things right with the world? Hardly. Most days it felt as if they were lucky if they made any difference at all. Certainly there were the glory days when the villain, or villains were caught, confessions were secured, evidence gathered and the end result was taken out of their hands and became the property of the legal system.

All they could hope for was that they had crossed all the 'Ts', dotted all the 'Is' and put together a sufficiently watertight case so that the Crown Prosecution Service could secure a conviction and suitable punishment in the far from certain world of defence counsels, juries and judges.

There were times when it seemed like a strange game where opposing teams had different rule books and the referees, the judges, had another book of rules that bore no relation to the rules that the opposing teams were using.

However, that was the situation in which they found themselves and it was up to him and his teams to make the best of it. There was little point in crying foul. Nobody was listening. The media seemed intent on damning them if they did, and damning them even more if they didn't.

On a sunny morning in Yorkshire Sutherland decided that none of it mattered. What mattered was getting on with the job to the best of their ability. Catching the bad guys.

He wondered what Young Eric's technical solution might throw up. Eric constantly surprised him.

He was the future of police work. Eric and his computers, just like Ed Richardson, the head of the Scene of Crime unit, and his experts were the cutting edge of forensic detection, and the Home Office Appointed Pathologist, Dr Helen Ellis over at Rochfield Infirmary and the ever more sophisticated analysis of tissue samples, wounds, toxicology and all that went up to make a watertight analysis of the cause of death, if murder was under investigation.

Together the sometimes frustrating, often mundane, aspects of police detective work, when put with the science succeeded in making it all worthwhile.

He pulled into his parking space round the

A DEADLY ACCOUNT

back of the building and let himself in through the rear security door with his swipe card, took the stairs up to the CID room to see who was on duty, to catch up on any overnight crime that needed to be brought to his attention before continuing up the stairs to his office.

He would return to CID later for the morning briefing only if his presence was required. Most mornings he left that to his Inspectors while he caught up with the paperwork.

Although his shift didn't start for another ten minutes, it came as no surprise to Sutherland that Young Eric was already at his desk.

"I trust that you haven't been here all night, laddie," he said as he crossed the floor.

"No sir," Eric replied.

"Is it too early to ask if you've come up with anything?" Sutherland asked casually, more in hope than expectation.

Eric remembered what Inspector Simpson had said the previous evening – 'Unless he asks.' To Eric this sounded like a definite ask.

At that moment Inspector Simpson arrived.

"Morning sir. Better day by the look of it," he said as he hung his raincoat on his peg.

"Aye, Dean. I was just asking if Young Eric's system had found anything yet."

Simpson came over, giving Eric an imperceptible nod.

"A possible maybe, sir," Eric said handing the Chief Inspector the printout that he had shown to Simpson.

Sutherland scanned it rapidly, pulling the

salient facts off the page, the 'who' and the reasoning behind it. Who had the computer suggested and based on what information?

"Mmm. I'm impressed," he said handing the pages to Simpson. "What do you think?"

Simpson looked at the pages again. Another page had been added.

"How did you manage to get a name? I though it was going to take at least a couple more days."

"Remember I said that the more information it had the better the result would be?"

"Yes, I remember."

"Well Vikki and I managed to get a few more reports on last night, and I got some more done this morning. This is the result."

"A better than sixty percent probability! Is that enough to go on?" Simpson turned to Sutherland. It would be his call.

"Good enough for me, Dean," Sutherland said, "What do you think? Should we pay them a little visit, see what they have to say for themselves?"

"It would be better to do it early in the morning, don't you think. Less chance of their little band of look-outs being awake."

Simpson had a valid point. To pick them up successfully would require the assistance of uniformed constables and probably the dog handlers, something that couldn't be pulled together at a moment's notice.

The computer had thrown up the possibility that a family firm operating out of the Blackwood Estate had probably been responsible for a couple of recent crimes.

A DEADLY ACCOUNT

The Blackwood and the Oakridge Estates lay either side of a through route to the east of the town and probably accounted for half the crime in the district.

They were last resort council housing estates that were in the process of being re-developed, populated by those at the bottom of the socio-economic scale and new immigrants, those experiencing their first taste of the good life that Britain had to offer.

It always surprised Sutherland and his detectives that after a few months of exposure to the vicissitudes of living on these estates, frequently harassed by their often openly racist neighbours, that these people didn't run for the hills or retreat back to their homelands. Many, however, worked hard and saved what they could from what they earned and what they didn't send back to their mother country, and gradually climbed out of these near slum conditions to make better lives for themselves either elsewhere in Rochfield or by moving further afield.

With the upturn in the demand for fine worsted cloth from the Far East, both Croziers and Featherstones had increased their workforce and some of the residents of the Blackwood and Oakridge found themselves in a position to move up the property ladder, even if it only meant renting a better property in a better part of Rochfield.

Others, made redundant from earlier factory closures, who didn't wish to spend the rest of their days relying on benefits had been forced to find other work, or create their own employment. Sutherland admired the way that many had built up small businesses supplying the needs of their less enterprising neighbours.

"We'll discuss details after the morning briefing, and see if we can put it in place for first thing tomorrow," he suggested.

* * *

Richard Tillsworth arrived at the offices of The Mutual Cap and opened up as he did most mornings.

It was Thursday. The day when the expenses got paid. 'No matter what happens,' he thought, 'Thursday is a good day.'

He would spend the morning prospecting. The mining of information, of making phone calls to set up appointments for the following week. As an old hand in the insurance business had once told him – 'Prospecting is like shaving. If you don't do it you end up like a tramp.' That was something he had no wish to do.

For him, prospecting wasn't just about finding new clients; it was also about recruiting new sales people. He had heard a news item about a factory closure in Sheffield. He needed to start an advertising campaign in the local press. A two pronged attack. One to get people to invest their redundancy payments, another to trawl for likely sales people.

He had a couple of clients to see on the Saturday morning. Hard working people with long commutes who could not spare the time to see him during the week. He didn't mind putting himself out for clients like that. After seeing them, hopefully with some extra business in his pocket, the rest of the weekend was his. His and Rachael's, and the children.

The clocks went back on the Sunday morning, almost a week earlier than usual which was why the half-term break ended with Halloween, rather than starting with it. It did mean that they would be back at school for Guy Fawkes Night. He had arranged to take a few days off to look after them while Rachael worked. She had arranged to take the last three days off. They would do something as a family on the Wednesday, but hadn't decided what yet.

He collected the mail from the box in the lobby, made his way to the top floor, sorting the mail as he walked and unlocked the door that led past the reception area to the rest of the offices. There was less than usual.

That seemed to be the trend over the past couple of years.

He placed the general mail and the junk mail on the receptionist's desk. The sales mail he put on the table in the sales office and Harmsbury's mail he put in the tray that hung at the director's door.

Tillsworth unlocked his own door, went in and closed it behind him. He was always glad of the ten or fifteen minutes of peace and quiet at the start of the day. He stood at the window and looked out over Rochfield as he did most mornings. The day was sunny, and the forecast for the weekend was for dry weather. Maybe he'd take the kids for a walk along the river. They liked that, and there was always plenty of wildlife to look out for.

He heard footsteps in the corridor, and the door to Harmsbury's office being unlocked. That was his cue to take his seat behind his desk and open his mail.

He had barely started reading the material in front of him when there was a knock on his door.

"Come in," he said, looking up.

Harmsbury entered, "Have you seen Adams?" Harmsbury sounded troubled.

"The book keeper? No, his office was locked when I came past." Tillsworth looked at his watch. It was already after ten past nine, and the office staff should all be at their desks. "Have you asked reception?"

"He hasn't passed them," Harmsbury answered. "I've tried his door. It's still locked. Do you have a spare key for it?"

Tillsworth pulled the office keys from his pocket, selected a key and handed the keys to his boss. "This one should do it. Don't forget to bring them back. I'll need them to lock up. Oh, and you know I'm off on Monday, Tuesday and Wednesday?"

"Yes, I haven't forgotten. I'll unlock and take the Monday meeting. Anything special that I should know?"

"Keep an eye on Sally Pickton. I think she could be quite good with the right encouragement.

See what you think, okay?"

"Will do." Harmsbury departed with the key and was back minutes later.

He handed the keys back to Tillsworth, "Well he's not in his office. I'll have to phone his home. See what's keeping him. I need figures from him."

"Not to mention the expenses payments!" Tillsworth said under his breath.

He watched Harmsbury's retreating back and wondered what was so urgent that Harmsbury needed to speak to their temporary book keeper. With a shrug, he turned back to the latest sales literature from head office. More stuff to learn up on and to arrange training courses for. At least it promised some sort of future in the pipeline.

Jeremy Harmsbury returned to his office, pulled the sheet of paper that he had written Tommy Adams's details on towards him and reached for the phone.

The number rang out unanswered. After half a minute of listening to the brrr-brrr of the ringing tone, Harmsbury hung up. He checked his Rolodex and dialled the number for the Accountancy and Book Keeping agency that Adams worked for.

After a brief conversation with the head of the business he determined that they had not heard from Adams, and had no reason to think that he wouldn't turn up for work, albeit late. They suggested that Harmsbury phone the house again after another half an hour, and if they heard anything they would phone him.

Harmsbury explained that he needed figures

from Adams, and that Thursday was the day that the expenses were paid to the permanent staff.

The Agency agreed to send somebody competent round if there was no sign of Adams by eleven o'clock.

It was the best that Harmsbury could hope for.

After half an hour he phoned Adams's house again with no result.

He knew that Adams liked to walk to work if the weather was fine – which it was, so there was no suggestion that his car might have broken down.

He decided to go round to the house and see if there was any sign of a car in the driveway. At the same time he would be able to check if there was any sign of Adams.

He advised Tillsworth of his intentions, and told reception to put any calls from the Agency through to Tillsworth's extension until he returned.

Navigating his way through the maze of streets on the eastern side of Rochfield, Harmsbury arrived at Adams's house. The car was in the drive, its bonnet cold. It had not been driven that morning.

Harmsbury leant on the doorbell. He could hear the Westminster chimes echoing behind the door. There was no response.

He looked around to see if there was any sign of nosey neighbours, twitching curtains or anybody he could ask if they had seen Tommy Adams. There was nobody.

He took a walk around the house trying to see

in through windows. What little that he could see provided no evidence that there was anybody at home.

Reluctantly he returned to his car. He sat at the wheel, keys in hand, wondering what route Adams might have taken if he had walked to work and failed to arrive. He tried to visualise what the most direct pedestrian route would be, started the car and drove slowly to the end of the road. There he had a choice of right or left. He had come from the left so he decided to turn right and take the next left. That street crossed several other streets before reaching the main road that would take him back to the one way system above the office.

There was no sign of Tommy Adams. Not that he had expected there to be. There were no parks or open spaces that he had had to skirt that Adams could have walked across.

Back at the office, he phoned the agency and informed them that Adams hadn't turned up, and could the agency send somebody round. All he could do was to wait for Adams's replacement to turn up. Sorting out the expenses would take priority over the information that he had asked Adams to get for him the previous evening. Hopefully the information would be in the accounts office or on the computer. He would wait until the expenses had been done before asking the replacement book keeper to help him find it.

Chapter 6

The raid on the Blackwood had been planned on the previous afternoon and those taking part knew exactly what they were expected to do and when they had to be in position. For most it meant an early start, and some overtime.

The family whose door they were about to knock lived right in the middle of the Blackwood and were known to have a number of people on the look out for obvious signs of police activity. As every vehicle in the police compound was probably known to them, the obvious liveried vehicles as well as the unmarked and personal vehicles, the chances of catching the Talbots unawares was pretty slim, but at seven fifteen in the morning, there was always a chance.

Sutherland arranged for back up vehicles to be kept at a distance unless required. At this point he didn't have a warrant to search any property, and in law the Talbot family could refuse to allow a search of the house in which they lived.

Mindful of this, all Sutherland wanted to do was take them in for questioning.

He would post constables in the estate where the front and rear of the property could be observed, and where known lock-ups belonging to the family were located. That way he hoped to prevent the movement of any items that they might be storing that might be stolen or the proceeds of crime.

It wasn't a perfect solution, but it was the law.

However, if someone did attempt to remove anything from any of these locations, the police would be within their rights to stop and arrest that person and confiscate anything that might be found as the offence was now being committed on public land. The person or persons arrested would also be charged as accessories to the original crime, or to attempting to pervert to course of justice.

He almost hoped that they would be stupid enough to try it.

He sat in his car while Simpson and three uniformed officers approached the house. Two other officers had approached from the rear in a coordinated manoeuvre to prevent any attempt by the brothers to evade the police.

Inspector Simpson hammered the door with his fist, "Police, open up!"

He was somewhat surprised when Stephen Talbot came to the door, dressed in jogging bottoms and a singlet. He was broad shouldered, muscular and sported an assortment of colourful tattoos.

"Inspector Simpson, you're up early this morning!" Talbot surveyed the three officers accompanying Simpson with disdain. "Sorry gents, we don't have enough mugs to offer you all tea."

Simpson heard the commotion at the back of the house.

"I presume young Eddie has met our colleagues?" he said matching Stephen Talbot's look of disdain.

"What's this all about, Mr Simpson?"

"We thought that you and your brother might like to take a friendly ride down to the police station to answer a few questions, that's all," Simpson replied calmly.

"But we haven't done owt, Mr Simpson."

"Then you won't have much to say, will you?" Simpson looked at him. "Stephen, do yourself a favour, and your brother. Come quietly, or make trouble, it's all the same to me."

"Are you arresting me, Mr Simpson?"

"Do you want me to?"

"Yeah!" Stephen tried staring Simpson down.

It didn't work.

Simpson called to the back of the house, "Bring Eddie with you, lads."

The two police constables escorted the unhappy younger brother, already in cuffs, to the front door.

"What's he done to warrant the cuffs?" Simpson asked.

"Tried to take a swing at me," PC Elliott said. On every count, PC Elliott was every inch as big as Eddie, and almost as big as Stephen.

"Stupid bugger!" Stephen muttered to his younger brother. "Well Mr Simpson, are you going to arrest me or not?" Always defiant.

A DEADLY ACCOUNT

"Stephen Talbot," and turning to the younger brother, "Edward Talbot, I am arresting you on suspicion of theft, aggravated burglary, and assault . . ." he went on to recite the caution which both men probably knew by heart. "Whistle up the van, Charlie, will you. Take our guests down to the station; make them comfortable until I get there."

"Ma, make that phone call," Stephen shouted as he was led away down the short path with his brother towards the police van that had appeared from the Oakridge Estate.

Simpson knew that Mrs Talbot would phone the family solicitor as soon as nine o'clock came round.

She stood in the hall, hands on hips, "I take it you don't have a search warrant, Inspector Simpson?"

"I don't. Would you like to show me and my officers round while we're here? It'll save coming back later."

"Fuck off! Get the hell out of my house!" was the not unexpected response. Simpson laughed, turned on his heels and left without saying anything.

He didn't have to. The presence of a police patrol car at each end of the rear alley, and two police constables at the front of the house on the communal space told Mrs Talbot all she needed to know. Simpson would be back with his warrant. Just as well that her sons weren't stupid enough to stash anything under her roof.

She would make a few phone calls. One to

their solicitor who would delight in earning another hefty fee and others to people who could make stuff disappear.

Bad move, but just what Sutherland had been hoping for.

* * *

Back at Rochfield Central Stephen and Eddie Talbot sat in separate interview rooms waiting for the questioning to begin, to which their stock answer born out of years of practise that had started when they were learning their trade as juvenile offenders, 'No comment' would be iterated endlessly.

With their solicitors present, one for each of them, the cost of which would come out of the public purse in the form of legal aid, Sutherland and Simpson wanted to keep the process as short as possible.

After a few preliminary questions to establish identity for the taped records each brother was formally charged.

The formal proceedings were interrupted at one point when Sutherland was called out to take a call from Ed Richardson.

"Good news Andrew!" Ed rumbled down the phone.

"What have you found?"

"You were right about Ma Talbot trying to get rid of the evidence. A couple of their dumber lackeys were arrested in possession of stolen goods that matched the lists from the break-ins that you had suggested. Better than that, the boys' finger prints are on several of the items. Whether they did the actual break-ins I can't say for certain, but they certainly handled the items. So at worst you'll get them for receiving."

"Good to hear that, Ed," Sutherland said. Richardson was right on that score. The fingerprints didn't tie them to the robberies, and no fingerprints had been found at any of the crime scenes, but at one crime scene there had been a potential witness. A night watchman had been assaulted. He had made a statement from his hospital bed the following afternoon. What he had said was full of the usual if, buts and maybes, but he had said that he had heard two of the men speak and had a fair idea of their general build and another interesting item. He had seen the edge of a tattoo between one of the men's sleeves and the gloves he was wearing.

Whether the night watchman could put the positive bits of knowledge together to link Stephen Talbot with the crime remained to be seen. Sutherland was going to hold back on that piece of information for the present.

He would press charges against both men on the receiving at this stage. The men arrested trying to move the stolen property would be charged with possession of goods knowing them to be stolen, of being accessories after the fact, and of attempting to pervert the course of justice.

With any luck one of the minions would try and make a deal with the police and drop the brothers in it. However, he wasn't hopeful. The brothers had their own painful ways of inspiring loyalty. That was another reason for keeping quiet about the night watchman at this stage. He knew that the court would probably release them on bail for the lesser charge of receiving, and he did not want to stir things up about them being liable to interfere with witnesses. They had never been known to skip bail before, so he wasn't worried about that.

Model citizens in that respect.

They would be bailed to appear before the magistrates on the following Monday morning.

The three men arrested in possession of the stolen goods were remanded at a detention facility until the following Monday morning for a later hearing. Remanding them was as much to ensure their safety as to make things easier for the Rochfield police.

* * *

At Rochfield police headquarters on Monday morning Inspector Simpson was briefing Sergeant Cranfield for the Magistrates Court hearing of the cases against the Talbots that would take place in an hour's time. After briefing her, he turned to DC Jack Wilson to brief him for the hearings against the three men that had been arrested for trying to remove the Talbots' stolen property.

That hearing would follow immediately after the Talbots and it was important that the Talbots and their three accomplices should be kept apart.

Simpson was under no illusion that the Talbots

would have been made aware of the arrests of the other three, but their largesse did not extend to providing legal support to the lower ranks. All he was concerned with was preventing any direct contact between them.

With the briefings over, he headed upstairs to Sutherland's office.

At the Magistrates Court, the proceedings were routine. The defendants were asked to confirm their names and addresses. The charges were read out. Pleas of not guilty were entered. Sergeant Cranfield said that the police had evidence that linked the accused to the crimes. Because one of the charges related to grievous bodily harm to the night watchman at the warehouse the case would have to be heard in the Crown Court at a later date.

Bail was not opposed and the two brothers were led away and allowed to leave the courthouse with their family and hangers on.

Sergeant Cranfield watched to see that both Talbots had left the building and driven away before returning to the courtroom to watch the proceedings against the three defendants who were up on the lesser charge of handling stolen property. As they had been caught in the act all three pleaded guilty and, because they were previous offenders they were sentenced to six months detention.

It was a good result and suited the defendants and the police. It kept them away from the Talbots.

Sergeant Cranfield and DC Wilson walked the

half mile back to the police station rather than summon a police driver to collect them

"Do you suppose that we would have caught them if it hadn't been for Young Eric and his computers?" Wilson asked as they walked.

"In the end, maybe, but it would have taken longer and by then God knows how many more crimes they would have committed," she replied.

"Be nice if he could link a load more crimes to them," Wilson said, "That would help the clear-up figures a bit, wouldn't it?"

"Keep the Chief Constable happy, too."

They returned to the CID room to see if anything interesting had happened while they were at court.

Young Eric and Vikki Gibson were still working through the endless pile of case files.

"Anything strange or startling, Eric?" Wilson asked as he approached PC Young's desk.

Eric looked up, "Nothing so far. How did it go?"

"My three pleaded guilty and got six months. Couldn't get them to implicate the Talbots though. Just said that they had got the stuff off a guy they met in a pub and had been allowed to use the lock-up by Eddie Talbot."

"What did the magistrates make of that?" he asked.

"Seeing as they'd just heard the two brothers pleading not guilty to having stolen the stuff in the first place, raised eyebrows and sharp looks towards Sergeant Cranfield," Wilson told him with some glee.

"So the connection wasn't lost on him."

"No, I think they would have liked to have heard my three first, and then the Talbots. They mightn't have been so quick to grant bail."

Young Eric nodded, "But not a bad morning's work."

"Any chance that you can tie more cases into the Talbots?" It sounded more like a request than a serious question, and the implications were not lost on Eric or Vikki.

"We'll keep feeding the information in, and see what happens, Jack. That's the best way," he replied.

Wilson shrugged and went to his desk.

"I think that he . . ." Vikki began.

"I know exactly what he was on about, Vikki. I'm not going to play that game. We continue to feed the information in, just like I told DC Wilson," he whispered.

Sergeant Cranfield, seeing that Inspector Simpson wasn't at his desk asked DI Lawson where he was.

"Upstairs with Sutherland, Maggie. No doubt the SS are busy plotting something!"

Maggie laughed and headed to Sutherland's office to report on the morning's results.

* * *

The weekend had been showery and grey. Parents with children just starting half-term hoped that it would dry up for the coming week.

The local football team had won their home game by two goals to one. The local rugby league team had won their away game and climbed a little nearer to the promotion zone, but it was still early in the season. A better than average weekend for Rochfield sports fans.

Simpson sat across from Sutherland, catching up on the weekend reports, prioritising them for the week ahead.

DCI Sutherland was reading through his morning mail when the phone rang.

"Sutherland. Yes Alice," he wrote on a pad while she spoke, "Right away, thanks."

He put the receiver back on its cradle, pulled the sheet off the pad.

Sergeant Cranfield knocked on his door just as he was about to phone for her.

"Perfect timing, Maggie! A body's been found. Middle aged man in running gear. Found in the river below Meadowland. Caught up in some overhanging branches."

"Suspicious?"

"Could be. Won't know until we get there," Sutherland sounded almost pleased. Pleased to have something that might exercise the mind more than the endless paperwork and petty crime, not that some poor unfortunate was now dead instead of enjoying the rest of his life. "Doctor Ellis is on

A DEADLY ACCOUNT

her way," he said as he headed for the door.

"Who else do you want, sir?" Maggie asked.

"At this stage, nobody. Probably a bit premature for the three of us to be going, but I'm going stir crazy stuck in the office. I need to stretch my legs, get a bit of fresh air, enjoy a nice autumn morning. You can tell Dean and me how your court cases went while we drive," Sutherland said.

They took Sutherland's car. DCI Sutherland drove; Sergeant Cranfield sat in the front passenger seat and relayed the brief details of both her case and the hearing against the three stooges. Simpson sat in the back listening over her shoulder.

Sutherland complimented her on how well it had been handled, "So there was no chance that the Talbots could interfere with them?" he asked.

"No sir, but that probably won't stop them from trying once they are locked up," Maggie answered.

"A chance we'll have to take. I'll get on to the prison and request to be kept informed of any visitors they may have," Sutherland said.

"They probably won't be so direct," Simpson said from the back, "They'll probably know some of the other prisoners and use them to get at our trio."

"Aye, laddie, you're probably right, but that's beyond our reach," Sutherland said. "Looks like the media got here before us," he said. He could see the local hack, John Mansfield trying to blag his way past the constable on the police cordon.

He pulled up at the side of the road leading down to the riverside carpark.

Sutherland got out, waved his warrant card obviously at the constable, as did Simpson and Sergeant Cranfield. It was done more to emphasise to Mansfield that without a warrant card he wasn't getting any closer to the crime scene, than for the benefit of Constable Tom Jones who knew them all by sight.

Mansfield had chosen the wrong man to try and get past. Constable Jones had driven for each of them on different occasions, and wasn't going to risk getting on the wrong side of them for Mansfield. He lifted the tape, watched them bend under it and noted their names and the time in his log.

The three detectives approached the area car. Constable Tate was standing beside it waiting for them.

"Who found the body, Charlie?" Sutherland asked.

"Man walking his dog along the river path," he said pointing to a man with a black Labrador who was standing to the side of the other police car talking to Constable Gibson.

Also in the carpark were Dr Ellis's Land Rover Discovery and the mortuary van with its rear door open and the two mortuary attendants waiting for Dr Ellis's signal to come and remove the body.

"Well, we've come this far, we better go and have a look," Sutherland said. He turned to Constable Tate, "Do we have an identification?"

"No sir. He's wearing running gear and a good

pair of trainers. Better prepared for running than most of the joggers we see. I'd say he was doing some serious training."

"Pity he didn't think to carry ID," Sutherland grumbled.

"If he's into serious training, it won't take long to find out who he is," Simpson said. "A quick check round the gyms, sports clubs and the like should put a name to a face."

"I'll let you handle that," Sutherland said as they made their way down to the riverside.

Dr Helen Ellis, dressed in her white Noddy Suit and Wellington boots, was bending beside the corpse. She looked up as they approached.

"Welcome to the party," she said and stood up.

"I take it that he didn't just fall in?" Sutherland asked.

"Could have, I suppose," she replied in a voice that indicated that she thought that to be highly unlikely.

"Enlighten us, Helen," Sutherland said.

"He appears to have been hit quite hard on the back of the neck, and before you ask, it doesn't look like something that might have happened after he fell in, if indeed he did fall. I'll be able to tell you more after I've had a good look at him back in the autopsy suite."

"How long ago, d'ye think?" he queried.

"Four, maybe five days by the state of the body," Helen hazarded a guess.

"Nothing to indicate where he entered the water?"

"Probably not round here, further upstream,"

she suggested, "There's nothing immediately evident to suggest where it happened."

Sutherland knew what that meant. A lot of man hours spent searching along the bank from above the town, through the town and down both river banks to the point where the body was found.

Henderson would love that.

"Nothing more to be done here, I take it?" Sutherland asked.

"No. I'll get him moved to the Infirmary." Dr Ellis signalled her attendants to come down with the stretcher and collect the body. Sutherland, Simpson and Sergeant Cranfield took a good look at the deceased to see if he looked familiar.

Definitely not one of their acquaintances. Not one of the criminal fraternity that had met his end in the river.

They watched as the body was placed in the black body bag and lifted onto the stretcher and, with Dr Ellis, followed the attendants back to the carpark.

"When are you planning to do the autopsy, Helen," Sutherland asked.

"I'll get some lunch first, and be ready to start at two o'clock," she replied.

"I'll be there. Can you get a photograph, head shot, so that we can show it around, see if we can get an identification?" Sutherland asked.

"I'll do that before I go for lunch. It should be ready by three if the photo lab isn't too busy," she said as she got into her car, "See you later."

They watched her drive away before walking back to Sutherland's car.

Mansfield had remained standing by the tape hoping to get some first hand information.

Sutherland decided not to ignore him, "An unidentified male, aged early forties. We hope to have more for you after the body has been fully examined."

"How did he die, Chief Inspector?"

"Until the pathologist has done her stuff we can't say for certain, Mr Mansfield, but we can't rule out foul play at this stage."

"Will there be a briefing later?"

"Depends what she finds. Can't say more until then," Sutherland said.

Mansfield knew better than to press his luck. It was rare that the Chief Inspector gave him any information. He headed back to his car. The other police cars were let through the cordon. Constable Jones would remain on duty to prevent access to the public until all necessary searching had been completed.

Sutherland went straight to Henderson's office after returning to Rochfield Central. Henderson listened to his Chief Inspector's news and considered the implications.

"So, no chance that he fell in by accident?" Henderson asked, more in hope than expectation.

"Dr Ellis doesn't seem to think so. I'll know better after the autopsy," Sutherland informed him.

"Going yourself?" Henderson asked.

"I need Simpson and Cranfield to start organising the legwork. We need to find out who he is, where he went in, where he comes from, as much as we can about him. That way, if he has been murdered, we'll have some idea of why he might have been killed," Sutherland said.

"Going to take a lot of manpower to scour both riverbanks," Henderson said absently, "But, if it needs to be done, then we'll just have to hope we get lucky early on, Sutherland." Henderson would have liked to make that a direct order, but even he knew that luck didn't come to order, not even for Sutherland.

"Yes sir." There wasn't much more that Sutherland could say.

* * *

Sutherland arrived at the Rochfield Infirmary mortuary to witness the autopsy and protect the chain of evidence. DC Wilson accompanied him.

Wilson's sergeant, Jimmy Grieves was on leave and Sutherland was glad to have the extra manpower on his team. DI Peter Lawson and his DC, Eddie Fowler, were following up on new leads thrown up by PC Young and Vikki Gibson's work with the new computer system.

"Thanks for letting me come along, sir," Wilson said as they entered the room.

Helen looked up from her external examination of the body.

"Perfect timing, gentlemen. I'm just about to start," she said. "His clothes are on the table over there." She indicated the small pile of clothes with the trainers sitting neatly on top. "Nothing in the pockets."

"Nothing?" Sutherland was surprised, "No keys?"

"Nothing."

"Then there must be somebody waiting at home for his return, or at whatever sports club he might be a member of."

"But sir," Wilson said, "If somebody was waiting for him, you would have thought that they would have made enquiries when he didn't return from his run."

"Exactly, Jack," Sutherland said, "Unless the killer took them."

"Which means that the killer knew him or where he lived, otherwise what use would a set of keys be?" Jack Wilson said.

"Unless there were car keys and the killer wanted to steal the car?" Dr Ellis suggested.

"Ah, that's what I like to hear! Nothing has to be simple, does it? Always has to be some sort of mystery to give us extra work," Sutherland said.

"Come off it, Andrew. If it was simple we wouldn't need detectives!" Helen said with a slight laugh.

Sutherland nodded, "Jack, bag that stuff up and label it before we leave. Richardson and his SOCOs will need to give it a thorough going over to see if it tells us anything."

"Yes sir."

Sutherland and Wilson concentrated on the work that Dr Ellis was doing, listening intently to her commentary.

She had pulled the hanging microphone down, checked that it was on and began.

"The body is that of a white male aged late thirties to early forties. Weight 77.5 kilos, height 175 centimetres. Well nourished, no distinguishing features, birthmarks or tattoos. Dark hair, brown eyes. Muscle tone not well developed," she looked at Sutherland, "Which suggests that our victim along with his recently bought fancy trainers and running gear was a relative newcomer to the world of the healthy lifestyle."

The look was not lost on the Chief Inspector.

"Aye, Helen, point taken, but I think I'm a bit too old to be going down that road. I'll just try sticking to the diet."

Sutherland's wife, Jill, and Helen attended the same church, Rochfield Methodist. Jill and Helen were always trying to conspire to improve Sutherland's general fitness and waistline. As long as he passed the annual medical, Andrew wasn't as concerned for his health as they were.

Dr Ellis shook her head slightly and continued her examination of the body.

"There are no signs of defence wounds . . ."

"Which suggests an attack that was totally unexpected to the victim," Sutherland said.

"Looks that way," she said as she examined the hands carefully. "I'd say that our victim was in some sort of clerical job. No sign of the roughening of the skin that one would get with manual labour, and not over cared for either. Not likely to be a medical professional for example."

"But you've probably met most of the medical professionals in the district at one time or another,

Helen."

"Unless he doesn't come from here," she pointed out.

"In which case why would he be out running at night?" Sutherland asked.

"Maybe he's a visitor," Wilson suggested, "Staying at a hotel. That way, he wouldn't need keys."

"A possibility," Sutherland nodded, "Follow that up Jack. Get a copy of the photograph and hawk it round the hotels."

She continued her examination down to the feet and then, with her assistant, turned the body over and began the examination of the back from the feet up to the head. The only point of real interest was the wound to the base of the skull.

Helen pulled down the overhead lighted magnifying glass and started to probe gently round the edges of the wound.

The fast flowing River Roche, swollen by the heavy rain from the previous week and the heavy weekend showers that continued to drain off the moors above the town, had washed it clean.

"There are no traces of blood on the fabric of his jogging top collar, Andrew, but this injury is definitely ante-mortem, and the probable cause of death. I'll not know until I've had a good look at his lungs, but nothing suggests drowning as the cause at this stage."

"What sort of a weapon?"

"Not a bar or pipe, nothing smooth like a baseball bat. Whatever it was, it was used with some force, but left no traces. I'll need to open him up to see for certain what damage it caused, but it looks like his neck has been broken."

"What about the time of death?"

"The time spent immersed in cold river water plays hell with temperature readings. Hard to be precise, but I'm sticking with my original estimate of four to five days. I may be able to put a closer figure on it after I've examined the stomach contents, but don't hold your breath."

The long time window would only exclude a suspect whose whereabouts could be verified for the entire period.

"Pity he wasn't wearing a watch that stopped when it hit the water!" Sutherland said.

"He was wearing a watch," Dr Ellis said, "A good one. It's still going."

"No help there then." Sutherland was disappointed.

Dr Ellis completed her external examination.

This was the point where, had he been present; Inspector Simpson would have left her to it, content to listen in on the speaker in her office.

They were in a relationship that suited both of them, but nothing would induce Dean Simpson to stand and watch her delving into the inner workings of the human body.

Sutherland had seen it all before. Too many times to be queasy about it, but every time he watched he was amazed and saddened in equal measure. Amazed at the seeming complexity of the inner workings of the human body and amazed at what stories it could tell in death. Saddened that each time he saw a body on the

A DEADLY ACCOUNT

table it meant that another family had lost a relative in less than natural circumstances and it would be up to him and people like him to find out why and to secure justice for the bereaved and the victim.

DC Wilson stood back a short distance but was able to observe enough of the autopsy to be glad that it wasn't something he had to do on a regular basis.

At the end of the proceedings Dr Ellis was no closer to a more exact time of death. The deceased had not eaten since a lunch of pasta and salad, few traces of which remained. Not enough to determine how much time had elapsed between ingestion and death, and certainly no use in determining how long before the body was found and the time of death.

"Sorry, Andrew nearest I can say with any certainty would be Wednesday evening. I know how important a more precise answer would have been, All that I can tell you with certainty is that he didn't drown." she said.

"Not your fault Helen," Andrew said. "We'll just have to work harder at the coal face, see what nuggets of truth we can dig out."

Sutherland and Wilson left her to tidy the corpse and return it to the chiller.

Wilson carried the sealed bag into which the victim's few personal effects had been placed.

"I'll let Ed know that these are ready for collection," Wilson said as he placed the bag onto the floor between his feet.

Sutherland just nodded as he started the car.

Chapter 7

Detective Inspector Simpson, having been tasked with canvassing all gymnasiums, sports clubs and fitness centres put together a list and divided it up. He had grouped the facilities together geographically to keep the travelling to a minimum.

He gave half to Sergeant Cranfield and took the other half himself. Helen Ellis's photographer had managed to rush through a set of photographs of the dead man and get them to Rochfield Central before three o'clock.

Armed with a list and a photograph each, they headed out to cover their territories.

Simpson's first stop was at the new fitness centre. He pulled up outside the modern glass and block structure with its garish sign in bright lime green and pink declaring it to be Rochfield Gymnasium and Health Spa, and noted the preponderance of small sports cars and GTI hatchbacks in the carpark.

Rochfield's yuppies were clinging to their youth regardless of the cost.

The young, tanned, fit looking girl at the reception desk momentarily tagged him as a prospective new customer, but changed her mind when he produced his warrant card, "DI Simpson, Rochfield CID. I need to know if the gentleman in this photograph was a recent member here."

"Was?" The girl's interest was aroused.

"Yes. Was." Simpson pushed the glossy photograph across the counter.

She recoiled slightly, "He's dead!" It was a statement, not a question.

"Did you know him?"

"No, he's not a member here. I'm sure of that," she said.

Simpson sensed a 'but'.

"But?"

"I think he was here seeing about membership."

"When would that have been, miss?"

"About a week or two ago. Not sure. Last Saturday, or the one before, maybe. I'll ask Scott. He's our senior personal trainer. Scott usually talks to prospective clients."

"Thank you," Simpson said and stood with the photograph in his hand, while she put a call out for Scott to come to the front desk.

A couple of minutes later a tall, well muscled man close in age to Simpson, with a mane of blond hair approached down the corridor that obviously led to the inner workings of the enterprise.

"Hi, I'm Scott Nelson. Can I help you, Mr . . .?"

"Detective Inspector Simpson, Rochfield CID," Simpson handed Nelson the photograph. "Have you seen this man before?"

Nelson looked at the photograph, nodded and handed it back. "Yes, Inspector, he was here Saturday before last. Just making enquiries about the facilities and membership. He didn't join, though." And now he never will, Nelson rightly surmised.

"Did he give you a name?"

"No, as I said, he didn't join, so no form filling." Put off by the price, Simpson guessed.

"Right, thank you Mr Nelson. I'll not take up any more of your time."

Back in his car, Simpson looked at the next address. Rochfield Boxing Club. He knew it of old, had trained there himself when he was a boy, and remembered it with fondness. He hadn't been back through the doors in years, and wondered if any of the old gang continued to use it.

The club, housed in a disused church a few hundred yards from the gates of Featherstone's Mill, as it had been for over forty years, had a small carpark at the front. Simpson pulled up outside, got out of the car and looked around him. There was more ivy clinging to the building than he recalled, and the place looked in need of a coat of paint. The double front doors, once a bright blue were a faded relic of their past. He could see where a bodged repair had been done round the lock, and remembered hearing about a break in over the summer.

He pushed open the door and walked in. The well remembered smell of warm bodies, sweat, liniment, and leather all mingled together. That

A DEADLY ACCOUNT

and a faint trace of cigar smoke. Castellas, if he remembered correctly.

'Blokes' Pringle was in his office.

'Blokes' was the club's owner and trainer's nick name. He called everybody a bloke – even the few girls that he now trained. Simpson wasn't sure what Pringle's real given name was. Everybody called him 'Blokes'.

Pringle looked up at the sounds of approaching footsteps. To nobody in particular, since the place was empty, he said "Scarper blokes, it's the law!"

"Hi ya, Blokes. How's the fight game?" Simpson said.

"Bloody awful, Mr Simpson. The girls are better fighters than the boys these days!" He shook Dean's outstretched hand.

"What's with the Mr Simpson routine? Dean was good enough when you and I were a lot younger and you tried to teach me the noble art."

"Ah, the good old days. You could have been quite good if you'd stuck at it. Surprised you didn't keep it up in the force."

Most Police Divisions had their share of boxers in the ranks. They would compete as amateurs in the Police Boxing Tournaments each year, but Simpson hadn't been interested in being used as a punch bag. He knew his limitations. Sparring in a gym was one thing; fighting was another. Any fighting he had had to do was strictly street fighting. Not even a nod to the Marquis of Queensbury.

"What can I do for you Dean?"

Simpson handed the photo of the dead man

over. Blokes looked at it for several moments before handing it back with a shake of his head.

"Never seen him, Dean. I take it he didn't die of natural causes?"

"Looking like murder, Blokes. We pulled him out of the river."

"Sad," Blokes said shaking his head again. "Sorry I can't be of more help, Dean."

"Oh well, on to the next one. We're covering all training facilities in the district. Seems he'd recently taken up running."

"Oh? How can you tell?" Blokes asked.

"The equipment he was wearing was all quite new, which suggests that he's probably a recent convert to health and beauty!"

"I wish you luck! A lot of people are just taking it up for the hell of it. You don't need a gym for that," Blokes pointed out.

"Got to start somewhere," Dean said as he waved a farewell.

* * *

Detective Sergeant Cranfield wasn't having any better luck.

Her first visit was to Rochfield Rugby League Club's grounds and training facility out beyond the Meadowland Estate, not far from where the body had been recovered. It was located on a piece of flat land that had been graded out of the hillside the other side of the road from the river. Its sloping west side gave a natural bank of terracing. The terracing on the eastern side roofed over the offices, changing rooms, indoor training facilities and the club's bar and restaurant. The club was semi-professional and played in the Northern League, hoping someday to get to the top and break into one of the premier league divisions. Maybe someday they would get to play at Wembley.

The club was well supported and allowed full members to use the training facilities two days each week with the club's professional coaching staff to assist. Some of the full members had gone on in the past to play for the club.

The receptionist looked up, "Can I help you?"

Sergeant Cranfield flashed her badge, "DS Cranfield, Rochfield CID. I'm trying to identify a body. We think he may have taken up some sort of fitness regime recently. Is there anybody here who could have a look at a photograph, see if they recognise him?"

"I know most of the members here, Sergeant. They all have to check in here before using the facilities. Maybe I could help."

Maggie handed over the glossy print. The girl recoiled slightly.

"He's dead?"

Good observation.

"Yes. Does he seem familiar?"

"Sorry, no."

"We think he might be a fairly recent member, if he has been training here."

The girl shook her head slowly before handing the print back.

"We haven't had any new members join since

the April Big Sign Up. Places are limited."

Maggie remembered the campaign. It had come at the end of the season after the club had narrowly missed reaching the dizzy heights that would lead to promotion. The club hoped that, with more support and more funds, they could buy a couple of game changing players.

"Any chance that somebody who signed up then would only just have started using the facilities?"

"No. All of the men who were lucky in the draw for places have been coming regularly ever since. I'm sorry I can't be of more help."

"No worries." Maggie put the photo back in the envelope, thanked the girl and went back to her car.

Next on her list was the Hockey and Cricket Club. It was on her way back towards Rochfield, between Meadowland and the start of the town proper.

Unlike the rugby club its premises were very modest. A long low building housing an office, changing rooms, a kitchen for team teas – used mostly by Rochfield Cricket Club, and a small gymnasium with circuit training facilities which the players used when it was too wet to train outdoors. There was also a small bar and recreation area where members could hold entertainment evenings and invite their guests and enjoy a drink.

The only people on the premises at that time of the day were the Club Secretary and the caretaker who also acted as bar manager and was busy stocking the bar for the evening.

She showed the photograph to both men. Neither recognised the face.

After thanking them she returned to her car. Next on her list was the town's leisure centre.

* * *

After making sure that the bagged and labelled items from Dr Ellis's autopsy had been correctly signed for by one of the SOCOs, DC Wilson took one of the victim's photographs from the small pile on Simpson's desk and headed into the town to show it round the hotels. He started with The Lion and had some sort of luck.

They didn't have a name, the man hadn't been a resident, but two of the restaurant staff remembered seeing him dining with a guest about a week earlier.

It took some time to arrange for the information to be extracted that would place the victim with a specific guest, but the restaurant manager hoped that, if the meal had been put on a room account, they would be able to trace it and pass the information to CID.

"I know it's urgent, Constable, but the office staff have gone home, and I'm short staffed as it is. The best I can do is to get it to you tomorrow morning. It'll take time to go through all the receipts and check them against resident records."

Wilson had to settle for that. He looked at his watch. Half an hour to go until his shift ended. He wouldn't have time to go back to the station, get his car and drive out to the next nearest hotel. If the restaurant manager came up with the information he wouldn't need to.

* * *

Simpson's next visit was to the Golf and Country Club that also had a flourishing tennis club in the grounds. He drove in through the ornate gates, once the entrance to a large country house and cruised slowly up the drive, admiring the well kept grounds, the greens and fairways looking, as always, immaculate.

As a sport, golf held no fascination for Simpson. He admired the skill of those who excelled at it, much as he admired the skill of top snooker or darts players. As a sport though, he considered it on a par with chess.

He parked his Sierra Cosworth between a Jaguar XJ6 and a Porsche 911. It didn't look out of place.

As with the posh new health and fitness establishment that he had visited first, this place reeked of money. It was hard, looking round, to get any impression that most of the country was going through one of its routine periods of recession in the boom and bust economy that had become the norm. The current upturn in the fortunes of the local textile trade being a bit of an exception.

The boxing club had shown the other face of the coin.

Most of the members that he passed gave him a

A DEADLY ACCOUNT

cursory glance and typecast him as staff, or not one of them. One or two knew him by sight.

Whispered comments. Wild speculations. They assumed that his visit had something to do with the Country Club.

As with the first two places on his list, The Rochfield Country Club was a dead end.

Simpson returned to his car and headed across town to the grounds of Rochfield Athletic, the town's Division Three contenders.

Like many of the football clubs in Britain it had been set up during the latter half of the Industrial Revolution. As factory employment became the way of life for the greater mass of the working population, and various Acts of Parliament had gradually reduced the length of the working week to the point where most workers had free time on a Saturday afternoon, enlightened and well meaning employers had started to provide sports facilities for their workers and others living in the vicinity.

With four main employers at that time, two had banded together to provide Rochfield Athletic with grounds and facilities. One of the companies had been Featherstone's Woollen Mills, but with a Rugby League Club of that name already playing in Yorkshire it had been decided to call the football club after the name of the town.

The other two major employers had provided the cricket club and the rugby league club.

That all four were well supported a century later was commendable and now, with a greater emphasis on fitness and participation were enjoying something of a revival. This was less evident at the grounds of Rochfield Athletic where the active participation was limited to a select few. Their revenue came from the league and supporters and tended to reflect the team's fortunes. If the team was doing well, the club was doing well.

To judge from the new building work going on, Rochfield Athletic was in the ascendancy once again.

Simpson followed the temporary signs, weaving his way round scaffolding and down passages lined with polythene sheeting behind which construction was noisily taking place, to the temporary offices.

It took a further five minutes to find anybody and that was the bar manager. He looked at the photograph but did not recognise the dead man.

"Sorry, Gov, but if he's new here I wouldn't necessarily get to see him – unless he were a regular in't bar, like. You'd need to talk to t'training staff, and they's all gone for t'day. I reckon thee'd need t'come in't morning."

Another dead end, until the morning that was. He thanked the bar manager and left, hoping that Maggie was having better luck.

* * *

Maggie looked at her list, two more to go. The town's Municipal Leisure Centre and Rochfield Harriers, the town's running club. Knowing where their premises were located, but being unsure that they had any full time staff, she decided to try the leisure centre first.

Located down a side street near the bus station, she had to negotiate her way round the one way system. Being the middle of Rochfield's rush hour, this was a slow and frustrating journey. The road works that had sprung up in the town to effect repairs and upgrading to the town's Victorian sewerage system didn't help.

She carefully checked her rear view mirror and signalled before darting down the side street, carefully avoiding the pedestrians streaming towards the bus station. Rush hour was always the worst driving time. People more anxious to get home to a hot meal and the telly than to get there safely seemed to think they were invincible.

She pulled into the Leisure Centre carpark and headed into the 1960's glass and concrete building. She held the door open as a party of school-aged children, hair still damp, emerged and rushed past her, screaming and laughing. They were followed at a more leisurely pace by a gaggle of harassed looking mothers loaded down with games bags.

'Oh, the energy of youth!' Maggie thought as one of the mothers gave her an apologetic smile.

"Bloody birthday parties! I swear that every year will be the last one," she said by way of explanation.

"Rather you than me," Maggie replied.

The sugar rush and E-numbers of a birthday tea had not worn off by the look of it.

Maggie went up to the reception desk and

explained her presence.

The receptionist, one of three on duty looked at the photograph, shook her head and called the other two over.

"Yes, I think I've seen him here recently. Doesn't look very well in that photo, though,"

"Course not, he's dead isn't he!" the first receptionist informed her colleague.

"You'd best have a word with Gordy," the girl who recognised the dead man suggested. "He's our head instructor. He'll be able to give you all the details."

"And where will I find him?"

The girl looked at the clock, "At this time of the afternoon he'll be in the cafeteria most likely. Stoking up on his carbs before the evening crowd arrive. You can't miss him. Look for a big blond guy wearing a lilac and green track suit." Lilac and green were the town's corporate colours. The girl pointed to the sign to her left and Maggie retrieved the photograph.

"Thanks," she said and headed in the direction of the centre's cafeteria.

The description was sufficient to guide Maggie directly to the instructor's table.

He looked up as she approached. A slight look of annoyance crossed his face.

"DS Cranfield, Rochfield CID," Maggie said as she took a seat, "Sorry to have to interrupt your break. It'll only take a moment."

She pulled the photograph out of her folder and slid it across the table, watching the face all the time.

She saw him start as he picked up the glossy print. He looked up at her.

"He's dead?"

She nodded.

"Can you tell me anything about him? His name, anything?"

"How did he die?"

"We pulled him out of the river beyond the Meadowland estates earlier today. No ID on him, nothing to say who he was. All we know is that he's recently started exercising and was dressed in running gear."

"Let me finish this, and we'll go to my office. Do you want a tea or coffee?"

"I'm alright, thanks," she answered. "I'll need your name and address in case we need to get back to you."

"Gordon Tripp. Call me Gordy, everybody else does. The idea of a fitness instructor called Tripp tends to put some people off!"

She caught the humour in his voice, "Okay Gordy. Call me Maggie. Makes life easier." She wrote down his name and address and a contact number. "Can you remember his name, off hand?"

"Tommy something. I'd need to check his card. It has all his personal details," Gordy shovelled the last remnants of his pasta and sauce into his mouth, wiped the plate with a crust of bread, finished his power drink and stood up. "Follow me Maggie."

Passing the end of the serving counter he put his plate and cutlery down, and flipped the drink bottle into the recycling bin.

Maggie followed him down a short corridor and up a staircase to an upper corridor lined with doors. Gordy opened the third one and held it for her. It was a small office, the far wall taken up with a picture window looking out over the gymnasium and a door leading directly to it.

Everything was bathed in stark high-bay lighting. The room was as functional as an aircraft hanger and about the same size. Men and women of all ages and shapes were working out on equipment under the watchful eyes of three instructors.

Gordy crossed to a filing cabinet and opened a drawer.

"We file them by joining date for the first six months. After that we have usually got to know them or they've left. The cards go into either the dead file or into alphabetical order."

It seemed a very sensible system.

After a few seconds of flicking through the cards, Gordy extracted one.

"Thomas Adams," he passed the card over. Maggie wrote down all the details in her folder before handing it back.

"No next of kin?" She had noted that the space was empty.

"Divorced. No children. I think that he may have been getting back into shape to start the dating game again, but I could be wrong," Gordy said, "We chatted for a bit while I filled this in. I like to have some idea of what motivates a person to come here. It helps with training and with marketing."

"Did he say he had a specific reason?"

"Wanted to get fit and then try his luck with one of the Sunday League teams. Strictly amateur stuff. Seems he used to play a bit before he got married. I remember that he seemed rather bitter about it all."

Maggie sensed that Thomas, or Tommy Adams's marriage had gone really sour at some point and wondered who had been to blame.

"Right Gordy, thanks for this. At least we can now put a name to the face and start filling in the background. You don't know where he worked, do you?"

"Sorry, no. We didn't get round to talking about anything like that. Office type, I'd guess. Definitely not manual worker. Probably not executive or professional – they tend to go to that fancy new place or the Country Club."

She sensed a tinge of jealousy.

"Not thought of getting into that yourself?"

"Occasionally," he smiled. "Is it that obvious?"

"But you like your job here and your customers, those that stay, are really dedicated and not trying to impress anybody?"

"Something like that," this time he laughed, "My guess is that you are very good at your job, Maggie!"

"I try to be. Thanks again."

She left him to continue his evening's work and retraced her way back to her car.

"Delta Sierra Three-Seven to control," she said into her police issue radio.

"Come in Three-Seven," the static laden voice

came back.

"Can you contact Delta India Two-Four and ask him to meet me in the carpark of the Municipal Leisure Centre? Over."

"Roger that, Three-Seven,"

"Three-Seven, over," she said.

"Go ahead Three-Seven."

"You might like to inform Big Top One that we have a name, and let him know where I am in case he wants to follow this up, over."

"Roger that, Three-Seven."

"Three-Seven out." Maggie hung the microphone up and sat in her car looking at the photograph of the dead man for whom they now had a name and an address.

"Control to Three-Seven, over."

"Three-seven go ahead."

"Big Top One and Delta India Two-Four will join you at your location shortly."

"Three-Seven, Roger out."

It wasn't long before DCI Sutherland's car pulled in to a space beside her. Inspector Simpson was beside him.

Inspector Simpson indicated that she should join them in Sutherland's car.

"Seems that you've struck gold, lass," Sutherland said as she got in.

"Well, I have a name and an address." She handed over her notebook. Sutherland read it out.

"I take it you've locked your car, Sergeant?" he asked.

"Yes sir."

"Good. Wouldn't do to have it stolen, Maggie.

Let's go and see what we can find at his address."

Sutherland checked round him before pulling out and heading to the carpark exit.

* * *

Back at Rochfield Central Wilson heard that DS Cranfield had come up with a name and an address and uniforms had been called out for a house to house.

That suited Jack Wilson. He went up to the CID room, empty except for Young Eric and Vikki still working at their computers.

"No home to go to, Young Eric?" he asked as he entered.

"Just finishing up here," Eric said.

"Any further leads from your program?"

"Nothing yet, but it's early days."

Wilson put his notebook in his desk and locked it, "Right, that's me for the day. See you in the morning folks."

"Bye," they chorused and turned back to their computers.

* * *

Five minutes after leaving the Leisure Centre carpark Sutherland was pulling up outside Tommy Adams's house.

"We don't have any keys to get in," Simpson said as he got out.

"True, laddie, but I have a feeling that we might not need them," Sutherland replied.

"You think the murderer got here before us?" Sergeant Cranfield asked.

"I think somebody did. Whether it was his killer, I don't know." Sutherland stood and looked across the lawn at the chalet bungalow with its neat lawn and well tended shrubbery.

"Dean, take a look round the back," Sutherland said. Simpson peeled off and headed round the side and through a low gate between the garage and the house.

Sutherland and Cranfield walked up the short driveway, squeezing past the car that they assumed belonged to Adams, to the front door and rang the bell. It chimed unanswered in the background. Sutherland took out a handkerchief and tried the door handle. It was locked.

Simpson appeared on the other side of the door and, wearing his latex gloves, opened it and let them in.

"Better call SOCO, sir. Somebody has given this place a going over."

Sutherland pulled his radio from his pocket and contacted control, issuing instructions and asking for uniforms to conduct a house to house to see if anybody saw or heard anything.

That done, the three went slowly through the building without touching anything.

"Somebody was very anxious to find something," Maggie said.

It wasn't the complete shambles that Sutherland has expected, but drawers had been emptied into piles that had obviously been gone through carefully.

A DEADLY ACCOUNT

The master bedroom was like the aftermath of the January sales. Clothes everywhere as though desperation had been setting in.

There was no obvious point where the searching had stopped.

They returned to the hallway just as the police mini-bus was parking across the road.

Sutherland went out and spoke to Sergeant Ferris, explaining what he required from the uniformed officers. Ferris briefed the constables and watched as they spread out.

In the distance the sound of Ed Richardson's new SOCO van could be heard. A specially converted ex-army vehicle that housed all of the SOCO team's field equipment and could carry a full team of six forensic scientists.

Always impressed, Sutherland, Simpson and Cranfield watched the team go into action dressed in white disposable Noddy-suits, over boots and purple Nitrile gloves.

One of the team started by examining the car, carefully dusting for prints.

Ed approached, "Evening, Andrew. This to do with your body in the river?" he rumbled.

Sutherland nodded, "Victim's name was Thomas Adams, known as Tommy. Other than that he was divorced and had recently taken up keep-fit, we know nothing about him. Where he worked, what he did, nothing."

"He was a good gardener, though," Ed said looking round in the half light.

"Unless he had a gardener," Simpson said.

"We'll soon know," Richardson said and

walked over to try the garage door.

It was an up-and-over door and not locked. Well maintained, it slid up almost silently revealing a chest freezer, switched off, lid open that had obviously not been used for some time. An electric hover mower, bright orange, hung from a hook, beside it, along the same wall was a carefully arranged selection of garden tools all in good order, all obviously well used.

"So, no hired help, then," Richardson said. "Somebody's given this place the once over too," he pointed to the tool drawer that had been emptied on the floor.

"The rest of the house is the same," Simpson said. "We don't think that they found what they were looking for," he added.

"Came in through the side door," Richardson said putting down his case and extracting his finger-print kit. They watched as he puffed the grey dust over the surfaces round the door and began lifting prints.

"We'll leave you to it, Ed," Sutherland said.

"Don't think we're going to find much other than the victim's and any previous occupants," Ed rumbled.

"Oh?"

"Some of these prints are recently smudged. Somebody was wearing gloves when they searched this place."

"Nothing's ever easy, is it?" Sutherland said. To the others he said, "Let's go and see how Sergeant Ferris is getting on."

Chapter 8

It was now full nightfall, and with it a noticeable change in the weather. The sunny day had given way to a windy night laden with cloud and the probability of rain.

The constables were returning to the mini-bus with nothing significant to report.

No sightings of strange cars. No strange people. No strange noises. No unexplained lights on in Mr Adams's house. Unless you happened to know that your neighbour was already dead and that whoever was using lights behind closed curtains wasn't Mr Adams.

One neighbour who had been giving his dog a late evening walk had noticed lights on downstairs at about ten thirty on the Wednesday night, but with the car in the drive had thought nothing of it. He had noticed lights on upstairs half an hour later and had merely assumed that it was Tommy Adams going to bed.

The police now knew that Adams had been killed on the Wednesday.

Another neighbour had seen Tommy Adams setting off on his run at eight o'clock, as he had done for the previous evenings. He had once been observed returning about an hour and a half later, letting himself in through the back door – well, he had disappeared round the side of the building and lights had come on inside, the neighbour had said. She hadn't actually seen him enter the house.

They now knew that he had probably been killed some time between eight and nine thirty.

All of this was relayed to Sutherland.

"Right, thanks folks. Let Sergeant Cranfield have your reports in the morning," he said. "Home time everybody."

The mini-bus pulled away with a rattle of diesel and a trail of exhaust.

He was about to start the car when there was a tap on the driver's window.

He turned and looked up, surprised to see John Mansfield, ace reporter for the local evening paper looking down at him

Swearing under his breath, Sutherland lowered the window.

"Detective Chief Inspector Sutherland! I though it was you. Must be important if you're here." He nodded across to Simpson, "Inspector Simpson, too. What's going on?"

"Who tipped you off that we were here?" Sutherland asked.

"One of your constables. And before you ask, I don't know his name. He knocked on my door and started asking questions."

"Your door?"

"That one," Mansfield said pointing across the road.

"You live here?"

"Everybody's got to live somewhere, Mr Sutherland," Mansfield said. "I don't crawl out from under a rock, regardless of what you're thinking."

Sutherland laughed, "Point taken. What can I tell you? This morning, as you know, a body was pulled out of the river a mile or so below Meadowland Two. Until a short time ago we were unable to identify him. Turns out he was your neighbour. . ."

"Tommy Adams?" Mansfield had the good grace to appear shocked.

"But you knew that from the question the constable asked," Sutherland retorted.

"Yes, but I didn't know he was dead. Your officer only wanted to know if I'd seen or heard anything suspicious. I thought there'd been a break-in, some trouble in his house, something like that."

"Well, sorry then. No, Tommy Adams is dead, and it's looking like murder. We'll be carrying out more interviews tomorrow to see if anybody remembers seeing him leave the house on Wednesday evening, or while he was out running."

"It didn't make the local news," Mansfield was surprised.

"No name for the victim at the time of autopsy. It was only declared an unlawful death after the autopsy was completed, and we don't like upsetting people until we have a few more facts to go on."

"Understood. Will there be a formal press

briefing?"

"Tomorrow morning. Eleven o'clock. Maybe we'll know more by then," Sutherland said and started the car. Mansfield took the hint and stood back.

"Thanks, Mr Sutherland," he said to the already closed window.

Mansfield watched them depart. His story of a body being pulled from the river had gone below the fold in the evening edition. His editor didn't want to run it as a headline without more information. Usually in the case of murder the media were briefed early on, but, as the Chief Inspector had revealed, they hadn't known that for certain until a short time ago.

Sutherland drove Sergeant Cranfield back to the Leisure Centre carpark and waited until she had driven off before asking Simpson what his plans were.

"Fancy a dram, Dean?"

"Sorry, Andrew, I've promised Helen to cook the dinner tonight. She's working late."

"Anything special?" It was unusual for Dr Ellis to have to work late.

"The food or the work?"

"The work."

"Fatal traffic accident out towards Ilkley. Dry road, no other vehicle involved. Accident investigation could find nothing wrong with the car and wanted to know why a forty year old father of three was wrapped round a telegraph pole on a bend that didn't require much driving skill to negotiate."

A DEADLY ACCOUNT

Sutherland nodded slowly. As a father of three, himself, he felt sympathy for the family left behind.

Sutherland turned to Simpson, "I'll drop you back at the factory. We'll set up the incident room in the morning and see where we go from here."

* * *

Andrew Sutherland watched Dean Simpson drive away before parking his car and entering the Headquarters building.

The Chief Constable had already left the building so Sutherland phoned his home. Henderson's long suffering wife, Marjorie answered the phone.

"Andrew, I'm sorry, George isn't home yet." She did not elaborate and Sutherland knew better than to press her. "I take it that it's urgent, otherwise you wouldn't be phoning."

"Aye, Marjorie. Look, I'm heading home myself now. Could you make sure he phones me as soon as he gets in? I just need to run something by him."

"I'll tell him as soon as he comes through the door. I was going to tell you to enjoy your evening, but I rather think you're going to be working."

"Yes. The body we pulled out of the river this morning. We've put a name to the face. Now we have to fill in the gaps."

"Not an accident, I take it," she said.

"Doesn't look like it," Andrew replied.

"I'll let him know. Good bye Andrew, give my regards to Jill."

"I will thanks." Sutherland put the phone down. It was time to go home, spend some time with his family, enjoy some good home cooking and relax before the hard work started.

The rain was blowing in gusts, born on a cold north east wind giving an early warning of winter's approach. Halloween and Guy Fawkes, the fireworks were already going off round the town. Sutherland pulled into his driveway, waited a few minutes until the worst of the rain had passed before making a dash for the front door.

It was on nights like this that Andrew wished that he had kept the garage. A garage with automatic doors and a side door into the house, which was his idea of luxury.

Jill Sutherland came out of the kitchen drying her hands on a towel. She looked up at him as he bent to give her a kiss.

"Rough night by the look of it," she said noting the rain on his coat. "Tea will be ready in about ten minutes."

"Perfect timing then!"

It gave him time to go upstairs, look in on his children as they struggled with homework, or not as it turned out. Jamie was playing a computer game in his bedroom, Sheenagh was reading a fan magazine in her room, and their youngest, Peter, was sitting on the floor in his bedroom listening to his Walkman.

Monday evening, half term, no homework. Andrew went into the bedroom, hung his jacket up, and had a quick wash before pulling on a thick fairisle jumper that his mother had knitted some years before and was one of his favourite garments for loafing about the house in.

He joined Jill in the kitchen and helped lay the table. It was a chore that the children usually were dragged out of their rooms to do, but tonight, he was happy to keep his hands occupied while he mentally put together a plan for the investigation.

The action wasn't lost on his wife. "So, I take it that something major come up?"

"Afraid so, darling. A murder. Body pulled out of the river this morning. It's taken us all day to get a name and address. He was dead before he entered the water and his house has been turned over." It was a concise summing up of the day's events.

He was about to call upstairs to the children when the phone on the hall table rang.

"Andrew Sutherland," he said.

"Henderson here, Andrew. Marjorie tells me that you were looking for me. About this murder, is it?"

"Yes sir," Sutherland spent the next five minutes bringing the Chief Constable up to date. "I'll need to get the Incident Room opened up and to get what little information we have entered on the new computer system. I'd also like to hold a press briefing at eleven to get the public racking their brains to see if anybody spotted the victim prior to his death. It looks like it occurred last Wednesday evening."

"What else will you need?" Henderson asked.

"Lots of boots on the ground checking the river bank to see if we can locate where he went in."

Henderson digested this information and the financial implications. It would probably mean overtime, which, on restricted budgets, was always a worry, but murder tended to overrule such considerations.

"Alright. Do what you have to do, Andrew. Will you need me?" Henderson and his wife had been invited to lunch at Rochfield Golf and Country Club. He was to be the guest of honour and to give an address. To him it represented good public relations, as well as a welcome change from the usual weekday activities.

"No, sir. I'll handle it. We'll have to bring in a few extra bodies to man the phones in case the briefing produces any results."

"Good man. I'll leave you to it. Anything significant comes up and you can brief me when you see me."

Andrew put the phone down, and gave a bellow up the stairs, "Come on you lot, hands washed, quick, quick."

There was the usual stampede from Jamie and Sheenagh. Peter followed at his own pace.

Sutherland ruffled his youngest's blond curls as he passed, "Good day today Peter?"

"Good," Peter replied without stopping.

After his evening meal, Andrew headed down to his study with a mug of coffee. Jill had put the fire on earlier and the room was cosily warm.

While he had the opportunity, Sutherland used the phone in the study to let his team know that they would be required first thing in the morning. It didn't come as a surprise to any of them except Young Eric.

"I'm going to need you in the Incident Room from the start. I think we should use your system to collate all the reports and see what it throws up."

"That's not a problem, sir. Will you need Vikki Gibson?"

"Not at this stage. I think it would be better if she concentrated on putting more of the files on the system while you work on this."

"Understood, sir. I'll see you in the morning."

"Thanks Eric," Sutherland moved on to the next call.

When he had finished, he poured himself a small whiskey and turned the television on before settling down in his favourite button back leather armchair to drink his coffee, which had cooled down considerably and sip the whiskey.

It was Andrew's custom to sit there, the television or radio on as background noise, often just staring into the fire, watching the artificial, gas flames create patterns while his brain mulled over the day's events. Occasionally he would pull a legal pad towards him from the table beside his chair and scribble down a point or two, something for the morning briefing, or something to chase up the next day.

The ten o'clock news came on and woke him from his reverie. There was a brief item, probably phoned in by Mansfield about the death of Tommy Adams. The usual hype about shocked neighbours, and sufficient detail for the news reader to speculate about the police's suspicions that the death might not be accidental, and asking for the public's help in tracing the victim's last known movements.

Sutherland grunted.

The story was now in the public domain.

The killer would know that Rochfield police would be out in force the next day. As no attempt had been made to hide the body, throwing it in the river meant that it would be found sooner or later.

Would it make a difference to the killer that Tommy Adams had been found sooner rather than later? Probably not, after all, the best part of a week had already elapsed.

It would depend on the killer's agenda. The motive for the murder, Andrew decided. He turned the television off.

The fire turned off, Sutherland picked up his mug and glass, turned the lights out and took them to the kitchen and put them in the dishwasher.

He joined Jill in the living room to watch the rest of the local news before they headed upstairs to bed.

* * *

Across town, Dean Simpson had gone to Helen's house via his own bachelor flat where he had showered and changed and gathered up the main ingredients for their evening meal. Salmon steaks and a bottle of wine. Helen's fridge freezer and well stocked condiment cupboard would provide everything else that he would need.

He let himself into her house and was greeted by the comforting warmth of her central heating. Working such erratic hours, she had long abandoned any pretence that an open fire was more homely. By the time she had got a good blaze going she had usually been too tired to enjoy it. And central heating did not require clearing grates, lugging coal scuttles around and endless dusting.

Helen would phone when she was about to leave the hospital. That would give him time to start the cooking. By the time Helen had got home, freshened up, and they had shared a drink, it would be ready for the table.

Cooking was Simpson's aid to relaxation. Like Sutherland he kept a pad handy to jot down ideas to follow up.

The phone rang. It was Andrew Sutherland. Sutherland informed Simpson that the Chief Constable had agreed to let them open up an Incident Room, and to providing extra officers to conduct searches and house to house questioning if it was required.

No sooner had he put the phone down after taking Sutherland's call than it rang again.

This time it was Helen.

They chatted briefly, and then Dean started preparing and cooking the salmon steaks, boiled potatoes, frozen peas and carrots.

"That smells good," Helen said as she came in, gave him a quick kiss and went upstairs to shower and change.

Her return to the kitchen was perfectly timed. She accepted the martini that he had prepared and sat at the kitchen table sipping it while he put the finishing touches to their meal before carrying both plates to the table.

There was a dining room in the house, but they seldom used it unless they were entertaining, something they rarely did, preferring their own company. Because of the nature of both their jobs, time together was cherished, and frequently interrupted.

They compared notes on their working days while they ate.

To some it would be seen as talking shop, but for Helen and Dean it was often a way of easing the tensions and the mysteries out of their work. They found that it helped both of them as their work often overlapped.

"What about your car crash victim?" Dean asked.

"Heart attack. Sudden, massive. If coming off the road hadn't killed him, the heart attack would. Maybe, if he'd been in the town, close to the hospital and hadn't crashed his car he might have been saved," she said.

"But maybe if he'd been in the town, in his car he might have hit pedestrians and killed them," Dean countered.

"Sad all the same," she replied. "A husband, and father, leaves for work in the morning. Looking forward to the rest of his week, his children on half term, Halloween, bonfire night and all that. Now this time of year will be marked as the time they lost their father and his wife lost her husband."

"Has she been told what happened?"

"Yes. The police family liaison officer was given the details as soon as I had them. She did the hard bit." Dean knew from experience what that entailed. He knew the liaison officer and admired her ability to deal with other people's suffering so calmly and with utmost sincerity.

Like his boss, Dean settled down to watch some television before the news came on. With Helen snuggled up beside him on the sofa, sleeping peacefully. She was rudely awoken when Dean gave a start at the news item about their murder victim.

"What's up?" she exclaimed, now fully awake. She concentrated on the news reader's words. "Does that help or hinder your investigation?"

"Probably won't make much difference either way. It'll just lead to endless speculation from the media and the locals. Is there a crazed killer on the loose? That sort of thing. Whether it helps the killer or not, there's no way of knowing."

Helen stood up, turned the television off and pulled Simpson to his feet, "Bed time, Dean. You've got work tomorrow."

Chapter 9

Tuesday morning saw a hive of activity within Rochfield Central as the Incident Room was set up in the conference room. The sign was changed, the room re-arranged, Eric's computer was installed with its printers, the extra phone lines that would be required were instated.

The Murder Board was attached to the wall with a dry-wipe board to one side and a cork board to the other side.

A photograph of the victim was attached to the Murder Board and Tommy Adams's name was written above it.

On the dry-wipe board Simpson wrote in the left hand margin, roughly half way up the board the time that Adams had last been seen and at the bottom the time when the body had been pulled from the river. The implication was clear. They had to fill in the gaps before and after those two times.

What had the victim been doing before he left his house, and everything about him? His whole background would have to be looked into to see if it would give the police any reason for his death – Motive.

A DEADLY ACCOUNT

Establish a motive and you're half way to finding the killer, provided that it is the right motive. Get the motive wrong and it can lead to fruitless hours of wandering down blind alleys. They had all been there.

What had happened between the two time points, other than floating down the River Roche? – Opportunity.

Somewhere along that time line his killer had met with him:- by design or accident? Narrow that time down to a point where one suspect's path above all the others could have crossed with that of Tommy Adams.

Finally, and this would require as much luck and forensic evidence as could be gathered, what had been the weapon? – Means.

There was a chance that they might be as sure as they could be what weapon had been used to deliver the fateful blow, but if they didn't know where it had occurred, or the weapon had been thrown into the river after the body there was a bigger chance that they would never find it. Even if it was found there might be nothing by way of evidence to link it to a suspect.

Sutherland and Simpson were pinning their hopes on motive and opportunity. There was no smoking gun, no serrated knife that matched a wound.

The victim had been hit from behind. A single blow that killed him before he was pushed into the river. Dr Ellis's examination had determined beyond doubt that Adams was dead before he entered the water.

Closer examination had also determined that while the blow hadn't exhibited signs that extreme force had been used, it did show that the blow had been very well aimed; but was that by luck or design?

They probably wouldn't know that until they had a definite suspect.

Sutherland stood beside the Murder Board and called the morning briefing to order. The babble of noise died away. Every person in the room was seated and looking at him.

"Our victim is Thomas Adams. Tommy Adams, aged late thirties to early forties, killed some time between eight thirty and ten thirty last Wednesday night by a single blow to the base of his cranium at the back of the neck. It has not been possible to determine what was used to inflict the lethal blow, and our chances of finding the murder weapon are very remote. Until we can establish where the body entered the water we won't know where to start looking," Sutherland said. "Whatever it was, was probably chucked into the river with the body."

He looked round at the upturned faces.

"In order to have some idea why Adams was killed we need to know as much as we can about him. What he did for a living, where he did it, who he worked with. We need to know about his private life. We know that he was recently divorced. Look into the ex-wife and her life. Has she re-married? Has she a new partner? Speak to his neighbours – one of whom just happens to be our favourite reporter, John Mansfield. Be careful how you question him. Try to ask questions without revealing too much about the line of enquiry." There was a muffled laugh. "Yes, I know, a tall order, but do your best. Dean, I think you and Maggie should interview him. He'll be here for the press briefing at half ten. Grab him before he leaves. He'll be anxious to get back to the Echo to file his copy so he may be off his guard, but don't count on it."

They nodded their assent.

"I want everybody back here by twelve thirty for a de-briefing. Young Eric will act as collator. If somebody rushes up to you and confesses, drag them down here pronto and let's see if they are telling the truth or just pissing us about. Okay?"

Heads nodded.

"Right, go to it. Get round to where he lived. Ask the neighbours about him. Try and sort out the facts from the gossip, ye know the routine. Dean, Maggie, stick around. I'll need some back up for the press briefing."

The three of them, and Eric watched the rest of the detectives leave.

"Ideas, anybody?" Sutherland asked.

"About the case?" Maggie asked.

"I was thinking more about the briefing. They have most of what we know already: the victim's name, where he lived and when he died, and the fact that he was pulled out of the river," Andrew said.

"We need information. I think we reiterate what they already know, giving them as much of the facts as we know, then ask for help to fill in the gaps," Dean said.

"Eric, can you use your computer to print out some sort of a script?" Sutherland asked.

"Yes sir."

"Good lad," Sutherland said by way of thanks.

For the next ten minutes they sat round Eric's desk and dictated the memo, making adjustments as they went until Sutherland was satisfied that he had something that was well thought out and achieved their aims.

There was a knock at the door.

"Who is it?" Sutherland called out.

"Press officer, sir," William Franklin called from the door.

"Right, come on in William."

The Rochfield Divisional Police Headquarters was lucky to have a full time press officer to handle all of the arrangements for press briefings, dress the set, introduce the speakers and generally vet those who were attending, including the media, the police and any relatives to make sure that everything ran smoothly, that the right signals were being given and the correct message was being put forward.

William Franklin asked them how they were going to go about the morning's briefing. Eric printed out the prepared statement and handed it to Franklin. He read it through rapidly, nodded his approval and handed it back.

"Everything's ready in the Media Room," he said.

The Media Room was more usually in use as a training room. Using a mock up of a real

A DEADLY ACCOUNT

interview room which was at one end and hidden behind a curtain, and role playing, the Media Room was used to improve interrogation techniques.

There were full video recording and playback facilities.

The other end of the room had a long table for microphones. It was back-dropped by the force insignia, a theme which was carried down the front of the table. Running down an outer wall, the room had feed points for television companies, and multiple power points. It also had an emergency exit along that wall which was opened to allow the media to enter and leave the building without having to come through the front entrance.

Rochfield Division were able to set up well presented, well run press briefings without it interfering with the daily workings of the police headquarters. It was better than the ad hoc briefings on the steps of the police headquarters that occasionally happened.

Franklin looked at his watch, "Five minutes to go," he said, "Let's get into position."

The detectives followed him to the Media Room. Their door entered by the side of the briefing table. They took their places before the assembled reporters from the print and audio-visual media. Sergeant Cranfield led them on and sat to Sutherland's left. Sutherland sat in the middle, Simpson to his right. Franklin stood at one side.

"Good morning ladies and gentlemen,"

Franklin began, "Detective Chief Inspector Sutherland will read a prepared statement. You may then ask questions. Detective Inspector Simpson and Detective Sergeant Cranfield are also present to answer them where possible. I must stress that this case is at a very early stage. Chief Inspector Sutherland."

That was Sutherland's cue to read the prepared statement which he did while remaining seated.

"Any questions?" he finished by asking, hoping that their statement had covered most, if not all, of what they were in a position to disclose.

"John Mansfield, Rochfield Echo. Chief Inspector, have the police any idea why Tommy Adams might have been murdered?"

"At this stage, none. This is where we need the help of the public, including your good self, to fill in the gaps, to tell us about Mr Adams. Who he was, what he did, and where he might have been in the hours before his murder. Until we have that information, I'm afraid to say that we are as wise as you are."

There were one or two more questions, but it was soon obvious to the media that they had been given all they were going to get for the moment.

They were preparing to leave. Maggie left her seat and went to the emergency exit. She managed to attract Mansfield's attention as he approached the door.

"We need to speak to you, Mr Mansfield, just briefly, since you were a neighbour of the deceased."

That caused some of the other journalists to

take note, "What you been up to, John?" a reporter from one of the national dailies asked.

"Did you know the deceased?" another asked.

"He was just a neighbour, alright. Nothing more." It wasn't often that Mansfield was on the receiving end of questions. He wasn't happy having to follow Sergeant Cranfield, but it was preferable to having to field inane questions from his fellow journalists.

He got the distinct impression that she was enjoying his discomfort.

"Sorry about that, Mr Mansfield," Simpson said, coming up to him, "We are talking to all of his neighbours, trying, as I said, to find out as much about the man as possible. As you are here, and not at home we hoped you could give us five minutes to tell us what you know of Mr Adams."

"Here?" Mansfield wanted to file his story.

"We can use one of the interview rooms if you like." Simpson said.

"Yes. It'll be a new experience!" Mansfield followed Simpson and Cranfield out of the side door and down the corridor to Interview Room One.

Sutherland went back to the Incident Room with Franklin after watching the last of the media personnel leave and closing the emergency exit doors.

"That went well enough," Franklin said. "I saw Inspector Simpson take Mansfield inside. What's that all about?"

"Coincidence," Sutherland said, "He happens to live in the same street as the victim. Simpson and Cranfield are going to ask him the same questions that the rest of the team are asking on the ground. We really don't know a thing about Adams. Until we do, we've got nothing to work on."

"Will you be having another briefing today?" Franklin asked.

"No William. Tomorrow will be soon enough, unless we get very lucky," said Sutherland without much optimism.

"Keep in touch, Mr Sutherland," Franklin said

and left Sutherland to stand staring at the Murder Board.

"What did you do to deserve this?" he asked the photograph of the dead man.

"Sir?" Young Eric said from behind his computer screen.

"Eric, sorry. I'd forgotten you were here." Sutherland said and wandered across to Eric's desk. "Any further revelations from the files?"

"Nothing as definite as the Talbots, sir. A few cases are starting to flag up, but it's too early to say," Eric answered.

Sutherland was tempted to ask further questions, but Simpson and Cranfield arrived.

"How did it go with Mansfield?" he asked.

"You were right, sir. He was more interested in his surroundings and in getting away to file his story than the questions," Maggie said.

"What does he know about Adams?" Sutherland prompted.

"Very little, as it happens," Simpson said, "Adams was living there before the Mansfield's moved into the Close. Mansfield and his wife moved there two years ago. It seems that Adams and his wife kept themselves to themselves. They were in to ballroom dancing. Probably her idea, from what Mansfield gathered. In the end, seems she went off with her dancing instructor. The Adams's divorced a few months ago, which we already knew."

"I take it he didn't know where she'd moved to?" Andrew asked.

"No, sir. Maybe one of the others can answer

that," Maggie replied.

Gradually the team reassembled in the incident room. Sutherland let them get refreshments and then the de-briefing began. Eric put the information straight into the computer. Each time a new name cropped up the computer asked for more information on it. Occasionally Eric had to ask one of the other detectives a follow up question. Finally, by one o'clock he was finished.

"Okay Eric, what do you have?" Sutherland asked.

Eric stood up, "These are under a number of headings, sir," he began, addressing Sutherland, "Personal: Tommy Adams was thirty nine years old. It would have been his fortieth birthday at the end of November. He had been married to his wife, Doreen, for twelve years. They separated in August last year and their divorce came through a year later on the grounds of her infidelity. It seems that she was the dominant partner in their relationship," he consulted the printout before continuing. "One neighbour, who seemed to know both of them quite well, and had known Adams before they were married said that he did what she wanted at all times, and lost all of his old friends as a result. There were no children. The house was his, and he kept it after the divorce."

He paused again, "Occupation: This is a complete blank. We haven't a clue at the moment. Nobody has come forward to say that he's not turned up for work. The autopsy rules out his having been a labourer, or in manual work, so he was probably managerial, clerical or retail.

"Leisure activities: Adams was a keen and accomplished gardener and sometimes helped his neighbours with their gardening problems and bit of landscaping. Before he married he was a keen footballer, and quite good by all accounts. The neighbour who supplied this bit of information had been chatting with him at the start of the week. It seems that Adams had decided to get fit again and try his luck with one of the weekend warriors, to see if he could get a game or two."

Eric had finished his briefing and sat down.

Sutherland stood up.

"Thank you Eric," he said, "So, the next thing is to fill in the background. DI Simpson will allocate tasks. First thing will be to find out where he worked."

He turned to Simpson, "I'll leave you to it, Dean. Let me know when anything significant comes up."

Sutherland headed back to his office.

Simpson listed the various items of information that they required and allocated them to different members. The phone calls could begin.

The first call would be to the Inland Revenue to see if they could provide information on the victim's employment status.

The first call did not have to be made. One of the dedicated Incident Room phone lines lit up. Jack Wilson snatched the handset from its cradle and pressed the winking button. "Rochfield CID, DC Wilson. How can I help you?" He started to scribble down the caller's information.

The others watched. He raised a thumb,

"Thank you for calling. That has been most helpful. We may have to send somebody out to talk to you and your staff if we need further information. Thank you. Have a good day."

He put the phone down and looked over at Inspector Simpson, "Result, boss," Wilson said. "That was the City Secretarial and Book-Keeping Agency in Leeds. Tommy Adams has been working for them for a few years. They were wondering what happened to him. Seems he was working locally. The Mutual Cap's book-keeper had gone off sick and he was asked to fill the gap until she returned. When he didn't show up on Thursday they had to send somebody else out to cover for him."

"Good result, Jack," Simpson said. "You and Sergeant Cranfield head down there and have a chat with them. You'll find it easier to walk than trying to find somewhere to park."

Simpson watched them go. "That's one question answered. Let's try and locate the ex-wife."

That was going to be more difficult. They knew her former married name. They didn't know her maiden name, her new boyfriend's name, whether they were married, anything.

"Start with ballroom dancing. We know they have that in common," Simpson suggested. He then phoned Sutherland's extension with the news.

Sutherland arrived a few moments later. "Bring me up to date, laddie."

"We know where he was working," Simpson began. He filled Sutherland in on what little they had to go on.

"Nobody come forward with any sightings of him out running?" Sutherland asked.

"Nothing so far. The uniforms are out in force scouring the river banks. We're lucky in a way," Simpson said.

"In what way?"

"When you think about it, there aren't that many places where there is access to the river bank that isn't in a fairly public place." Simpson took a pointer and used it to demonstrate on the large scale Ordnance Survey map that was pinned up with its Dry Wipe covering. On the map the location of Adams's house was clearly marked, as was the location where the body was found. Sutherland looked at the map with Simpson and noted that, as Dean had said, there really weren't that many places.

There were several points above the town, the nearest being about two and a half miles from the house. The next nearest location was in the town itself. After that, below the town there were several places where he could have gone in. A pathway ran close to the river, sometimes right beside it, at others several yards from it, for the whole distance to where he had been found and beyond. A favourite place for walkers, joggers and cyclists, and the source of friction between the various users as they vied for space.

"Be different if he'd been found in the canal. The tow path runs right beside it for the full length," Simpson said.

"Then thank God he wasn't! I dread to think

how many man hours would be needed to search that," Sutherland said. He continued to study the map. "Do you suppose that he ran the same route every night?"

"Maybe, if he was timing himself and wanted to see how he was improving," Simpson said, "That's the sort of thing a runner does after a while. Trouble is he'd only just started the keep fit routine."

"Another thing for the briefing then. We need to find out if anybody spotted him on any other evening. See if the guy at the leisure centre can shed any light on that. He may have been asked for ideas about places to run. Just a thought." Sutherland suggested.

"I'll get it checked out sir," Simpson replied.

"I'll leave you to it. If you're looking for me, I'll be in my office," Andrew said and left the Incident Room.

Chapter 10

DS Cranfield and DC Wilson walked down to the offices of The Mutual Cap and into the building through its imposing front door, flanked on one side by an empty retail unit and on the other by a charity shop full of second hand clothes, books and toys.

The gloomy hallway led to stairs and a lift, the light above the door signalling that it was on the top floor.

Jack Wilson thumbed the button as Maggie Cranfield made for the stairs.

"Four floors up, Sarge!" he said, "You must be joking!"

"Not asking you to take the exercise, Jack. I'll see you at the top," she laughed and started to climb, two steps at a time. Being over six feet tall and very fit had its advantages. Along the way she could hear the lift slowly descending to the ground floor, the doors rumbling open, then closing. She could hear it starting to make its ascent as she passed the third floor and was standing, barely stretched by her use of the stairs at the lift doors when they finally opened. She was looking out of the landing window at the view over Rochfield when Wilson joined her.

"Let's see what we can find out about the late Mr Adams," she said as she pushed the door marked 'Reception' on a modern adhesive plate that seemed curiously out of place on the solid Victorian door.

Paula Lewis looked up, noting the tall redhead approaching and the man beside her who was pulling out a police warrant card and holding it up.

"DC Wilson and DS Cranfield, Rochfield CID, miss. We need to speak to your boss."

Without thinking Paula gave the stock reply, "Mr Harmsbury is in a meeting."

Maggie Cranfield looked down at her and said quietly, but firmly, "Then do us a favour, love; get him out of it. Now."

Paula Lewis pressed the call button for Harmsbury's phone, "Mr Harmsbury, there's police here wants to speak to you."

Maggie couldn't hear the reply, but Paula Lewis reddened, unplugged her headset, stood up and said, "Follow me please," in one fluid motion. She came out from behind her reception desk and led them down the corridor to Harmsbury's office and showed them in. Harmsbury was on his own, which didn't come as a surprise to DS Cranfield.

He stood up.

Jack Wilson flashed his card again and repeated the introductory mantra.

"Is this about Mr Adams?" Harmsbury asked.

"It is, Mr Harmsbury," DS Cranfield said. "Before we go any further I need you to tell your staff not to leave the premises until we've had a chance to speak to them. How many are in the building?"

"Most of our sales associates are out on the road. One or two may be in the sales office. Our book-keeper's not in. We have a replacement temp."

"Can you ask any of your sales people to stay here for a while, please? We'll try not to keep them any longer than necessary," DS Cranfield instructed.

"Would it help to talk to them first? Then they can get back out where they belong, keeping appointments."

It made sense.

They followed Harmsbury down the corridor to the sales office and Harmsbury introduced them to Richard Tillsworth.

"Richard will introduce you to the others. These people are from Rochfield CID. They're investigating the death of Tommy Adams. Give them all the help that you can," Harmsbury said, "I'll be in my office when you need me."

The two sales associates in the room with Tillsworth were Mike Blandford and Sally Pickton.

For the next half hour Cranfield and Wilson interviewed the two sales associates, and got details of the rest of the current associates from Tillsworth.

After taking details of names, addresses and contact numbers they asked each individual what their movements on the Wednesday evening had been, and details of anybody who could corroborate their statement. They asked whether the individual had had any contact with Tommy Adams while he had been working at The Cap, or at any other time.

The only person who had had any proper dealings with Adams had been Richard Tillsworth, the sales manager.

The sales associates had only exchanged pleasantries with him usually when handing in their CAPS or being issued with company stationery.

DS Cranfield asked the questions, Jack Wilson wrote down the answers. Occasionally he would ask a supplementary question to clarify a point.

After each individual had been questioned they were allowed to go, either back to the sales office or out to keep appointments.

After speaking to Tillsworth they returned to Harmsbury's office.

Harmsbury stood when they entered.

Without being asked DS Cranfield pulled up one of the two guest chairs. Taking his cue, Wilson took the other and sat down pulling his notebook from one pocket and a ball-point from the other.

Harmsbury sat back down, collapsing like a deflating balloon.

"We'll need to speak to your office staff as well, but let's start with you shall we?" Maggie began.

Harmsbury nodded.

"Full name, and address please."

A DEADLY ACCOUNT

"Jeremy Harmsbury, 147 Keighley Road, Rochfield."

"And your position in the company?"

"Managing Director."

"Thank you, Mr Harmsbury, Jeremy. Now, how well did you know Tommy Adams?"

"Hardly at all. He had only been here for a few days. He was a temporary book-keeper. Our regular book-keeper is off sick."

"And your regular book-keeper is who?"

"Hilda Hackett. Miss Hackett has been here as long as I have. This is the first time I've ever known her to be off sick," he said in a rush.

"And where does she live? We'll need to speak to her too at some time, probably."

"She's not at home. She's in The Rochfield Clinic. You'll find her there."

Wilson scribbled the information down.

"Thank you," Cranfield continued. "So, back to Tommy Adams. Tell me about him?"

"What do you mean? What do you want to know?"

"What were his duties, what was he like, was he any good at his job?" DS Cranfield asked, "Mr Harmsbury, we know nothing about the man, other than that he's dead. Talking of which, I'm sure you saw it all on the news. . ."

"Yes, yes I did," Harmsbury said, wondering where this was leading.

"I was just wondering why you didn't pick up the phone and tell us that he worked here." Cranfield said.

"I assumed that the agency would have called

you. I'm sorry, didn't they?"

"Eventually, yes. That's how come we happen to be here, Mr Harmsbury," she said. "So, tell me what Mr Adams did here before his untimely death."

"He dealt with the staff payroll, expenses and the agents commissions, handed out the company stationery, promotional material, that sort of thing. Pretty simple stuff really."

Wilson wrote it all down, "Simple for Adams, or just simple?"

"It used to be a much bigger job in the past, but with so much computerisation and fewer staff since we were amalgamated, it has become simpler," Harmsbury didn't elaborate further.

* * *

Back in his office, Sutherland pulled out the sheet of legal pad onto which he had scribbled notes the previous evening and reached for the phone.

"Sheelagh, DCI Sutherland here, can I have a wee word with Ed Richardson, please," he said and waited. "Ed, have your people finished with Adams's house?"

"No, Andrew, not yet. Why"

"Find out if anybody has come across any correspondence with a solicitor at all. We know he was divorced. There may be paperwork relating to that. Better still if you come across a copy of a will. Let me know will you?"

"Will do, Andrew," Richardson said and hung up.

Sutherland ticked the item off his list.

The next item on Sutherland's list might prove trickier to get an honest answer to.

What did they know about The Mutual Capital Life Assurance of Rochfield? Could that have a bearing on the death of Tommy Adams?

One thing that Andrew Sutherland had learnt over the years was that the value of conferences was more often in the contacts one made than the lectures one sat through. He pulled his personal diary towards him and looked up 'F' for fraud in the address section at the back. It was where he stored an assortment of names, contact details and other bits of possibly useful information.

Somewhere in the back of his mind he recalled an interesting encounter with one of the Met's top fraud investigators. An unassuming lady, he remembered, called Janet something or other.

Janet Black. The name came back to him before his eyes focussed on the page. He remembered an evening spent in the hotel bar with Janet and one of her colleagues discussing the many ways that fraud was becoming the fastest growing crime in the country. Millions of pounds were being cleaned out of accounts, both corporate and personal, each year by criminals using modern technology, credit cards, cold calling and other techniques, and Janet Black was of the opinion that they were only seeing the tip of an ever growing iceberg.

He dialled the number for the Metropolitan Police switchboard and asked to be put through to her extension.

"Janet, Andrew Sutherland. Don't know if you remember me or not?"

"Of course, Andrew! Congratulations on catching Hydinge, by the way," she said.

"Teamwork, Janet. Teamwork and my tame computer guy." Sutherland gave a quick explanation of the work that Young Eric had done.

"Sounds like the sort of talent we are in short supply of," Janet said.

"Aye, and don't be trying to poach him!" Sutherland replied swiftly.

"Wouldn't dare! When he's learnt all that he can from you then I'll poach him," she laughed, "Anyway, I take it that's not why you've phoned?"

"No. I don't know whether this comes under your area of expertise, but I have a murder up here . . ."

"Tommy Adams?"

"Yes, how . . ."

"We do get the news down in London, you know," She said.

"It's early days yet, but it doesn't feel like a random killing, if any murder can ever be random. We know very little about him other than that he was working as an agency book-keeper for a clerical services firm in Leeds. His most recent job was with a local life assurance company, The Mutual Capital Life Assurance Company of Rochfield – to give it its full title – known hereabouts as The Mutual Cap. Does it ring any bells with you?"

There was silence from Janet Black.

Sutherland waited.

"Janet?"

"I haven't gone away, Andrew. I'm just looking something up. Look, this may take a few minutes. Can I call you back?"

Sutherland gave her the station number and his extension, "I'll wait for your call Janet, thanks."

He hung up, dialled the switchboard and told Alice that he was expecting a call and was heading to the canteen to get a coffee.

* * *

DS Cranfield and DC Wilson questioned all of the staff present at The Mutual Cap, but none were able to expand on what they had already learnt from Harmsbury and the sales people.

They returned to Jeremy Harmsbury's office.

"We'll need a list of all your recent sales associates, ones who have left in the past couple of years and their contact details," Cranfield said.

"But they wouldn't have had any dealings with Adams," Harmsbury said.

"Probably not going to be of any use, but we'll need the information anyway," she replied.

"I'll ask head office to get that for you. Is there a fax number where they can send it? It would be quicker than the post."

Cranfield gave him the number.

"Than you for your time Jeremy. We'll not keep you any longer."

Cranfield and Wilson stood and left the office.

Outside on the street Maggie turned to Jack,

"He was a bit helpful, wasn't he?"

"Think he's hiding something?"

"Something, yes. Not sure what though. Let's get back to the factory and feed this lot in, see where it leads us."

"Do we really need all the information about former associates?" Jack was puzzled.

"Probably not; I just wanted to get under his skin. Make him do some work. Means he'll have to talk to somebody in head office, that in itself might stir something up."

"Just fishing then, Sarge!"

"Yeah, got to have some fun in this job!"

Back in the Incident Room they sat with Eric at his computer and watched while he took the information from Wilson's notebook and rapidly, with practised ease entered it onto the system.

Once he had finished, the computer digested the information for a short time while a small cartoon policeman started walking across the screen.

"What does that mean?" Maggie asked as she followed the jerky movements of the figure.

"He's thinking," Young Eric said, "Ah!"

"Ah?" Maggie repeated.

The little pixelated policeman had stopped pacing and a blinking square lit up over the helmet.

"With better resolution and a colour monitor, I could have a flashing blue light," Eric said and clicked the mouse over the flashing box. "He's found something."

A new screen opened up.

"A couple of interesting things," Eric said, turning the monitor slightly towards Maggie. "Their book-keeper is staying at the Rochfield Clinic which is one of the places where the victim's route could have passed by if he was keeping close to the river. I don't know if there is access from the grounds of the clinic to the river path though."

"We'll get it checked out. What's the other thing?"

"Probably irrelevant, but the two company sales reps live close to each other in Rochleigh. Mike Blandford and Sally Pickton. They mentioned being in each other's company briefly on the Wednesday evening. That's all so far."

Cranfield and Wilson returned to their own desks.

"We'll have to go round the other associates individually," Maggie said.

"How should we handle that?" Jack Wilson asked.

"I think we had better start by phoning them and arranging a time to see them face to face," Maggie said. She photocopied Wilson's notes and said, "You take the top half, I'll take the bottom half and then we'll work out who will interview them."

* * *

Sutherland took his mug of coffee along the corridor to the Incident Room. There had been no call back from Janet Black yet. He wondered if that was significant.

"Anything new?" he asked as he entered.

Young Eric looked up and nodded. Sutherland walked over.

"DS Cranfield and DC Wilson's visit to The Mutual Cap has yielded a couple of points."

Eric gave Sutherland a quick run down.

"Leave the Clinic with me, Maggie," he said and jotted down Miss Hackett's name on Eric's pad and tore the sheet off. "Anything else seem interesting from your visit?"

"We think Harmsbury is hiding something, but we're not sure what."

"I'm waiting for a phone call that might shed light on that," Sutherland said.

As if on cue, the phone on Simpson's desk rang. Dean picked it up, listened and nodded to Andrew, "I think this might be your call, sir."

Sutherland took a sip of his coffee as he crossed to Simpson's desk.

"Janet? Thanks for getting back to me. Did you find anything?"

He listened for a couple of minutes, making a few notes on the page he had torn from Eric's pad. The rest of the room watched in silence.

"Thanks Janet. That's useful to know." Sutherland put the phone down. He stood up and looked at the expectant faces. "I think we may have some sort of a motive. That or a monumental red herring. It seems that The Mutual Cap may be the first prize in a take over battle. That was a contact in the Met's Fraud Squad."

"Why should that be a motive to murder

Adams?" Simpson asked.

"Maybe Tommy Adams found something fishy in The Cap's books."

"As in?" Maggie asked.

"As in 'I haven't a clue', Maggie!" Sutherland said, "There may be nothing wrong with their books at all, but it's an idea that might be worth pursuing. Anything more from the public?"

"A couple of possible sightings," Simpson said, "I've asked uniform to follow them up and get back to us."

"Good. I'm going to phone the Rochfield Clinic and see if I can get to have a wee chat with Miss Hackett. Can I use your desk, Dean?"

Simpson nodded.

Sutherland looked up the number, dialled and waited. A very professional sounding receptionist answered the call, "Rochfield Clinic, how may I help you?"

"Detective Chief Inspector Sutherland," he replied, "You have a patient, a Miss Hilda Hackett in the clinic, I believe."

"I'm sorry Mr Sutherland; I'm not able to answer your question."

"Then put me through to somebody who is able to answer it, lass, and don't waste my time," Sutherland said quietly.

"I'm sorry Mr Sutherland, but we have a patient privacy policy and . . ."

"Sorry, lass, but a murder investigation takes precedence over your privacy policy. I don't want to arrive on your doorstep to interview Miss Hackett only to find that I've been misinformed by her employer and that she isn't there. Just answer the question or put me through to somebody who can."

Sutherland was not going to be put off, and the receptionist sensed that this was above her pay grade.

"Putting you through to the Clinic Administrator, Mr Sutherland," the girl said and her voice was replaced by a musak version of Pachelbel's Canon in D Major. Sutherland was only kept waiting for a couple of bars before a man's voice replaced the receptionist's.

"Tony Carmichael, Clinic Administrator. Mr Sutherland, what can I do for you?"

Sutherland was minded to reply 'Answer a simple question,' "I've no doubt that your receptionist was only following orders, but, Mr Carmichael, when a senior police officer asks whether you do or do not have a patient, a simple yes or no would suffice."

"You must understand that as we have never spoken to you before we have no way of knowing that you are who you say you are."

"Point taken, Mr Carmichael. When are your visiting hours? I'll come down and show you my warrant card. Will you tell me then?"

"Probably. The hours are open to family visitors between eleven in the morning and after nine in the evening unless the patient is undergoing treatment. If there are special reasons those visiting hours might be extended."

"Understood, Mr Carmichael," Sutherland said, "I'll be there tomorrow at eleven if that's alright. I will need to interview Miss Hackett. It is a murder investigation, and it does concern her. I will need to speak to you as well."

"We will see you then Chief Inspector," Carmichael said.

Sutherland looked at his watch. It was nearly four o'clock.

"Press briefing in five minutes, Dean. Anything you want to bring up?"

Simpson thought for a moment before answering, "I think we need to make it clear that we still need people to come forward who knew Adams, or who may have seen him out running, or anybody who may have seen him about the town for whatever reason. As things stand, we don't know that much about him or his movements."

Sutherland nodded and stood up, "Right, let's go and ask for help. The vultures might as well earn their keep."

The press briefing lasted less than ten minutes. The death of Tommy Adams was fast becoming yesterday's news. The deepening recession, news of more pit closures and job losses in the steel industry were uppermost in people's minds, especially in Yorkshire.

Sutherland and Simpson reiterated their call for people to come forward with information, while emphasising that they had no reason to believe that this was a random killing, or that there was any threat to the wider public.

Chapter 11

Wednesday morning, almost a week after the murder of Tommy Adams, and Rochfield CID were no further on in establishing his movements prior to his death, or a motive for it.

After the press briefing of the night before, they had decided to leave it until there was anything new for the press before holding the next one.

Inspector Simpson took the morning briefing with the team.

"We've been provided with a list of the past and present associates of The Cap. For the time being we'll concentrate of the current crop of associates. Maggie, you take Jack and interview them. There are only four that we haven't talked to so it shouldn't take too long."

"Already in hand, sir. We phoned them yesterday afternoon and have arranged appointments to see them."

"Good work. When are you seeing the first one?"

"Half ten, sir."

"You and Jack better go now then."

Sergeant Cranfield and DC Wilson left the

A DEADLY ACCOUNT

briefing and headed to the carpark.

Simpson continued his briefing. "There are half a dozen probable sightings of Adams from the night he was killed and previous evenings. Eddie," he beckoned to DC Fowler, "I need you to follow these up. Sergeant Ferris is going to let you have a couple of his people to share the leg work. If I'm out when you get back, give all the information to Young Eric and let him work his magic."

Fowler took the list and headed to reception to locate Sergeant Ferris.

"Vikki, can you keep on at the files. If anything comes in about the case, Eric, you handle it. If it's significant, get hold of me or the chief. And while you're waiting, I want you to enter the names of the recent past associates into your computer. See if any of them crop up on any other data base. Can you do that?"

"Yes sir."

Dean left the Incident Room to go and see Sutherland.

He outlined where the investigation was going and what avenues were being pursued.

Sutherland listened and took some notes.

"Right, let's go and see Miss Hackett," Sutherland said, "While I talk to her, I want you to take a wander round outside. See if there's any way of getting onto the river path from the grounds. Also, see if there's any way that a patient could leave the building unobserved."

"You think that Miss Hackett had something to do with this?" Simpson was surprised.

"Probably not, but I don't want to find out later that she had free run of the place, had heard about Adams taking over her job, knew what he looked like, any of that. I want to rule her out completely before we move on to the next person who might have had a reason to kill him."

"Okay," Dean said shaking his head.

"You're not convinced?"

"That a woman who is undergoing tests for goodness knows what in a private clinic would lie in wait on the river path in the hope that Tommy Adams, a man we don't even know that she knew by sight might chance by so that she could bop him over the head and pitch him in the river . . ."

"Okay, I agree. A bit far fetched," Andrew acknowledged, "But let's go and see her anyway and see what she has to say for herself."

They informed the rest of the team where they were going and headed down the back corridor to the rear exit.

"You drive," Sutherland said and followed Simpson to his car.

"Have you ever been to this place before?" Simpson asked as he started the car.

"Been past the entrance, that's all. You?"

"Same. Looks pricey!"

"I'm sure it is, Dean. Mostly paid for by private health insurance, I expect."

"What does Jill think of that?" Dean asked. Jill Sutherland had been a NHS casualty nurse when Andrew had first met her. There hadn't been so much of the ever-growing private sector then outside London and some of the other major cities.

"Och, I think she's sad to see so much money going to the private sector, but is realistic enough to know that it's the way things are moving. I think that her biggest problem with it lies in the work done by doctors and consultants trained up by the taxpayer. She said once that they should be compelled to work for a specified number of years in the NHS before they could work abroad or in the private sector. It's not something we talk about much."

The clinic lay to the north of the town so they had to negotiate the one way system to get there. Their route passed The Mutual Cap's offices.

"That must have been some business in its heyday," Sutherland said looking up at the imposing Victorian edifice.

"I remember the man from The Cap being a common sight when I was a kid. They used to knock on doors to collect premiums on a Friday evening after the mill workers got back home, full wage packets in their pockets."

"At the rate things are going, there soon won't be any mills left," Sutherland added.

"Our two seem to be doing alright at the moment."

"Aye, but for how long?" Sutherland mused.

The entrance to The Rochfield Clinic reminded Simpson of the Golf and Country Club. The landscaping and well manicured lawns were evidence of the money going into the clinic.

He found a vacant visitors' parking space in the small carpark across the tarmac driveway from the clinic's entrance and waited until Sutherland had got out before locking the car and catching up with him.

"Do you still want me to take a look round the outside?" Simpson hadn't changed his view that it was an unlikely scenario.

"Yes, laddie. The fresh air will do you good!"

Simpson snorted his derision but set off at a tangent to his boss, heading for the right hand side of the building while Sutherland made for the front door.

Like the SOCO building outside Rochfield, the clinic's origins were built on the shell of an industrialist's mansion. In this case the home of one of the old wool barons, but Sutherland didn't know which one. It had done service as a local government office for a while and then lay empty for several years. The clinic had been in operation for the past four years.

The door opened automatically and he entered what had been the grand hallway of the mansion now tastefully decorated in pastel shades, modern art on the walls along with the clinic's name and mission statement picked out in gold letters on the sage green wall behind the reception desk.

"May I help you?" The same voice that had answered Sutherland's phone call.

Sutherland produced his warrant card and held it up for her to see. "I've come to see Miss Hackett. Her boss told us that she was here." That stalled any suggestion of the receptionist trying to fob him off.

"Mr Carmichael said you would be coming, Mr

Sutherland. I'll get somebody to show you to her room."

The receptionist pressed buttons and spoke into her headset, "A visitor for Miss Hackett, Charlene. Can you show him to her room please?"

She returned her attention to Sutherland, "One of our nurses will take you down, Mr Sutherland, if you'd like to wait over there. The nurse will have to check with Miss Hackett first."

Sutherland nodded and crossed the hall to the easy chairs in the corner and sat down.

On a coffee table to one side were several glossy brochures produced by the clinic, detailing their areas of expertise.

He picked one up and started to flick through it but was interrupted by the approach of a tall thin man in a charcoal grey suit.

"DCI Sutherland? I'm Tony Carmichael, Clinic Administrator. Pleased to meet you."

Sutherland stood up and shook the well manicured outstretched hand.

"Miss Hackett is looking forward to seeing you. She tells me it will brighten her day!" he said and indicated that Sutherland should follow him.

"Does she have many visitors?" Sutherland asked.

"She's had one or two that I'm aware of. Neighbours mostly. Her employer, Mr Harmsbury visited her the other evening," Carmichael said.

That bit of information might prove useful. Sutherland filed it away.

* * *

Simpson rounded the side of the main building. A couple of acres of well tended lawn sloped gently towards a seven foot high beech hedge that bordered the river walk. A thick hedge that protected the privacy of the clinic. There was no sign of any way through it that he could see from where it stood, but as it followed the line of the river path there was a section that was out of sight. He walked slowly across the lawn towards the bend in the hedge.

Looking to his left he could see the new building at the back of the old mansion. A two storey addition ran the length of the building; and then a single storey extension, running some twenty to thirty yards beyond the building.

He noted that the rooms on the ground floor under the two storey section each sported a pair of French windows. The ground floor rooms had direct access to the spacious garden. A covered veranda separated the building wall from a path that bordered the lawn and flower beds. Alternating beds of roses, a few of which were still in bloom, and beds of late flowering bedding plants providing a colourful display.

On the other side of the lawned area a long Victorian greenhouse ran the length of a brick wall. A wheelbarrow sat at the door to the greenhouse.

As he continued towards the bend in the hedge he observed a man dressed in green bib-overalls come out of the greenhouse and look in his direction before striding across the lawn to intercept him.

"Oy! You. Where do you think you're going?"

Simpson continued his walk towards the hedge, walking slowly enough for the man to catch up with him.

"I asked you a question. Where d'you think you're going?" the gardener demanded breathlessly.

"Detective Inspector Simpson," Dean said looking down at the rotund gardener whose face had turned very red with the exertion of hurrying across the grass. Simpson produced his warrant card, "Is there a way through the hedge to the river walk, Mr . . .?"

"Bill Wharton. I'm the gardener here. Yes, there's a gate just this way. Is this to do with that body?"

"Tommy Adams, yes," Simpson said and followed the gardener.

There was an ornate black wrought iron gate set in a brick arch well hidden in the hedge.

It was padlocked, but was obviously in use as the padlock was well oiled as were the hinges and the locking bar.

"Who has the key to this gate, Mr Wharton?"

"I have one. There's another in reception and I think that Mr Carmichael has one. We open it in the summer during the hours of daylight. Some of the more mobile patients and their relatives like to go and sit by the river. There's benches along this stretch. Nice in the summer, watching the river. Very relaxing."

"When was it last used?" Simpson asked.

"End of September. We lock it for the winter from October through to the end of March," the gardener said.

Simpson examined the padlock closely without touching it.

It wasn't a particularly secure brand. Simpson knew from experience that locks of this kind could be opened quite easily with a little knowledge, but doubted that Miss Hackett would be likely to have that knowledge.

"I'd be obliged if you could make sure that nobody comes near it until our forensic people have had a good look at it and the gate, Mr Wharton."

"I'll make sure of that, sir, don't you worry," Wharton said. "Shouldn't be nobody out here at this time of year 'cept me."

The two men walked back across the lawn towards the greenhouse.

"Do you grow vegetables here?" Simpson asked, more out of interest than a need to know.

"Oh yes. There's a walled garden through there. Was all overgrown when the clinic took it over, but I used to work here as a lad when it were a family home. Been a labour of love bringing it all back to life. The produce is used in the kitchens. All organic, like."

Simpson was impressed.

* * *

Tony Carmichael knocked on the second door along the corridor, "Miss Hackett, you have a visitor."

"Come in," a firm female voice commanded.

Sutherland followed Carmichael into the room.

Miss Hackett was sitting in the armchair at the side of her bed, a small, immaculate lady attired in sensible day clothes.

Sutherland introduced himself, including showing her his warrant card.

"I'll leave you to it, Mr Sutherland," Carmichael said and pulled the door closed behind him.

"Good morning Chief Inspector. Do take a seat. It saves me from having to strain to look up at you." Miss Hackett said. A bemused smile played over her lips. "I feel honoured!"

"Honoured? That's not a response that I usually hear in my line of work." Sutherland pulled up the other armchair and lowered himself into it.

"I've been a great fan of yours for a number of years! You and Mr Simpson. I take it that he is lurking about somewhere?"

"Aye. He's taking a wee wander round the garden," Sutherland replied.

"Ha! Checking to see if there's an easy route from my bedroom to the river path, I presume!"

"And there is, I take it?"

"Oh yes. Out through the French windows, across the lawn, down to the left, the gate in the hedge is almost obscured from here, but it is there, and as far as I know, it's locked at this time of year," Hilda Hackett informed him.

"And I've no doubt that Inspector Simpson will confirm all of that when I speak to him."

"I certainly hope so Mr Sutherland. I would hate to think that you thought that I might be capable of murdering poor Mr Adams, even if I had a motive for doing so."

"At this stage, Miss Hackett, we're just talking to everybody who either knew Mr Adams or who work for The Mutual Cap in any capacity."

"Did you think that I might be concerned that he may be after my job and that I might do him in to be sure of getting it back, or something?"

"And are you concerned?" Sutherland asked.

"Heavens no!" Miss Hackett laughed. "Chief Inspector I haven't been told what is wrong with me yet, but I have a nasty suspicion that losing my job is the last thing that I should be worried about. Somehow, I don't think that I will be seeing the inside of The Cap again. A pity, I would have liked to reach my retirement and maybe received a clock or something equally useless."

She sounded bitter and sad at the same time.

Sutherland decided that a direct approach was called for, "Miss Hackett, what is your impression of the state of the business of The Mutual Cap?"

Hilda Hackett raised an eyebrow, "That's an interesting question, Mr Sutherland. Let's just put it this way: if I had any more money to invest, it wouldn't be in The Mutual Capital Life Assurance Company of Rochfield, that's for sure."

"Oh?"

"But then you probably know that already."

"Know what?"

"The business is barely viable. The parent company is trying to sell it off."

"Is that common knowledge?" Sutherland asked.

"I doubt it. I'm sure that I'm not supposed to know, but when people start asking odd questions one can usually work out what's going on more by what information they don't ask for than the information that they do ask for."

"You would have made a good detective Miss Hackett."

"Maybe in another life, Chief Inspector." She gave a rueful smile, "When Tommy Adams was sent to take my place I did wonder if he had been deliberately chosen for the job."

"Why should that be?"

"He's used to be a fully qualified accountant, at least that's what he trained at."

"You knew him?"

"No, not really. I knew of him. He used to have a furniture shop in the town. I knew his uncle quite well."

"His uncle?" Sutherland wasn't sure where this was leading.

"Tommy inherited the business from his uncle. Samuel Adams was very proud of his nephew, spoke very highly of him."

"Who else knew that he used to be an accountant?" he asked.

"Jeremy Harmsbury for one. I mentioned it when I last saw him. He seemed rather put out by the news," Hilda Hackett answered.

"And when did you last see Mr Harmsbury?"

Miss Hackett confirmed what Sutherland already knew.

"He was here on Wednesday evening. He left just after I mentioned Adams's background."

"What time would that have been?" Sutherland asked.

"I'm not absolutely sure. Half seven, eight o'clock. I remember him saying something about having a client to see at eight thirty and leaving rather hurriedly. At least that's what it seemed like."

There was a knock on the door. Miss Hackett looked at Sutherland, wondering if he was expecting Simpson to join them.

"Come in," she said.

It was Inspector Simpson.

Sutherland rose from the armchair and looked down at Miss Hackett, "I hope things don't turn out as badly as you anticipate, Miss Hackett. It's been a pleasure to meet you." He shook her hand. "Come on, Inspector, we have a person of interest to have a wee chat with."

"The pleasure was all mine, Chief Inspector. Inspector Simpson, it was nice to meet you too, even if we didn't get to talk!"

Simpson nodded, "Maybe another time, Miss Hackett."

Chapter 12

On their way back to the car Sutherland asked Simpson what his findings had been. Dean confirmed what Hilda Hackett had said. There was a gate and it was padlocked. The gardener held one key, the Administrator, Carmichael, held one and there was a third in a key cupboard at reception.

"Is it a locked cupboard?" Andrew asked.

"No Andrew. Anybody could remove it if there was nobody there to stop them," Dean answered.

"And is the reception permanently manned?"

"They have one receptionist who works from eight to three thirty, and another who works from three to nine thirty. They overlap by half an hour to allow for late arrival or if the morning girl needs to go early," Dean told him.

"We may have to have a word with her at some point," Sutherland said.

Simpson unlocked the car. Before starting the engine he asked, "Do you think Miss Hackett had anything to do with it?"

"Probably not." Sutherland shrugged and pulled his seat belt on.

"Any idea what she's in the clinic for?" Dean

asked.

"She hasn't been told, but I got the impression that she thinks she may have some form of terminal cancer," Andrew informed him.

"That's tough," Simpson said and started the car.

"Aye. She's a feisty lady. Beneath that demure exterior I think there lurks a rather wicked sense of humour."

They reached the end of the driveway. Simpson stopped to watch the traffic.

"Where to next, sir?"

"The Mutual Cap. I want to speak to Harmsbury, find out exactly where he went after leaving Miss Hackett."

Simpson waited for a taxi to turn into the clinic's driveway before pulling out and heading into the town.

"By the way, get Reg to send one of his constables to take a look at the river bank behind the Clinic. Just in case!" Sutherland said.

* * *

While the SS were heading towards The Rochfield Clinic, DS Cranfield and DC Wilson were following up on phone calls to the sales associates that hadn't been available when they had visited The Cap's offices.

They had arranged to meet the second person on their list at his home in Keighley. The first person they had spoken to had not added to their knowledge.

A DEADLY ACCOUNT

"A nice day for a drive in the country," Wilson remarked as he headed north out of the town.

"Not bad for the time of year," Maggie agreed.

"Sarge, what do you think of Young Eric and his computer program thing?" Wilson asked.

"I think it's the future of policing. At the moment we're relying on the memories of those who've been around a long time. They won't be here forever, and memories aren't always accurate. You've got to admit that it produced some useful info very quickly," Maggie said.

"Yeah, but maybe that was just luck."

"Maybe. Only time will tell. At the end of the day it's only as good as the information it's given. Given good information even us dumb humans can come up with the answers sooner or later."

"So why do we need it?" Wilson wasn't convinced.

"To me it's the sooner bit that counts."

Twenty minutes later they were parking up outside a neat stone house on the outskirts of Keighley.

Their conversation with the sales agent produced nothing of note. He hadn't done anything more than say good morning to Tommy Adams on the one occasion that he had seen the murdered man, and hadn't formed any opinion about him.

He could see no reason for anybody working for The Cap would want to murder Adams.

They thanked him and returned to the car.

"That was another waste of time," Wilson muttered as he climbed in behind the wheel.

"Maybe the next one will produce a gem."

"I admire your optimism, Sarge!" He started the car, did a U-turn and headed back over the hills, bypassing Rochfield on the way to Bradford to see the third person on the list.

The village of Guisewick was right on the south western edge of the Rochfield policing area. It was a strange mix of housing types to no particular order or pattern. Local stone bungalows next to all brick detached houses next to half-brick half-rendered semis that had sprung up haphazard as the village had grown over the years to become almost a small town.

"Any idea where this address is?" Wilson asked as they reached the centre of the village, itself a mixture of local independent shops struggling to keep up with the brand supermarkets that they had passed on the way in.

"Pull in over there while I get a look at the directory," Maggie said.

She thumbed through the well worn area directory that she carried in her handbag.

"Bloody useful having that handbag, Sarge. Got any sandwiches hidden in there?"

"No such luck, but I'll treat you to a pub lunch after we've talked to this bloke."

"You're on. Now, where are we going?" he asked.

"Take that street over there. There's a T-junction at the top. Turn right and then the next left. We're looking for number sixty-four," Maggie instructed after consulting the map at the end of the directory.

A DEADLY ACCOUNT

Jack Wilson started the car again and pulled out into the lunchtime traffic, such as it was. There didn't seem to be much activity in the village of Guisewick.

Following Sergeant Cranfield's directions they found the house, a brick semi near the far end of the crescent.

There was no sign of a car either in the driveway or parked nearby.

"I just bloody hope he's in," Jack grumbled.

"I thought that you had spoken to him on the phone."

"No. I spoke to his wife. She said he was out but always came home for his lunch. We'd get him in any time between twelve and two."

Maggie looked at her watch, "It's just gone one, so he should be here."

She set off up the short drive and rang the doorbell.

A nervous looking woman in her late forties answered the door, "Are you the police that rang?"

"Yes, and you are?"

"Mabel Crossley. I'm Fred's wife."

"Detective Sergeant Maggie Cranfield," she showed the woman her warrant card, "And this is DC Wilson."

Jack Wilson held up his card, "Is your husband in, Mrs Crossley?"

"No. That's just it. He didn't come home last night." The woman was beginning to sound on the verge of hysterics.

"I think we better come in, Mabel, while you

tell us all about it," Maggie said.

Mrs Crossley showed them into the front room. Sunday best, weddings and funerals only, the room screamed. The furniture looked twenty years old but brand new. The wall paper was of the same era as was the carpet. All brown and beige, not helped by the cream net curtains and the heavy brown Dralon curtains hanging at each side of the bay window.

They all sat. Mrs Crossley in one of the armchairs and the two detectives uneasily on the settee opposite.

"I take it that this is not a regular occurrence, Mabel?"

"It's never happened before, not in all the time we've been married. The only time we've been apart is when I've been in the maternity hospital having the children."

Photographs either side of the tiled fireplace showed there to be two children, a boy and a girl. The most recent ones showed the son in full graduation regalia holding the obligatory fake diploma, and the daughter in the uniform of a prefect at Bradford Girls Grammar.

There was a wedding photograph at one end of the mantelpiece. A young Mabel Crossley in a white wedding dress beside a smiling Fred Crossley in a formal regimental dress uniform on the steps of a country church. A group photograph of proud parents and in-laws in a matching frame at the other end.

"When did you last see your husband, Mrs Crossley?" Wilson asked.

A DEADLY ACCOUNT

"Yesterday lunchtime. He had appointments for the afternoon and said he'd be late back as he had a presentation to do the other side of Halifax. He works for The Mutual Cap, but you know that anyway."

"Yes. Tell me," Maggie asked, "Is a late night a common occurrence?"

"Quite regular, I'd say. About every other week. Sometimes two in the one week. Usually he's home by half ten, never later than eleven-thirty though."

"How long has Fred been working for The Cap?"

"Oh, must be three or four years by now. He joined them after leaving the army. He's been doing ever so well. It's all his ex-army pals and their relatives that's his client base mainly."

"Any chance that he was visiting one of them last night and it turned into an old pals drinking session?"

Mabel gave a weak laugh, "Oh no, nothing like that. My Fred's on medication that doesn't allow him to drink. Not like the old days though. In his day he were a right one for going out with the boys and knocking it back."

"Why did he leave the army, Mrs Crossley?" Maggie asked.

"His time were up, and they were cutting back so he decided not to sign up for a further term. I'm glad. Didn't want to see him doing another tour of Northern Ireland."

They could both understand that.

"Did he have a drink problem?" Wilson asked.

"No, not really. But he did have an ulcer. That's why he had to give it up. He's alright if he sticks to his medicine, his diet, and doesn't drink."

"Mabel, do you know who he was visiting yesterday evening?" Maggie asked, getting back to the subject.

"No, sorry. He always took his appointment book with him."

"What sort of a car does he drive, Mrs Crossley?" Wilson asked.

"A red Vauxhall Cavalier," she answered.

"You don't happen to know the registration number?" he asked.

"G43 MUM. Easy for me to remember. I was 43 that year, and he always calls me Mum."

"Mk 3 red Cavalier, registered in Leeds. Do you have a recent photo of your husband?" Wilson asked.

"There's one on the table in the hall. It was taken last year on holiday."

"Right. May I use your phone, Mrs Crossley? I'll contact our headquarters and get them to keep a look out for the car and him. I'll phone Bradford too and give them the information."

"Oh thank you. The phone is beside the photograph," she breathed a sigh of relief. "I'm so worried about him," she said to Maggie after Wilson had left the room.

"We'll do all we can to track him down for you, Mabel, don't worry. We do need to speak to him you know," Maggie said.

"Is it about the man they pulled from the river last week?" Mabel asked.

A DEADLY ACCOUNT

"Yes. Tommy Adams. Did your husband mention him at all?" Maggie asked.

"Only to say that he was filling in for old Miss Hackett while she's off sick. Said it made a change not having her querying everything. She gives the sales associates a bit of a hard time from what I can gather. Look, can I get you a cup of tea or something?"

"No thanks. As soon as my colleague comes back, we'll have to go. We have a couple more associates that we have to speak to before the end of the day."

"I understand."

"We have your phone number. If we hear anything we'll let you know, and if Mr Crossley returns please give us a call. If you phone Rochfield Central, they'll contact us and we'll be right back as soon as we can." Maggie handed Mabel one of her cards.

Wilson returned, "That's all in hand, Mrs Crossley. Soon as we know anything we'll get in touch."

Back in the car Maggie asked Jack what his impressions were.

"For her sake, I hope he isn't found upside down in a ditch," Wilson said as they drove back towards Rochfield for their next appointment, "There haven't been any reports of RTAs in the district or from Bradford."

"You know how the boss hates coincidences," Maggie said.

"Yeah, but you don't seriously think that her husband worked out that today would be the day we came looking for him and decided to do a runner?"

"Bit far fetched, isn't it!" She agreed, "After all, he only had to say what the last bloke did, 'I only said 'Good morning' to him once,' and we'd have no way of proving him wrong unless his alibi for last Wednesday evening didn't check out."

"Maybe it didn't. Maybe he has done a runner."

"In that case we better widen the search for the red Cavalier." Maggie lifted the radio handset and instructed control to widen the search, "Control, it may be completely unrelated to our enquiries, but until we find him we can't rule it out. Better make it a 'Wanted in connection' alert," she said.

"Roger Delta Sierra Three-Seven, Control out."

"Nice one Sarge. Keeps us right."

"Be even better if it's true!" she said. "Here, there's a pub up the road that does a good ploughman's."

"That's what I like to hear. I'm bloody starving," Wilson said with feeling.

"You always are!"

* * *

"Park up at the factory, Dean. We'll walk the rest of the way. It'll be quicker. Not to mention less grief from the yellow hats," Andrew instructed as they rounded the one way system at the top of the town.

The day remained dry but, not taking chances, they pulled raincoats on for the walk down to The Mutual Cap. The north east wind was rising again

A DEADLY ACCOUNT

and more rain was forecast for the evening.

They didn't hear the APB being put out for the missing sales associate.

Unlike Sergeant Cranfield, both men chose to take the lift to the top floor. From it they entered the door marked reception and confronted the receptionist.

"We're here to see Mr Harmsbury," Sutherland said, flashing his warrant card under the girl's nose. Simpson held his up.

"He's not in," the girl said in a rush, "Hasn't been in all morning. Don't know where he is."

"Oh! And no appointment book to tell us where he might be?" Sutherland asked."

"I don't know. I mean, his office is locked."

"Somebody must have a key," Simpson said.

"Richard has one. That's Mr Tillsworth, but he isn't here either. I mean, he was but now he isn't."

Patiently Simpson asked if she knew where he was.

"Out seeing a client, I expect."

"Did you phone Mr Harmsbury's home when he didn't show up this morning?" Simpson asked.

"Yes, but there was no answer."

"Have you tried it since then?" Sutherland asked.

"Oh yes! Every hour. Still no answer," she said.

"Is he married?" Sutherland asked.

"Yes. I think Mrs Harmsbury works, but I don't know where."

"Right, you'd better give me his address and we'll go round there and see if there's any sign of him. You don't happen to know what sort of a car he drives, do you?"

"A black Audi, that's as much as I know, sorry." She wrote down Harmsbury's address on a yellow Post-it note and handed it to Sutherland.

"We're doing well!" Simpson remarked dryly as they entered the lift.

"We'll see what we can turn up at his house," Sutherland said. "Get on to Swansea and see if they can come up with details of any vehicles registered at this address or at The Mutual Cap's address in case it's registered through his work."

"Better try their head office address as well, in case he has a company car bought by them," Simpson suggested.

"Get Young Eric to phone them and find out. It'll save time. Tell him to contact you when he has a result."

The two men walked swiftly back up the hill to the factory. Sutherland checked his watch. "You take the Incident Room, I'll check the canteen. If Eric's there I'll send him to you."

They went in through the front door and separated.

Young Eric and Vikki Gibson were at a table together. They looked up when Sutherland approached.

"Sorry to disturb your lunch, laddie, but I need you to get back to the Incident Room. Inspector Simpson has a very urgent job that needs done, and he and I have to head out to locate a suspect."

"Yes sir." Eric took a longing glance at his pasty and chips, and the steaming mug of tea.

"Take them with you, laddie. No point in letting good food go to waste." It wasn't strictly permitted to take food out of the canteen or to eat in the Incident Room. "Anybody objects; tell them you're doing it on my orders!"

"Thank you, sir." Eric put the plate and the mug back onto his tray and navigated between the tables with the grace of a top class waiter.

"Vikki, when you've finished your lunch, go and give him a hand. As soon as he's finished eating, do me a favour and bring his tray back here."

"Yes sir."

"Thanks. Right, I must collect Inspector Simpson and head out into the country."

He made his way along the corridor to the Incident Room.

Simpson was just coming out, "Ah, good. This has just come in from Maggie." He passed over the report about the missing sales associate.

Sutherland read it, "Might be something or nothing."

"No such thing as coincidence?" Simpson prompted.

"Aye well, not in my book anyway. Eric knows to contact us if anything crops up?"

"Yes sir."

"Right, let's go and see if the elusive Mr Harmsbury is lurking at home, or whether we've now got two manhunts on our hands."

Ten minutes later they were pulling up on the raked gravel drive of Harmsbury's house on the outskirts of Rochfield.

There were no cars in the driveway, but an impressive double garage the size of a small bungalow, stood to one side of the main house.

Sutherland rang the doorbell. Chimes echoed from within, but there was no answer.

"Take a look round the back, Dean. I'll stay here in case anybody comes to the door."

From its location the ground fell away from the rear of the house giving a panoramic view over the Roche Valley.

'There must be money in the life business,' Dean figured as he peered in through the downstairs windows. Inside the house were neat rooms. Everything was neat. The kitchen looked almost new and unused. The dining-room with its long teak table, six matching chairs and two carvers, and matching sideboard looked equally unused.

The living room, or was it a drawing room in a house this big, had a three-seater settee and two armchairs, occasional furniture tastefully scattered round the airy room. Double French windows led out onto the well kept garden.

Was it always like that or had they done a good tidy up before doing a disappearing act?

He continued round the house and the double garage. Through the window at the rear of the garage he could see that it was empty, but obviously used for cars not rubbish. There was a connecting door into the house that was closed.

Sutherland heard him approach, scrunching across the gravel.

"Well?"

"Place is like something out of House and Garden. Totally immaculate, the house and the garden. No sign of occupancy at all. Garage is empty."

At that moment a silver Honda Civic came up the drive. The right hand garage door opened as the car approached but the driver stopped short and got out.

"Can I help you?" Lydia Harmsbury asked as she climbed out and walked towards them.

Sutherland and Simpson produced their warrant cards and introduced themselves.

"Lydia Harmsbury," she replied.

"Mrs Harmsbury, we're looking for your husband. He hasn't been seen at his office and they haven't heard from him," Sutherland said. "Do ye happen to know his whereabouts?"

"As far as I know he's in London. He got a phone call yesterday evening and said that Head Office wanted him first thing this morning. Is this to do with the death of the book-keeper?"

"Aye, we need to ask him a few more questions."

"How did he travel to London?" Simpson asked.

"I imagine that he flew down. That's how he usually travels."

"Did he say that he was flying?"

"No, but he left early this morning. I expect he's caught the 7.40. It's the flight he always uses, but you could check with BA."

"Thank you, we will. Do you have a mobile number for him?" Simpson asked holding his notebook ready.

"Oh, he won't have taken it with him. Never does when he goes to London."

"I'll need the number anyway," Simpson insisted. He wrote it down as she read it from a small diary that she retrieved from the car.

"Thanks, Mrs Harmsbury. If he contacts you, can you ask him to give me a call," Sutherland handed her his business card.

"Certainly, Chief Inspector."

"You have a lovely house, Mrs Harmsbury," he said, looking along the building, "We'll no doubt be seeing you again."

Lydia Harmsbury watched the two men return to their car and drive away, noting with gratification that the young Inspector resisted the temptation to scatter the gravel.

Her prime concern was where her husband was.

Yes it was true that he had got a phone call the previous evening, but at nine o'clock. Not the time of day Head Office would have phoned no matter how urgent things were. They would have phoned earlier in the evening.

Yes it was true that he had left early in the morning, but even with modern airport security she didn't think he would have had to be there at five o'clock.

And he had taken his phone with him, so no doubt the police would be ringing it, but knowing her husband he wouldn't answer a number that he didn't recognise if there was a problem.

A quick phone call to British Airways or any

of the airlines that flew out of Leeds-Bradford would probably reveal that he hadn't flown anywhere, but then, he hadn't confided in her.

She didn't know where he was.

Chapter 13

Following their pub lunch, a shared jug of orange juice instead of the beer that they both would have preferred, ham and cheese sandwiches with home-made chutney, Maggie and Jack were on their way back towards Rochfield for their next interview.

Maggie kept an ear open for the radio.

Jack Wilson concentrated on the driving.

They reached the address on Maggie's sheet without getting a call from control. It would appear that there had been no sightings of Crossley's car or of the man.

"Pull in over here," Maggie said, pointing to a space in front of a terraced house in what had once been a row of mill houses.

Just as they were about to get out of the car they heard the call for all cars to be on the look out for a black Audi Quattro, the driver was to be detained for questioning in relation to DCI Sutherland's murder investigation. Suspect not believed to be armed or dangerous, but exercise caution.

"Whose car is that?" Wilson asked.

"They didn't say, but I'll bet it's Harmsbury's. I

take it the boss knows that Crossley is missing too."

"Do you suppose there's a connection?"

"Bound to be. Probably some ex-military connection."

"Ex-military?"

"The pictures in Harmsbury's office," she reminded him. "He was in the Paras."

"Was Crossley in the Paras too?" Wilson asked.

"The only photo was of him in formal uniform at his wedding. I didn't recognise it."

Maggie picked up the handset.

"Delta Sierra Three-Seven to control"

"Come in Three-Seven."

"Three-Seven, can you patch me through to Young Eric?"

"Roger. Wait, over."

There was a short delay before Eric came on the radio.

"Go ahead Three-Seven."

"Eric, I want you to phone Mrs Crossley. Try and find out what regiments he served in, right from when he joined up to when he retired, and get back to me as quick as you can.

"Roger Three-Seven. Wait. Out."

Maggie and Jack sat in the car, the engine still running.

A few minutes later Eric came back on the radio and informed Maggie that Fred Crossley had served in the Paras, and had been serving in Northern Ireland up to his retirement. He'd joined an infantry regiment to do his basic training and then volunteered for the Paras after a couple of years as a squaddie in Germany.

"Roger, Eric. Can you raise Mr Sutherland and let him know. I take it he knows that Crossley is missing too?"

"Roger, Three-Seven. He is aware of that."

"Thanks Eric. We're just going to conduct an interview with Peter Jordan – provided he hasn't disappeared too!" she couldn't help adding.

They could hear a slight laugh just before the radio went dead.

"Right, let's go and see what Mr Jordan has to say for himself."

They locked the car and crossed the pavement to try the door-bell.

The door was opened by a short, slightly balding man with a moustache who peered at them through thick glasses, "You must be the police."

"Yes Mr Jordan, can we come in?" Maggie held up her warrant card. "Detective Sergeant Cranfield and this is my colleague, Detective Constable Walker."

The small man ushered them in to the through living-room. Originally it would have been two rooms, but most of these old terraces had had returns built at the rear for a bathroom and a kitchen, and a new staircase and landing to give the houses a modern interior.

The interior was tidy, recently decorated and through the open door Maggie could see evidence of a new kitchen. It looked as though this property had been recently renovated.

A DEADLY ACCOUNT

"We're here in regard to the murder of Tommy Adams," she said as they sat, "Did you have any contact with him at The Mutual Cap, or anywhere else?"

"Not really, no. Other than to speak to him on the phone. But I did know him from the furniture business a few years back. Furnished my last house from him, you know."

"Mr Jordan, would you have any idea why somebody would want him dead?" Wilson asked.

"Goodness, no! I mean, what possible reason would anybody have for murdering a temporary book-keeper? I could understand somebody wanting to have a go at old Miss Hackett!"

"Oh! And why would that be?" Maggie asked.

"Oh, only joking, but she did make our lives a bit of a misery at times. Queried everything! Very thorough she was."

"Good at her job, then," Maggie said.

Jordan gave a nervous laugh, "Yes, from the bosses' point of view. Us associates didn't always see it that way though," he said, "Kept us in line like a mother hen with her chicks."

"But you had no contact with Adams while he was at The Cap?"

"No, sorry. Like I said, I spoke to him on the phone. We all did. Had to ring every day with our CAPS. I take it that somebody has explained all this to you?"

Maggie nodded.

"He wasn't there very long," Jordan added.

Maggie and Jack stood up. There was nothing more to be gleaned here.

At the door Maggie turned back to Jordan, "How well do you know Fred Crossley?"

"We chat occasionally at the Monday morning sales meetings. Not really my type."

"How did he and Harmsbury get on? Do you know?"

"Oh, they were thick as thieves. Ex-army. Well, Crossley was. Mr Harmsbury was only National Service, but he played on it. I'm fairly sure he recruited Crossley when he left the military."

"Is Crossley a good salesman?"

"Has a lot of ex-army contacts, seems to get quite a bit of business from them. He's lucky that way."

"In what way?" Wilson asked.

"This business is about networking. If you've got a good network, you've got a good business. Most of us struggle after we've tapped our family and friends. We have to work a lot harder to build a good client base." The man sounded bitter. "That's why most associates don't last too long. Not prepared to put the effort in."

"Well, thanks for your time. We'll leave you to get back to work," Maggie said.

"Oh, I do most of my work in the evenings. Not being married, I don't have to lead a normal nine-to-five life. Most of my clients work during the day. It's easier to talk to them after work."

He closed the door behind them and called up the stairs, "It's okay Nigel, they've gone."

Back in the car Maggie looked at the last name on the list, "Mrs Elizabeth Crouch. You spoke to her?"

"Yes. She's expecting us at four o'clock," Jack said, "Lives in Rochleigh. Shouldn't be hard to find."

Maggie crossed Jordan's name off the list, "I don't think he liked Crossley, do you?"

"I think he was dead jealous of him and not just because he was ex-army and a pal of Harmsbury."

"A bit too 'masculine' eh?"

Wilson laughed and pulled away from the curb.

* * *

Back at the factory the SS went straight to the Incident Room.

"Eric, any news?" Sutherland asked.

"No sightings of either car, sir."

"Get on to British Airways at Leeds-Bradford and see if Harmsbury took the early flight to London, or any where else for that matter."

"Dean, give his mobile a call, in case he does have it with him."

Simpson tried the number. It rang but wasn't picked up.

Sutherland turned to the other members of the team, "One of you get on to Airport Police and get them to check the carparks if they haven't already done that, and all the fly-drive carparks. I want to know if Harmsbury's car is there, and get them to check on that red Cavalier while they're at it. The rest of you start checking the other airlines at Leeds-Bradford. If everything comes up blank, spread the net wider. Try Manchester. I'm going to phone The Cap's head office and see if he's down there."

"But you don't think he is, do you sir?" Simpson asked.

"Damn right I don't. I think he's up to his neck in this, him and his ex-army pal."

Sutherland left them and went up to his office.

Simpson looked at his watch and headed to the canteen.

In his office, Sutherland reached for the phone and, realising that he didn't have the number for The Mutual Cap's parent company he rang their Rochfield office.

The same receptionist that he had spoke to earlier confirmed that there had been no word from Harmsbury. Sutherland didn't mention that they were also looking for Crossley. She gave him the number for their London headquarters.

Sutherland dialled it and was answered by a machine that provided him with what seemed like an endless selection of menus before allowing him to speak to a human being.

The girl who answered the phone was more than a posh accent for window dressing.

"Detective Chief Inspector Sutherland, Rochfield CID," he said.

"Cathy Gates, Chief Inspector, how can I help you?"

"I was wondering if you would happen to know if a Mister Jeremy Harmsbury is in the building?"

She was able to answer his question.

"Yes Chief Inspector, Mr Harmsbury arrived first thing this morning. I believe that he drove down. He's been in a meeting with the senior directors all morning. They broke for lunch at one o'clock and expect to resume at two-thirty."

"Where is Mr Harmsbury now, do ye know?"

"In the executive dining room with the directors. Would you like me to ask Mr Harmsbury to telephone you before they return to the board-room?"

"No thanks lass, that won't be necessary. If you could get him to give me a call before he heads back to Rochfield, I'd appreciate it."

Sutherland hung up.

"Bollocks!" he muttered out loud.

He went back down to the Incident Room, "Eric, cancel the alert for Harmsbury's car. It's in London. Harmsbury's in a meeting."

"Yes sir." Eric left his desk and went down the corridor to the control room and spoke to the duty controller. While there he asked if there were any sightings of Crossley or his car.

There weren't.

Young Eric reported back to Sutherland.

"Thanks, laddie. I'm going to get some lunch. I take it that's where Inspector Simpson is."

"I think so sir."

* * *

Sergeant Cranfield checked in with control and got the information that the search for Harmsbury's Audi had been called off.

"Well, there's a turn up," Wilson said. "The boss'll be livid when he hears that."

"Still leaves Crossley unaccounted for. Head back to the factory. I want to phone his house and see if he's turned up."

"Surely she'd have phoned?"

"I don't know about that. If she thinks he's in some sort of trouble she might do anything to protect him."

"Then she's not likely to say, is she?"

"No, that's why I'm going to find out what his rank was when he left the army and get Inspector Simpson to phone looking for him. I figure that if Dean asks for him by name and rank it'll throw her off the scent. He can pretend to be an old army pal looking for a pension or something!"

"I like it! You have a devious streak, Sarge."

Wilson lost no time in getting them through the evening rush hour and back to Rochfield Central.

They entered through the back of the building and went straight to the Incident Room.

Simpson wasn't there.

"Any ideas where Inspector Simpson is?" Maggie asked.

"Upstairs with the chief," Eric said.

"Any sign of Crossley yet?"

"None. I think that's what they're discussing."

"I'll be up there with them if anybody is looking for me."

"Right Sarge." Eric turned back to his computer.

Sergeant Cranfield entered Sutherland's office on his command. He and Simpson were standing

A DEADLY ACCOUNT

looking out of the window at the encroaching darkness outside.

"Maggie, any developments?" Sutherland asked.

She brought them up to speed on her interviews.

"Sir, I was wondering if Inspector Simpson would like to do a bit of play acting."

"What do you have in mind, Maggie?" Dean asked.

She outlined the idea she had put to Wilson in the car.

"I think it's a great idea," Sutherland said. "Let me know how it goes."

Simpson and Cranfield went down to the CID room to make the calls. It would be quieter than the Incident Room.

Simpson put a call in to Army Pensions and found out that Crossley had retired as a Colour Sergeant.

"Good at his job then!" Simpson said as he relayed the information to Maggie. "He was in 2 Para. If I get hold of him, I'll tell him I was in 4 Para. That's the reserves, so there's little or no chance that he'll know of me anyway."

"Here's his number." Maggie handed over a slip of paper and watched as he dialled it. "Do you know the correct form of address?"

"I suppose that depends of whether I'm pretending to be an officer or a squaddie," Simpson said, "What do you think?"

"Be a squaddie. It's more anonymous, and call him Colour Crossley."

"You sure?"

"Yes. Richard was in the Royal Navy. I remember him calling one of his mates who was in the Marines, Colour Elliott once and asked him about it."

"Okay. In for a penny!" Dean dialled the number. It rang for a couple of rings before being answered. "Is that Mrs Crossley?" he asked.

"Yes, who's calling, please?"

"Corporal Simpson, ma'am, I'm looking for Colour Crossley. Is he about?"

There was a silent pause before Mabel Crossley spoke again, "Do you know my husband Corporal Simpson?"

"No ma'am, never had the pleasure. I was 4 Para. He was two. I got his number from a mate. Said he was the right man to talk to about fixing me up with a private pension."

Again the silence, and then Crossley came on the phone.

"Corporal Simpson?"

"Call me Jim, Colour. I've been out of the reserves for a couple of years."

"And I'm Fred. How can I help you?"

"I've started up my own business, a small taxi firm, just me so far, but my accountant said I should put any spare money into a pension. What do you think?"

He gave a thumbs-up to Maggie. She nodded and went down to the Incident Room to phone a former colleague in Bradford to get a car out to lift him as they were much closer to Crossley's house.

Simpson continued his conversation with Crossley, and arranged to meet with him on Monday evening. Simpson even provided Crossley with his own address. Since his initials were DJ, he could always pretend that he used his middle name. Dean James, he could just about remember his mother saying 'Dean after Dean Martin, and James after James Dean.'

He hated it.

He suggested that Crossley pay him a visit around eight on Monday evening when things were quiet, and repeated his address. That way, if Crossley looked him up in the phone book he would see the name D J Simpson at that address and hopefully assume that Simpson preferred to use his middle name. And if spending time looking it up gave Maggie's strategy more time to work, they would have their man.

Chapter 14

When Jeremy Harmsbury came out of his meeting with the directors of the parent company he felt drained. The meeting had been called at nine o'clock the previous evening. In itself an unusual request.

The reason had not been stated which gave him no opportunity to prepare, and the timing of the meeting was such that he would have no chance to get there on time even if he could have got a seat on the early flight.

It wasn't often that he got the opportunity to thrash the Quattro down the motorway, but that is what he had done, getting up very early for the drive down, stopping once for petrol and coffee..

He had arrived at the company headquarters with less than twenty minutes to spare, just enough time to grab another coffee, use the toilet facilities and tidy himself before taking the lift to the top floor with its panoramic view over London. Not that much of it was visible in the grey early morning overcast.

The board had one item on their agenda – the untimely death of the temporary book-keeper of their northern subsidiary.

A DEADLY ACCOUNT

Their preferred buyer was asking awkward questions. Questions that they had hoped Jeremy Harmsbury might be able to answer.

Harmsbury was at a loss to understand why this could not have been done over the phone instead of dragging him all the way down to London.

The reason was simple. While he was there they were able to go over the books of The Mutual Cap in minute detail to see if there were any irregularities there that might explain why the book-keeper had been murdered.

Much the same questions that the police would no doubt be asking.

There seemed to be a shortfall in one of the accounts, but Harmsbury covered that by showing that they had spent extra money on recruitment costs during the year.

An ugly rumour was already beginning to spread that there was something fishy going on. That the end of year figures for The Mutual Capital Life Assurance Company of Rochfield might not be as healthy as they were being held to be.

Could Mr Harmsbury shed any light on why such a rumour should be circulating?

And so it went on.

By the end of the afternoon, Harmsbury felt that he had been put through the wringer, and that he was lucky to still be employed.

However, search as they might, they were unable to confirm the suspicions. The only thing that was clear was that the subsidiary was not performing to expectation and that a substantial improvement would be required in the last quarter if they were to get the sort of money for the business that they were anticipating.

Harmsbury was left in no doubt that his neck was on the line.

As he passed reception, heading for the exit he was called back.

"Mr Harmsbury! Glad to have caught you, sir. You had a phone call while you were in your meeting."

Harmsbury turned to see who was calling him.

"Ah, Cathy, a phone call, you say?" He crossed the busy foyer, collecting interested stares from others who were leaving to go home for the evening.

Cathy Gates was coming towards him with a yellow note in her hand. She passed it to him, "I didn't think you would like me to shout it out, but a Detective Chief Inspector Sutherland from Rochfield CID was looking for you. Here's his number. He asked if you could phone him before heading back home."

Harmsbury took the note.

"You might like to use the office over there, sir." She pointed to one of half a dozen small offices on the ground floor that were used by visiting executives wishing to carry out private or company business while in London.

Harmsbury thanked her and crossed the floor to the indicated office. He closed the door behind him, opened his briefcase and took out his mobile phone. There were several missed calls, mostly from his wife and mostly from after the time that Sutherland must have called at the house.

He used his mobile to phone Rochfield Police Headquarters, not wishing to have any possibility of his call being monitored by his parent company.

While he waited for his call to be put through to Sutherland, Harmsbury glanced at his watch. It was just after four-thirty. Outside, the sky was darkening and it looked like being a long, wet drive back to Rochfield.

"Sutherland here," the soft Scots voice said in his ear, "Good of you to phone Mr Harmsbury."

"I'm sorry I wasn't available in Rochfield, Chief Inspector, but when one's lords and masters phone up and demand an immediate meeting, I for one, don't raise objections."

"I quite understand."

"What can I do for you, Mr Sutherland?" Harmsbury asked smoothly.

"When will you be returning to Rochfield?" Sutherland asked.

"I had wanted to stay overnight, but it seems that the men upstairs want me back at The Cap rallying the troops," Harmsbury said.

"Can we meet tomorrow some time? There are questions we need to ask you."

"Of course, Chief Inspector. Would eleven o'clock be soon enough? It's just that I'm going to have to spend some time reviewing associate performance and getting them to see the need for speed."

"Eleven o'clock would be fine, Mr Harmsbury.

Will all the associates be at The Cap tomorrow?"

"I hope so. I'm going to phone the office next and get the staff on to rounding them up. I don't see any reason why they shouldn't all be there."

"I'll see you in the morning. Drive safely," Sutherland said.

Harmsbury laughed, "You're beginning to sound like my wife!"

"You should give her a call too. I think she's a wee bit worried about where you might be."

"I will. See you tomorrow, then." Harmsbury killed the call, phoned the office and issued instructions, "I don't want any excuses Miss Lewis; I want everybody in the training room at nine-thirty, is that clear?"

"Yes Mr Harmsbury." Harmsbury could visualise Wendy Lewis making a rude sign at the phone as she hung up.

His next call was to Lydia.

"Where the hell are you Jerry? The police were here. Why didn't you return my calls?"

"Oh calm down, Lyd! I'm at Head Office. I've just spoken to Sutherland. What's he like? I've only seen him on TV."

"Big, calm and dangerous, I'd say. Are you involved in Adams's death, Jerry? You would tell me, wouldn't you?"

"Of course I'm not. I hardly knew the man."

He could hear an audible sigh of relief from his wife, "So what did the directors want?"

"For a while it looked like my head on a plate, but they've settled for better results in the final quarter. I'm heading home now. I'll see you about ten."

"Do take care, Jerry," she pleaded.

"I will, pet, don't worry," he said and switched his phone off.

Harmsbury had hoped to be able to spend the night in London and drive up the following morning after a good meal and a better night's sleep. He settled for a traffic clogged run into North London and the M1, a stop at the first Motorway Services, an indifferent, alcohol-free meal and two cups of strong coffee before filling the car to the max and heading back onto the motorway, thankful for the Quattro's wet weather performance and handling as he sped northwards.

* * *

Fred Crossley made a note in his diary, Jim Simpson, the address and time.

"Who's Jim Simpson, dear?" Mabel asked. She didn't often ask about his clients.

"New prospect," Fred said, buoyed by the possibility of a sale.

"Did he say where he was phoning from?"

"He's ex-army, recently started a taxi business in Rochfield. Could be quite a bit of business in it if I handle him right."

"What if he's police?"

"Oh for goodness sake, Mabel. Just because a couple of coppers come calling, looking for me, doesn't make everybody a copper," Fred said with more than a hint of exasperation.

"But you haven't told me where you were last night? It's not like you to stay out all night. You haven't done that since before your ulcer," Mabel said.

"If you must know, I got into a card game. While the others were drinking and playing, I was just playing."

"And?" Mabel asked anxiously, fearing the worst.

Fred Crossley pulled a wad of notes out of his back pocket.

"I wanted it to be a surprise, love. I know I said I'd give up the cards, but it was just too good an opportunity. I'd sold three of them policies and collected their first premiums. They wanted to try and win it back. They'd already had a few jars while I was giving them the pitch. It was like

A DEADLY ACCOUNT

taking candy from a baby."

"Oh Fred! You should have told me! I've been worried sick. I thought you might be involved in that man's death."

"Who? Adams? I only met the bloke the once to get more leaflets and policy forms. Is that what the police were here for?"

At that point there was a rap on the door, "Police, open up!"

Swiftly, Crossley slipped the wad of notes into the drawer below the telephone, before opening the door.

Two uniformed policemen stood blocking his path.

"What can I do for you, gentlemen?"

"Mr Frederick Crossley?"

"Yes?"

"We need you to come with us, sir. Rochfield CID wish to interview you in connection with a serious crime."

"Am I under arrest?"

"No sir, but they would appreciate it if you came voluntarily to help with their enquiries."

"No problem. Can I get a coat?"

"Where is it, sir? Perhaps your wife could get it for you."

"Mabel, love, grab my parka from the under the stairs could you?"

Mabel, eyes wide with fear, did as her husband asked.

"Look, don't worry pet. I'll be back before you know it. Save me some supper, would you?"

She nodded as she handed him the coat. They

exchanged a quick kiss and she watched as her husband was led to the waiting patrol car, its blue lights cutting through the darkening sky.

She watched as it turned at the top of the road, drove back past her and turned right onto the main road. Briefly, she caught a glimpse of her husband in the back, and of the neighbours watching from behind their net curtains.

* * *

DS Cranfield and DC Wilson were waiting in reception when the Bradford City Police area car arrived and Fred Crossley was handed over.

"Sergeant, this is all a bit over the top isn't it?" Crossley said as they led him down to Interview Room 1.

"For your sake, Mr Crossley, I certainly hope so," she said as she showed him in and watched him as he pulled a chair out and sat.

"I should remind you that you are not under arrest. You are not under caution. You do not have to answer our questions, but it would help if you did. We've questioned all of your colleagues, and we would have asked you the same questions this afternoon if you had been at home as your wife expected you to be when we made the appointment."

"Yeah, well, I was a naughty boy, wasn't I? Stayed out all night."

"You had her worried, you know. We had to put out an alert for you," Wilson said.

"Used to do it all the time when I was in the

army. She never seemed to mind then."

"So what were you doing?" Sergeant Cranfield asked.

"I doubt if it's any of your business, but I was playing cards with a few old mates after selling them insurance."

"Well, it's not last night we're interested it. It's last Wednesday night" Sergeant Cranfield said, "What were you doing then, between the hours of seven and eleven?"

"Working probably."

"Probably?" Maggie asked.

"Hang on a minute," Fred Crossley fished through his pockets and pulled out a well thumbed pocket diary, "It'll be in here. Getting old, you see. Have to write everything down!"

He opened it with the little tape book-mark and turned back a page, "Right, Wednesday of last week, let's see," he said. "Seven-thirty appointment with CB. Life policy with profits. I was there until eight-thirty. Nine o'clock presentation GF. His and Hers." He looked up, "That would have ended about half-ten and then I'd have gone home. Not a bad night's work, if I remember."

"We'll need a fuller record – names and places," Wilson said.

"No problem. The first one was a guy called Charlie Beddowes, lives the far side of Bradford – Queensbury. I'd need my files to give you the exact address. The presentation was in Birkenshaw, Brown Hill Drive." He was able to reel off the exact address and the names of the couple.

"Strange that you remember those details so well, and not Beddowes' details," Maggie said.

"Not strange at all. I'd served with Geordie. Always fancied his wife!"

"And the other?"

"Just another appointment. I do three or four of them a day when things are going well. Only tend to remember the details if I've sold them stuff. Got to go back to do that. He used to be Light Infantry. Never met him before."

Either Crossley was a well prepared, accomplished liar or he was telling the truth. Without anything else to go on, Sergeant Cranfield was inclined to go with the latter. "Can you wait here for a few minutes, Mr Crossley? If this checks out, as I'm sure it will, we'll see that you get back to Guisewick. Detective Constable Wilson will keep you company."

While Maggie got the phone number for the address in Birkenshaw and spoke to the occupant, getting confirmation of everything that Crossley had said, Wilson watched the other man.

Crossley seemed totally unconcerned.

"How well do you know your boss, Harmsbury?" he asked.

"Oh, top bloke. He was National Service but saw action in Egypt. Me, I was stuck in wet bloody fields in South Armagh!"

"Don't envy you!"

"It had its moments."

"Did Harmsbury bring you in to The Cap?"

"Yeah. He called one night to sell me a policy.

We got talking. I needed a job, and that's how it started. Been good that. Good job."

The door opened and Sergeant Cranfield returned, "Thanks for your time, Mr Crossley. If you can get us the details of your first call that night we'd appreciate it."

"Not a problem. If your driver wants to hang on when I get home, I'll give it to him."

"That would be most helpful. I'll arrange your transport."

Maggie went and found Tom Jones, "Drive him home. Get the details. Make sure there's a phone number. Call it in as soon as you have it, Tom. I want to get this Beddowes chap on the phone before Crossley gets a chance to ring him."

"Got you, Sarge." he said.

Jones collected Crossley from the Interview Room and drove him back to Guisewick. He got the details and radioed them in.

Maggie put a call in to the number she had been given. It was picked up by an answering machine after four rings.

Maggie cursed her luck. Either it had gone through to the answering machine because the phone was already in use, or there was nobody in. She had to hope that Beddowes was out and not being briefed by Crossley.

It was nearly the end of her shift. She wandered along to the Incident Room for the evening de-briefing.

Sutherland was sitting beside the murder board listening to the various progress reports. He looked up as Maggie entered.

"Sorry I'm late sir," she apologised as she took a seat with the rest of the team.

"To judge from the long face, Sergeant, I take it that we can't pin this on your man Crossley."

"No, sir. Not yet anyway. I couldn't reach the man he says he was with between seven thirty and nine on the night in question."

"And we can't pin it on Harmsbury either," Sutherland informed her.

"Oh?"

"For one thing, he hadn't done a runner. His head office directors were giving him the third degree over The Cap's figures."

"What about the night of the murder, sir?" Maggie asked.

"We've spoken to the person he says he went to see after leaving Miss Hackett. According to him, Harmsbury arrived on time for their meeting, at eight thirty, and seemed a bit edgy. Harmsbury left their meeting at quarter past ten."

"Would he have had time to track down Adams, kill him and get to his meeting on time?" Maggie asked.

"Not a chance. His appointment was in Harrogate. He would have needed a clear run just to make the meeting on time."

"Back to the drawing board, then," Maggie said.

"Unless Crossley's alibi turns out to be a fabrication."

"I've left him a message to phone me as soon as he gets the message sir, but we'll have no way of knowing whether Crossley got to him first."

"It's a chance we'll have to take. However, if push comes to shove and you suspect that he's providing Crossley with an alibi that's false, then you may have to gently remind him of the penalties for aiding and abetting. And if that doesn't work . . ."

"Be a bit less than gentle, sir!" Maggie suggested.

"Aye. I leave it up to you sergeant," Sutherland said. "Moving on, has anybody got any suggestions where we go from here?"

Maggie spoke up again, "Have we got anywhere with trying to locate the ex-wife?"

"Good question. Who was handling that?" Sutherland looked round the room.

DC Fowler raised his notebook, "I phoned round the place. Wherever the Adams's were ballroom dancing, it wasn't local. Nobody had heard of them. The only reaction to my questions was, you might say 'post-mortem'. They only knew of Adams because he was dead."

"And you've spread the net wider?"

"Yes sir. I've covered Leeds and Bradford to the south and Harrogate to the north. I'm waiting to hear back from a ballroom dancing school in York. All I got was a caretaker for the facilities they use. He was going to speak to the secretary when they meet tonight, and get them to ring me in the morning."

"And what about the sightings, any gems there?"

It was Fowler who answered again, "No sir, just people reporting seeing him on different nights along the river path. Sort of confirms that he ran the same course every time. Nobody has come forward who saw him on the Wednesday."

"Okay. I think that just about wraps it up for today. See you all in the morning." Sutherland rubbed a tired hand over his face. It seemed to have been a very long day with not a lot to show for it. But that was how it went sometimes.

He watched everybody file out.

Simpson came over, and as if reading Sutherland's mind said "Better luck tomorrow, eh?"

"Hope so. What are you doing this evening?"

"Helen wants to see Under Siege. She has a thing about Segal! Can't think why!"

"I believe it's quite entertaining. I wish you luck."

"And you?"

"Home for a bit of peace and quiet and to mull over what we know so far. Goodnight, Dean."

"Goodnight Andrew, see you in the morning."

Chapter 15

Before he could go home, Andrew had to return to his office for an hour of paperwork. The endless form filling that kept the administration of police forces around the world, and the sustainable forestry industry working. There was talk of a paperless office, but somehow, Andrew doubted if it would ever happen. People everywhere from the days of the Egyptian Pharaohs to Communist China with its billion-fold population loved their bits of paper.

'When electricity isn't available, where will your fancy computers be?' he mused as he signed off another arrest report and placed it in the Out-Tray.

Working that extra hour had one advantage. Everybody else had got home and was enjoying their evening meal or soap and game show television, or both at the same time. Andrew had the roads to himself. The evening entertainment rush hadn't started.

He parked in his driveway, checked that his car and Jill's were securely locked before going inside. Somewhere in the distance he could hear fireworks going off. The occasional flash lit the cloudy sky.

He was nearly knocked down by his eldest coming down the stairs and heading for the kitchen. Perfect timing. Jill must have just called out that tea was ready. He watched Jamie's retreating back and stood aside as Sheenagh followed.

Having waited for the stampede of his older siblings to subside, Peter made his way more cautiously down the stairs until he saw his father. Then he broke into a run and wrapped himself round Andrew's waist.

Andrew ruffled the blond hair, "Good day today Petie?"

"Good. Good." Peter unwrapped himself and followed Jamie and Sheenagh into the kitchen. Andrew hung up his coat, and after washing his hands, taking off his tie and pulling on his sweater went and joined the rest of the family.

Jill was at the cooker dishing up.

"That smells good," Andrew gave her a passing kiss on the back of the neck and took the proffered plate.

"How was it?" she asked.

"Long and fruitless. Every time we think we've got somebody we come up against seemingly unshakable alibis," he said as he took his seat.

"Do you want a beer to go with that?"

"Not tonight, lass, I'll settle for a glass of water. Are you in or out tonight?"

"In. Will you be free Monday night?" she asked, "It's just that I've got the MWI and we've got an interesting speaker coming."

"Should be okay. Dean and Maggie can handle anything that comes up," he answered.

After their meal was finished and cleared away, Andrew took his coffee down to his study and spent half an hour with the radio on in the background, scribbling notes on his legal pad.

Nothing leapt out at him.

Frustrated he switched everything off and took his mug back to the kitchen. The television was on in the living room. Jill was curled up on the settee watching the start of a documentary. He settled down beside her to watch but was soon asleep.

* * *

Dean and Helen enjoyed a Chinese at their favourite restaurant, Lee Cheong's, before heading to the cinema for the second house.

A couple of years previously, the enterprising owner of the cinema had decided to re-develop the theatre and gutted it out, replacing the old Victorian Music Hall style of one-screen and large auditorium-with-balcony theatre with a four screen set up on two levels. It gave him the opportunity of having longer runs of each film and of screening the occasional more unusual, off-beat films some of which Dean, an avid film buff, took in.

This time it was Helen's choice. They spent an entertaining, albeit not intellect stretching couple of hours watching Steven Segal save the world single handed.

"Bet you wish you could fight like that!" she said as they walked back to his car.

"No thanks. I'm happy that I don't have to!" he said, "These days I don't like the odds so stacked against me."

"So, how's the case going?" she asked as they drove back to her house.

"Full of dead ends, why?"

"You seemed a bit preoccupied during the film. Like you were running stuff through in your head."

"I was. I was trying to see if I'd missed something. Usually in an investigation some piece of information pops up, and like a key it opens the case wide open. This time, nothing. No sightings of Adams on the evening he died. No dodgy alibis that land somebody in it. No anonymous phone calls pointing the finger at somebody. Nothing. No motive as far as we can tell. Just a few vague rumours about the place he worked."

Simpson fell silent again.

"But it's only been just over a week since he was killed!"

"Seems longer."

"Oh cheer up! Something will come up."

"Oh, thanks Mrs Micawber!"

"I didn't know you read Dickens!"

"Seen the film. Great for education was Sunday afternoon television. Old black and white movies. All the classics. David Copperfield was my favourite."

"Well, you'll see, it'll all turn out all right in the end. If that doesn't work, there's always

A DEADLY ACCOUNT

Crimewatch!"

"It might come to that. A televised reconstruction. It would be more use if we knew where he went into the river."

"Maybe that's where you should start looking, Dean. Where's the uppermost place that it could have happened?"

"Top of the town. That's where the path starts."

"And I doubt if it happened more than a mile below that."

"Why?"

"It's the way that the Roche flows. The water moves quite quickly above where the canal runs parallel to the river. The canal and the river run side by side with only a low wall separating them for about half a mile and then the canal heads away while the river drops again. With the flow of the river at that time the water would have been running fast, the body would have gathered sufficient momentum to carry it through the level section before dropping again and gathering speed to end up where it was recovered."

"How do you know all this?" Simpson asked, genuinely surprised by her knowledge.

"I've walked or jogged the length of that path more times than I care to remember since I came to Rochfield. I do get my exercise in other ways, you know," she said squeezing his thigh.

"So why did the body stop where it did?" he asked to test her.

"The river widens out there. Remember that used to be water meadows before all the building work started. That's why they called it

Meadowland!"

"Right Miss Clever Clogs! I'll get the searchers out tomorrow morning."

He pulled in to her driveway.

"And tonight?" she asked.

"Oh, a bit more exercise, I think; don't you?" He turned and kissed her.

* * *

Thursday morning, Simpson was up early and glad that it was a dry morning. He didn't relish the idea of asking search teams to scour the riverside pathway in pouring rain looking for evidence that probably didn't exist, or had already been washed away, trampled over or generally contaminated.

He ran through Helen's analysis of the previous evening. If she was right, and she usually was, they would not be searching more than a mile of the path.

In reality, they only needed to search to the point where they could say with certainty that Adams had gone in. Having established that, with the right person to play the part of Adams, the police would be able to do their reconstruction.

Using the stores where Adams had bought his track suit and running shoes they would be able to dress the runner correctly.

He had a quick breakfast with Helen before heading to the factory. He wanted to catch the night shift coming off duty as well as the morning shift coming on so that he would be able to call on sufficient searchers to get the job done quickly.

Thirty officers, two minibuses, would give each man or woman less than sixty yards each to cover. One bus would drop half its officers at the top of the town, and the rest at the point where the canal runs beside the river began. The second van could drop its compliment in the middle, half to go upstream, and half to go down. That way nobody had more than quarter of a mile to walk to their search point.

He stressed to the sergeants who would be in charge that even if one of their officers found the probable site, the whole section was to be searched in case anything else came to light.

As soon as anything significant was found, that site was to be secured and SOCO brought in. If they ended up with multiple sites it didn't matter. SOCO could sort that out.

The inevitable question was asked, "What if we don't find anything, sir?"

"Search slowly, search carefully. I'd rather you got it right than missed something. Okay, go to it," he said and watched as they boarded the buses and pulled out of the station yard.

He followed the second bus to the middle location in his own car and sat in it with his police radio on, waiting for a call that confirmed that something had been found.

He was aware that it could prove to be a futile exercise, but it had to be done. Up until that time they had looked at only the most obvious locations, including the area behind the Rochfield Clinic and had found nothing of interest. They had also looked at locations below the point where

Helen had suggested was the lowest point where the body had gone in and found nothing.

He hoped that the morning's exercise would prove her right and justify the cost.

While he sat in the car he phoned Sutherland to explain what he was doing and why.

"Sound thinking. Maybe we should have done it sooner. I'll take the morning briefing and you can let me know if anything turns up."

"Thanks, I will," Dean said.

"Anything special for the briefing you wanted mentioned?" Sutherland asked.

"Could you see if Fowler has got any further with the ballroom dancer? I'm convinced that we need to find his ex-wife."

"Right. Anything else?"

"Only if Eric has found anything suspicious about the former associates that merits looking into," Dean suggested.

"Okay. Keep in touch laddie." Sutherland ended the call.

Simpson looked at the clock on the dashboard. The search had been going for nearly twenty minutes.

His radio burst into life. One of the constables was calling for his sergeant. He thought he might have found something.

Simpson tried to put a name to the voice and the call-sign, but couldn't. He did recognise the sergeant's voice, if only for the fact that it was Mary Proctor, one of the three lady sergeants in the uniform branch at Rochfield.

Simpson had seen her get off the bus that he

had followed to the river. He wasn't sure which way she had gone. A quick radio call got the answer.

He got out of the car, locked it, and walked to the riverside path. He headed upstream at pace, passing other constables who were meticulously examining the ground round them, prodding with staves, turning over leaves, stones and anything else that something important might be concealed under.

He saw the stocky figure of Sergeant Proctor, her uniform and stab vest bulking her out.

"Inspector, I think we may have something here," she said.

Simpson surveyed the scene in front of him. Crime scene tape was being staked out round an area of heavy shrubbery where the path had meandered some yards from the river bank. Even from where he stood he could see evidence of the bushes having been disturbed, but only because he knew where to look. A casual examination by a passer-by would not have spotted it.

Sergeant Proctor called the constable who had made the discovery over. Simpson recognised him. Dave Tanner. They had shared a beat together years earlier.

"Hi Dave, what have you found?" Simpson asked.

"It's looking like where he went in. I'm thinking he was attacked on the path and then dragged through the bushes. There's definite signs of heels being dragged, and some intact footprints. Whoever did it had to use some force to pull the body through there. There's signs that a bit of the bank gave way where something has gone in."

"Sounds good," Dean turned to Sergeant Proctor, "Mary, have you called SOCO?"

"Yes sir. They're on the way."

"Good. Keep everybody else looking in case we find anything else."

Simpson checked the time. Sutherland would be on the way to the factory to give the briefing. He wondered if Andrew had heard the radio exchanges.

In the distance, above the background noise of Rochfield's rush hour he cold hear the unmistakable whine of Ed Richardson's SOCO wagon, and in a few minutes the man himself leading his team up the path towards the taped off area.

"Morning, Dean. Bit early for you isn't it?"

"Like yourself, Ed. Leading from the front," Dean said.

"Andrew about?"

"He's doing the morning briefing. I've to let him know if it's significant."

"We better get to work then."

Simpson watched as the SOCO team were checked through the police cordon and stood watching while they spread out like a small platoon of polar bears each with their own distinct tasks.

Jimmy would take photographs. Alex would do plaster casts. Sarah and Michael would meticulously scour every surface for traces of fibres or anything that shouldn't have been there in nature.

Some of what they bagged and tagged would be totally irrelevant. Empty drink bottles and cans, discarded plastic bags that had blown in on the wind, empty crisp packets and take-away containers, cigarette and cigar butts, used condoms, all the usual detritus that a throw away society dropped as litter without a thought to the environment. In amongst it there might just be something discarded by the killer, or shed by the victim that would prove who did it and that they had the point of entry into the river.

If they came up empty handed it wouldn't be for want of trying.

Ed would oversee every minute detail and Colin, his number two, would record every location, leaving a trail of yellow plastic numbered markers behind him. Jimmy would photograph each item in situ before it was picked up and placed in a zip-lok bag and labelled.

Painstaking, methodical work that everybody hoped would bring the killer to justice.

Half an hour after Richardson and his team arrived it was obvious that no other sites of interest had been found.

Simpson dismissed the rest of the searchers, keeping Sergeant Proctor, Constable Tanner and two other day shift constables to keep the public away on site.

He used his mobile to call the Incident Room and give Sutherland an update.

"Keep me informed, Dean. Soon as Ed can give you some idea of what sort of a suspect we might be looking for, we'll be able to swing into action at this end."

Simpson put the phone away and continued to watch the area where the SOCOs were working, waiting for Ed to enlighten him.

An hour later Ed Richardson ambled over to where Simpson and Sergeant Proctor were standing. The small crowd of onlookers behind the police cordon further up the path looked on, straining to hear what was being said.

"Two people were involved. The bigger one did most of the work, but it looks as though the smaller one helped sling the body into the river."

"Are we talking man and woman or two men?"

"Too difficult to be sure just yet. We'll know better when we get the casts back to the labs and carry out some measurements. There's been a bit of distortion due to the rain over the last few days. It's hard to tell just by looking at them if it's a large woman's shoe size, say a six or six and a half, or a small man's, say seven or seven and a half."

"How long before you will know?"

"It'll take about another half hour to finish processing the scene. We'll head back to the lab and I'll give you a call as soon as we're sure. Probably round lunchtime."

"What's on the menu?" Dean asked; always glad of an excuse to eat in the SOCO headquarters' restaurant.

"Fish on Friday. Probably poached salmon."

"My treat. I'll come about one if that's alright."

"You better let Andrew know what we've

found."

"Heading back there now," Dean said, "Sergeant, can you stay on site until everybody has finished?"

"Of course. What about the public?"

"I think you can open the path now. Just don't let them into the crime scene area until after Ed goes. That alright with you, Ed?"

"No worries. We're nearly finished." He ambled back to join his team.

Simpson returned to his car and drove back to Police Headquarters.

"I take ye found something?" Sutherland looked up from his desk as Simpson entered his boss's office.

"A couple of sets of footprints. Ed's processing them now."

"How long will that take?" Sutherland asked.

"Twenty-four hours, apparently. The casts have to be fully hardened before they can take all their measurements. Then they have to apply a load of maths to determine what the corrected shoe sizes are."

"Do I detect a good Friday lunch coming on?"

"Salmon."

"Aye laddie. If this breaks the case, enjoy your meal. You'll have deserved it."

"Anything from the briefing?"

"Aye. Fowler has a lead on the ex-wife. He and Maggie are on their way over to York to interview her."

"When did they leave?"

"Twenty minutes, half an hour ago. Why?"

"Something I need Maggie to check on while she's there."

"And what would that be?"

"Shoe sizes," Dean said.

"Shoe sizes?" Sutherland was puzzled.

"Yes it could be a man and a woman, or it could be a man and a smaller man but I won't know until I've spoken to Ed. He still has to check those measurements."

"Try and get her on her mobile."

Simpson pulled out his phone and called up Sergeant Cranfield's number. There was a brief pause, "Maggie, are you with Adams's ex?

"Just arrived sir."

"Do me a favour; see if you can find out their shoe sizes without arousing suspicion, understood. Don't worry if you can't. It may turn out not to be important."

"Understood, sir. I'll get back to you."

Simpson put his phone away.

* * *

Sutherland stood up and came round the desk, "That gives us plenty of time to pay Harmsbury a visit and have another chat with his sales people." He grabbed his coat of the hook.

"What do you expect to get from them?" Simpson asked as they went down the stairs and out of the rear of the building.

"Probably nothing. I just want to see what they all look like. To put faces to names, you might say. See if any of them working together could have killed him and chucked him in the river. God knows why they would want to though," Sutherland said.

Chapter 16

Sergeant Cranfield slipped her phone back into her handbag and looked up at Ms Clarke.

She and Eddie Fowler were sitting in the front room of Adams's ex-wife's new home where she was living with her new partner George Barnes, her ballroom dancing instructor. George was at his day job. He was a bus driver for the York City Bus Company and wouldn't be home until after five.

"My boss," she said without explanation. "Sorry, where were we? Oh yes, as I was saying, Ms Clarke, we are investigating the murder of your ex-husband, Tommy Adams. We're trying to gather as much information as we can about him and people who knew him."

"What can I tell you? We were married, it didn't work out. I left him. Divorce, end of story." She was very matter of fact, abrupt to the point of callous. Maggie decided that Doreen Clarke was a selfish woman used to getting her own way and wondered if Adams had finally decided to stand up to her.

From where she sat she could see Doreen's shoes quite clearly. Doreen was tall, almost as tall as Maggie and had feet to match. Maggie wore a size seven and was equally at home shopping from the men's rack if sensible work shoes or trainers were required. She suspected that Doreen Clarke would do the same.

"When did you last see Mr Adams?" Fowler asked.

Doreen shrugged her shoulders, "I don't recall exactly. Must have been a month after the divorce. We met at the solicitors to sign some papers, so it would have been about four, five weeks ago. I haven't seen him since."

"And Mr Barnes, has he had any contact with your ex-husband recently?"

"Lord no! They couldn't stand each other."

"Not even when you were taking ballroom dancing lessons with him?" Maggie asked.

"Oh, it was alright at the start but after a couple of years, when it became obvious that Tommy just wasn't a team player things got a bit messy."

"They fought?" Fowler asked.

"Oh no, I mean not physically. More verbally."

"George wanted us to enter more competitions, to join the formation team. I was all for it, but my ex-husband had no ambition in that direction."

"And you?" Maggie asked.

"Oh, I wanted to go all the way. Come Dancing beckoned. We could have won, you know. We were ready for it. At least I was."

"Just a couple more questions, Ms Clarke, where were you and Mr Barnes last Wednesday evening. The night Mr Adams was murdered?"

"Here at home. I was putting the finishing

touches to my new gown," Doreen answered promptly.

"And one final thing, with all the media coverage since the body was recovered from the river, you didn't think to respond for our requests for information about Mr Adams?"

"Oh we hardly ever watch the news. So depressing don't you think?"

"And news papers? Radio?" Fowler asked following his sergeant's lead.

"Hardly bother with either, I'm afraid."

Maggie would dearly have liked this self-composed, self-centred, self-obsessed woman to be their number one suspect but it wasn't looking likely.

"Do you mind if I use your loo before we go?" she asked with a smile that she hoped didn't look too insincere.

"Oh not at all. It's the last door on the right down the hall."

Maggie stood up, took her bag and followed the directions. The downstairs toilet was part of the cloakroom. Neatly arranged along one wall was an array of immaculate dancing shoes. His and hers. As she suspected, hers were a size six and a half. His were a size ten. The sizing clearly marked inside the almost new footwear.

She flushed the toilet and washed her hands for effect before returning to the front room where they had conducted the interview.

"Thank you for your time, Ms Clarke," Maggie said as she re-entered the room.

More pointedly she turned to DC Fowler,

"Eddie, we need to be getting back to Rochfield."

DC Fowler stood up, put his notebook away and followed her back to the car.

Doreen Clarke watched them go and closed the door after them.

A look of concern crossed her face.

"What's up, Sarge?" Fowler asked as he drove up the road away from the house. "I thought we were going to visit Dancing George!"

"We are. I wanted her to think we'd been called back to the factory. That phone call was from Inspector Simpson. He wanted me to check on their shoe sizes. Seems his search of the river path came up with some foot prints."

"Theirs?"

"Don't know. He didn't say what size he was looking for. I've to ring him."

"What did you make of her?" Fowler asked.

"I think Adams stuck her for quite long enough. Pity he didn't get to enjoy it," Maggie answered.

"A right bitch!"

"Yes." Maggie pulled out her phone and rang Simpson's mobile.

Dean thanked her for the information, "I'll be seeing Ed tomorrow lunchtime. It'll be interesting what size the casts turn out to be. We can compare notes then. Where are you heading now?"

"York City Bus Company. We want to have a word with Mr Barnes."

"Who is Mr Barnes?"

"The dancing instructor with the size ten feet. Doreen Clarke's new partner."

"Good. See you later, Maggie."

"Bye." Maggie ended the call and put her phone away.

"How are we going to get to speak to Barnes?" Fowler asked.

"We'll try and get his route from their inspector's office and see what the best way of getting hold of him will be. With any luck they have some means of communicating with him and can help us out."

"That'll not be popular!" Fowler said.

"No, but they must have some contingency for swapping over drivers in the middle of a shift."

The bus company that George Barnes worked for had its headquarters close to the city's railway station. They followed the street signs to get there and found a place to park.

Inconvenient though it was, the duty controller was able to confirm Barnes's location.

"You're in luck. He's due in here for a break in ten minutes if you can wait. You'll be able to have half an hour with him if you don't mind sharing it with his lunch break."

"Not a problem," Maggie said. "We'll get a coffee while we wait."

There was a café on the station concourse.

"My treat, Eddie. Do you want a sandwich or anything?"

"Nah! Just a coffee. I try not to eat at lunch time. Trying to lose weight."

"You don't mind if I get one?"

"No Sarge, you enjoy yourself. I wish I could get away with it."

"Exercise, Eddie. That's the secret. Follow the late Tommy Adams's example and use the leisure centre. You'd be amazed what a few hours working out each week can do. Swimming is as good a way as any, unless you like running or circuit training."

"Can't swim," he answered.

"You could learn," Maggie said, "They run swimming classes for beginners early on Saturday morning. Quite a few blokes use it. You should try it."

"Might just do that. Finding it harder to meet the physical as each year goes by."

"Not good, Eddie. In this job you need to keep fit; if only to chase the occasional villain!"

For the next ten minutes they enjoyed their coffees. Maggie used it to wash down a tuna and salad sandwich.

With a couple of minutes to spare they returned to the bus depot's office and watched as a bus arrived, the passengers got off followed by the driver carrying his cash box. He exchanged a few words with his relief driver and wandered unconcerned over to the office.

The controller nodded to the two detectives.

They closed in either side of George Barnes.

"George Barnes?" Maggie asked.

"Depends who's asking."

She showed him her warrant card without making a show of it. "This is my colleague Detective Constable Fowler. We need to ask you a few questions."

"About Tommy Adams I suppose."

"Yes." They followed him into the rest area. He took a sandwich box and a flask out of his locker and apologised.

"No, you carry on, Mr Barnes. We'll not take up much of your time."

"Go ahead," Barnes poured vegetable soup into a mug and drank it slowly while they asked him the same questions that they had asked Doreen Clarke.

He answered between mouthfuls.

His answers tallied with hers.

* * *

Sutherland and Simpson walked down to the offices of The Mutual Cap and took the lift up to the top floor. They spent nearly an hour with Harmsbury and talking to the other employees present that afternoon but came away none the wiser.

"Maybe your footprints will produce something more useful," Sutherland said as they walked back up the hill to the factory.

"Or Maggie will come up with something in York."

* * *

At one o'clock the following day, Inspector Simpson parked in the visitors' carpark to the side of the imposing Victorian former mansion that was the headquarters of the Forensic Science Laboratories, the SOCO base, though they did a lot of private and commercial work.

He presented his warrant card at the front desk as a matter of routine and was signed in. They knew him well enough, "Mr Richardson is waiting for you in the restaurant, Inspector."

"Thanks." Simpson knew the way, and even a blind man could have found the restaurant in the rabbit warren of corridors by following the sound of cutlery and the rich aroma of well prepared food.

Ed Richardson was seated at a table with two of his technicians. There was an empty space. Simpson joined them.

"I've taken the liberty of ordering for you Dean," Richardson said. "You'll like the salmon, I think."

"I'm sure I will, Ed. Never been disappointed yet."

They made small talk until the meal arrived, and ate in silence, savouring the food.

Only when coffee was served did they get down to some serious conversation.

"Do you have a definite answer on the shoe size, Ed?"

"Like I said at the crime scene, there's been a lot of rain over the past week. The dampness in the air makes the prints distort so we have to use test results carried out by experimentation over years to give a reasonable answer, but it's not fool proof," Ed liked to make any report he gave backed up by as much fact and education as he could.

Simpson just wanted the answer. "I understand

that, Ed. What did you come up with?"

"You have suspects!" One of the technicians said.

"I have shoe sizes. I just need a match before I can call them suspects."

"Well, I don't know if this will help, but our figures suggest that you are looking for a ladies size six and a gent's size nine. Does that help?"

"How accurate is that?" Dean asked.

"Those are likely to be maximum sizes."

"Oh well, bang goes that theory. I was looking for 6½ and a 10."

"No, definitely not a 10, and not likely to be a 6½ either. The maths doesn't support that," Ed insisted, seeing the look of disappointment on Dean's face.

"Back to the drawing board, but at least we know were looking for a man and a woman. Or are we looking for a young adult male and an older male?"

"Could be, I suppose. Odd combination for a murder. Unless it was a mugging gone wrong."

"They stole his keys and ransacked his house," Dean said.

"They didn't take his expensive watch though," Richardson reminded him.

"Maybe they thought it was a cheap Hong Kong knock off, not the real deal," Dean suggested.

"A mugger would have taken the watch," one of the technicians said. "There's always a market for a good looking watch."

Dean finished his coffee and stood up. He laid

a couple of notes on the table. "Enjoy the rest of your day, gents. I better get back and break the bad news."

They watched him go.

"Seemed a pity to spoil his day like that," Ed said and scooped up the notes.

* * *

Back at the factory the team was assembling for the end of week briefing. The time when the entire case would be reviewed and decisions would be made as to where to go next and how many detectives and support staff would be required to carry it forward.

Simpson took a seat beside Sergeant Cranfield.

Sutherland took his place by the Murder Boards.

The room fell silent.

"Inspector Simpson, how did your visit to SOCO go?"

"The shoe sizes didn't match, sir."

"Oh well, at least you got a decent lunch for your trouble,"

There was a muffled laugh from the rest of the team. The news had come as an unwelcome surprise nevertheless. It would have been nice to go into the weekend on a high, knowing that they had probably nailed down the likely killer and his accomplice.

Now they were back to the beginning.

The only additional piece of information being the shoe sizes.

Sutherland continued to question the rest of the team as he went through every facet of the investigation to date.

"We still haven't established a motive, folks. I think until we do that we'll be hunting around in the dark. Any suggestions?" Andrew asked.

"I think it's something to do with the finances of The Mutual Cap," Maggie said. "He was an accountant. I think he found something out and somebody silenced him."

DC Fowler spoke up, "And we haven't managed to find out who the person he dined with in the week before he was murdered was."

"He wasn't a guest at the hotel, I take it?" Sutherland asked.

"No sir. A table for two was booked in the name of Mark Spencer. The meal and drinks were paid for in cash. No credit cards, no paper trail. Only a vague description. Man thought to be in his early fifties, over weight, wearing a dark business suit. Height about five foot ten. Brown hair. That's as much as I was able to get after speaking to the restaurant and bar staff."

"Mark Spencer probably isn't his real name then," said Sutherland as he wrote the name on the board. "Was he local?"

"Home Counties accent, sir," Fowler added, "Oh, that and the fact that the two men seemed to know each other quite well. The girl who waited on tables in the main bar got that impression."

Sutherland turned to Simpson, "Has anybody asked for Adams's phone records?"

"No sir, not that I know. Anybody?"

There were no answers of yes.

"Right, Eddie, get on to BT and ask for a record of all calls made to and from Tommy Adams's house in the four weeks prior to his death. That way we might be able to put a real name to this character. Do it now before they all go home and stress the urgency. They can fax it through."

"Won't that require a court order, sir?" Fowler asked.

"The man's dead, Eddie, we're not likely to be tramping on his human rights now, are we?"

"No sir." Fowler got up and went to use a phone at the back of the Incident Room while Sutherland continued with the case review.

"I'm more than ever inclined to go with Maggie on this. Find out what Adams uncovered and the motive will be there." He looked round the other detectives. "Jack, did you chase up Crossley's alibis?"

"Yes Chief. Without a good reason to doubt them, they backed up his story. Unless they are in it with him, there's no way he could have been visiting them and killing Adams."

"And as far as you could tell they were telling the truth."

"Crossley and Beddowes had never met before. The other guy served with Crossley, but lives in a wheelchair."

"Yeah, that would tend to rule him out!" Sutherland said, "Richardson didn't say anything about wheelchair tyre marks, I take it." He looked at Simpson.

"No sir."

"How did your visit to The Cap go, sir?" Sergeant Cranfield asked.

"Waste of time. They had nothing to add, but I did get a good look at them all."

"And Harmsbury, sir, what did you make of him."

"Smooth. Salesman. Too busy looking after his own skin at the moment. We could hear him going after his sales associates hammer and tongs while we were in the reception area. Sounded a bit like he was trying to get blood out of a stone if you ask me."

Sutherland turned back to the Murder Boards and studied them closely as if searching for inspiration. "I can't understand why there have not been any sightings for Adams on the Wednesday evening. Just about every other night at least somebody has mentioned seeing him. One man walking his dog reports seeing him on three different evenings."

It was Young Eric who spoke up from his computer, "Sir,"

"Eric?"

"The point where the body was thrown in the river is just through the hedge from the road."

Sutherland didn't need it spelt out any further. Neither did Simpson.

"There's a gap in the hedge there," he said. "Used to be just a muddy track that people used as a short cut until the council cut the bank away and paved it over, made it a sort of formal access point, put posts in, everything, even moved a lamp post if I remember rightly."

"Aye," said Sutherland, "And what's the betting that our victim didn't run that way, he wasn't attacked there. He was attacked somewhere else and transported there."

"That would suggest local knowledge, wouldn't it?" Maggie asked.

"Or careful planning," Simpson said.

"But this doesn't look like a carefully planned murder. At best it looks opportunist," Sutherland said, writing 'Vehicle?' on the board. "Not likely to have been carried all the way there, is he?"

"But they didn't use that gap, sir, they dragged the body through the bushes," Dean said.

"So, more than likely a spur of the moment thing; and people without local knowledge," Sutherland said.

He turned back to the team, "I put this up as a possible scenario: He gets a phone call arranging a meeting. We may get that confirmed when Jack gets hold of the phone records. Not wanting to change back into clothes more suitable for a meeting, or more concerned with keeping up his running, he arranges to meet the caller somewhere along the route. The caller meets him in a car or van, probably with the smaller accomplice. They lure him into the vehicle, might have been easy enough if it was part of the arrangement, they talk. Something Adams says upsets the other party . . . but that doesn't explain Dr Ellis's findings that he was struck with something like a bit of branch or a knobbly rock." Sutherland put the dry-wipe pen down. "Doesn't really stack up, does it?" He looked around, "Ideas anybody?"

"I don't suppose there are any security cameras operating along there, are there?" Maggie asked.

Sutherland wrote 'Cameras?' on the board, "Anything else we should be checking on?"

At that moment one of the Incident Room phones rang, "Get that, somebody," Sutherland ordered. He didn't like his Friday afternoon case reviews being disturbed.

Wilson reached for the phone, "DC Wilson," he listened for a moment, "I'll be there in a couple of ticks. Just hang on to them until I've had a word." He hung up the phone and stood,

Everybody looked at him.

"Somebody in reception with a bunch of keys. Seems they were fished out of the river near where the body was found."

"Check it out, Jack. See if it looks like being part of this or a coincidence," Sutherland said.

Jack Wilson left the Incident Room and walked down the corridor to the main reception.

A man in his mid twenties was standing there talking to Sergeant Ferris.

After careful questioning DC Wilson was able to determine that the man was a keen angler. He had been fishing from the bank and had hooked a good sized perch. To land it he had stepped down into the river with his landing net and it was as he was scooping the fish out to weigh it that he saw something shiny caught in the weeds.

It was a set of keys, but rather than give up the rest of his afternoon's fishing he had continued until the light became too dark to continue and brought the keys in on his way home.

DC Wilson took the keys from Sergeant Ferris after they had been logged in the lost property book along with the finder's details, thanked the angler and let him go on his way.

Back in the Incident Room he handed them to Sutherland.

The key ring contained a Yale type key, a mortise key and the car key for a car of the same make as Tommy Adams had driven.

"Okay, meeting finished. Jack, you come with me. We're going to go and see if these keys are what I think they are. The rest of you start work on Adams's phone records as soon as they get here."

Sutherland and Wilson headed out of the back and Wilson drove his boss to Adams's house.

The keys were for the Yale and mortise locks to the front door, and the car key opened the car that sat gathering dust and bird droppings in the drive.

"So what keys did the person who searched the house use?" Sutherland asked, more to himself than to Wilson, "And where did he get them?"

"You don't suppose the killer went down to the river and chucked them in, do you sir?"

"Does'nae seem the logical thing to do, does it?"

"No sir."

"I'm thinking that our killer visited Adams some time before he was murdered and stole a set of house keys. As we don't have Mr Adams to ask we can only assume that there was a set hanging up somewhere and Adams didn't notice that they went missing."

"Which suggests that he knew his killer quite well," Wilson said.

"Aye, which brings me back to the ex-wife and her boyfriend, no matter what SOCO say about the footprints. And who's to say that she didn't hang on to a set of keys after they separated?"

"I was talking to Eddie after they got back from talking to her. He thought she was a right bitch."

"Aye, Sergeant Cranfield wasn't too enamoured with her either." Sutherland pulled out his mobile and dialled SOCO's number and asked to be put through to Richardson. "Ed, it's Andrew. Did your people turn up any correspondence between Adams and a solicitor?"

"Sorry, Andrew, but we couldn't find any correspondence at all, other than from his bank and the people he worked for, the City Secretarial and Book-Keeping Agency. Pay slips mostly. There wasn't any private correspondence at all."

"Bit odd that, isn't it?"

"We'd usually expect to find something, yes, but with no children and only an ex-wife that we know about, maybe he wasn't the sentimental sort."

"Okay. Enjoy your weekend Ed."

"You too Andrew."

"Come on Jack, we might as well call it a day. Maybe something will break over the weekend."

Wilson dropped Sutherland back at the factory and then went home, glad to have the weekend off.

Some of the detectives on the team were on duty that weekend, those who wouldn't be required at the beginning of the week unless something important broke.

Chapter 17

Sutherland went in through the front of the building to reception and asked Sergeant Ferris for an evidence bag, filled the details in, put the keys in and sealed it.

"Stick that in the evidence locker Reg, please."

"Adams's keys?"

"Aye," Sutherland answered dourly.

Ferris sensed the frustration in DCI Sutherland's voice, "More questions than answers, sir?"

"Exactly, Reg. This case is like trying to catch Scottish mist. Just when you think you've got it, it evaporates before your eyes."

"Are you on duty this weekend, sir?"

"No, thank God."

"Then my advice would be to go home and put your feet up. Don't even try and think about it. Do something completely out of character. Take the kids to the fireworks display. Treat the wife to a night out."

"Completely out of character!" Sutherland laughed, "I think you know me too well, Reg!" he said, "But thanks for the suggestions. Anybody left in the Incident Room?"

"Not sure. I think most of them are away by now."

"I'll just check before I go."

"The Chief Constable's still here."

"Was he looking for me?"

"Not that I know of, sir."

"Let sleeping dogs lie, Reg. Be different if we had anything useful to report," Sutherland said. "I'll see you on Monday. Enjoy your weekend."

"Wish I could, sir. I'm on shift this weekend," Ferris replied, "Call it firework duty!"

Sutherland knew exactly what that meant. Fielding endless calls from disturbed citizens about overly loud bangs, frightened animals, firework accidents caused by malicious misuse and youthful high spirits. It was the same every year. His constables would also be responsible for policing matches, the council firework display, and the above average weekend revelry.

He didn't envy Ferris's weekend.

Inspector Simpson and Sergeant Cranfield were sitting in the Incident Room like naughty schoolchildren kept in after class.

"Any luck with the phone numbers?" Sutherland asked.

"He made a call to a mobile number at five twenty-five on the night that he was killed," Simpson replied.

"Don't tell me. It was a pay-as-you-go phone and we have no way of knowing whose," Sutherland said.

"Exactly. Only the network provider. But we do know where and when it was bought," Dean answered.

"Oh! Local?"

"London. Edgware Road to be exact," Maggie answered, "Bought a couple of weeks ago."

"Can we get phone records for the number?"

"A blank sheet. No calls have been made from it," Dean waved the paperwork at his boss.

Sutherland pulled out a chair and sat down, "When exactly was it bought?"

"Tuesday 20th. Why?" Maggie asked.

"That was the day after Adams started work at The Cap."

"Is that significant?" she asked.

"I think so."

"Because?"

"Let's get out of here and go somewhere more scenic and have a wee chat and a dram."

"Scotties?" Simpson suggested.

"My round," Sutherland said, "Just a quick one, then home and enjoy the weekend."

"You're on, boss!" they said in unison.

In the warmth of their favourite pub, Sutherland and Simpson, joined by Sergeant Cranfield sat in a quiet corner near the open fire sipping single malt Scotch whisky and talking in low tones.

"You have a theory Andrew?" Dean began.

"First: we need the Met to see if there is any CCTV footage from the phone shop on the Edgware Road for the day that the phone was bought. With that we may be able to get a face and the Met may be able to put a name to it. We may have a photo to show round, particularly in the Lion Hotel. See if it's the mysterious Mark Spencer."

"What else?" prompted Maggie.

"Second: I think that this Mark Spencer has a mole inside The Cap."

"A mole!"

"Think about it. The day after Adams starts work there somebody buys an untraceable phone in London. A week later Adams calls that phone. Now the only way he would know the number is if its owner gave it to him, yes?"

"They could have phoned him on a land line and given it to him."

"They could, I agree, but I think it's far more likely that he was given the number by Mark Spencer who will turn out to be the phone buyer and the other man eating dinner at the Lion, the night before Adams phoned the number. The same night he got killed." Andrew finished his drink and stood up. "Enjoy your weekend Maggie, Dean. Let's see what Monday brings."

When their boss had gone Dean turned to Maggie, "Want another?"

"Not for me, thanks."

"What did you think of his theory?"

"Makes some sort of sense. It would make more if we knew what Spencer's interest in The Cap is."

"Maybe when we know who he is we'll know the answer. You got any plans for the weekend?"

"Richard is flying in this evening. I'm picking him up at the airport. We'll probably go out for a meal, watch the fireworks tomorrow night, and spend the rest of the time slobbing about. He goes back to London on the early flight on Monday."

"Where's he working these days?"

"They've got some job on in the Thames estuary surveying some wartime munitions ship or something. We try to get together at weekends when I'm not working. And you?"

"Much the same! We'll probably see you at the fireworks."

They left together and walked up through the town to Rochfield Central to collect their cars.

* * *

While Jill stayed at home with Peter, Andrew took Jamie and Sheenagh in the car to the Botanic Gardens, the spacious park with its Victorian hot-house, undulating walks and wide open spaces where events such as rock concerts and the annual Halloween/Guy Fawkes firework display – depending on which event landed nearest to a Saturday on the calendar.

Burger bars did rapid business. The heavy aroma of cooking meat and frying onions filled the air. Andrew bought a burger for each of them and went in search of a good spot to view the event, eating as they walked.

At nine o'clock the loudspeaker system burst into life giving a lecture on firework safety and exhorting spectators not to cross the demarcation lines that were pegged at a safe distance from the display site.

The weather held. A clear, dry night, the

temperature slowly dropping as the event got under way.

It was spectacular. Everybody agreed that their council had put on a magnificent show.

There was further entertainment for those who liked rock music as a tribute band broke into song on the temporary stage in front of the hot-house.

Spectators drifted from one viewing point to another to join in the free event.

Andrew herded his children back to the car and home for hot drinks before bed. They didn't see Dean and Helen, or Maggie and Richard such was the size of the crowd.

* * *

It was with some relief that the team assembled on Monday morning not having been called out over the weekend.

The CCTV footage that the Metropolitan Police had managed to gather together and edit onto one DVD had been couriered up to Rochfield and was ready to view on Eric's computer screen.

Using footage from the shop's interior CCTV feeds and other public feeds that the experts in the Met had managed to examine, they were able to watch a montage of sometimes quite clear, at other times grainy images of a heavily built white male.

They were able to watch as this man came down the road from the direction of Hyde Park to the south, purchased the phone, paid for it with cash, exited the shop and headed north along the

Edgware Road from where he entered the Edgware Road tube station.

"And he could have gone anywhere from there, sir," said Young Eric.

"I take it that the Met have no idea who he is, do they?" Sutherland asked.

"No sir. He's not on CRO or any other database that they have access to. They've sent a still photo of the clearest image that they managed to lift." Eric handed it over to Sutherland.

Sutherland looked at it carefully before handing it round the room, "Take a good look people. I want this man brought in for questioning if he's seen on our patch. Wilson, take this down to the office and get them to run a couple of dozen copies, say about thirty to start with. Bring the original back here, keep one for yourself and go round to the Lion. Find out if this is the man who dined there with Adams."

"And the rest of the copies?"

"Give twenty to uniform. I'll decide the best use to make of the rest. Oh, and while you're at, see if they can blow it up to A3 size for the media room."

Wilson left the room while the rest of the team watched the DVD images again over Eric's shoulder.

Wilson returned after ten minutes with the A3 copy and the remaining copies. He handed the original back to Sutherland who pinned it on the board.

"Let me know as soon as you have confirmation, Jack. I realise that not all the evening staff will be on duty at this time in the morning."

"I have addresses for them here sir." Wilson tapped the pocket where he kept his police notebook. "Soon as I have an ident, I'll call it in."

Sutherland nodded, "Good man." As the door closed he turned back to the Murder boards and wrote 'Mole.'

"Have you had any more thoughts on that, sir?" Simpson asked.

"Aye, laddie. The one question we haven't addressed is 'When did each individual start working there?'"

Sutherland pointed to each name in turn.

"We can rule out Jeremy Harmsbury for the murder, but I'm of the opinion that his only crime is in doing some clever accounting of his own. He's been there longer than anyone. The next longest serving employee is Hilda Hackett, but she was definitely not in a position to kill Adams. Next is Richard Tillsworth. He's been there for twelve years. Michael Blandford has been there for over eight years, Fred Crossley for nearly four, and Peter Jordan has been there for over two years. Elizabeth Crouch has been there for just under a year; which leaves Sally Pickton. She's only been there for a matter of weeks. What do we know about her?"

"She and Blandford were together towards the end of that evening," Maggie said.

"Yes, but has anybody followed up on where she was for the rest of the evening? Did anyone interview the people she said she was with?"

Sutherland looked round the room. Nobody was providing the answer he wanted to hear.

"I take it from the deafening silence that we've dropped the ball," he turned to Maggie, "Sergeant, take Fowler with you. Find those people and talk to them."

"Right away, sir." Maggie grabbed her bag and her coat. Eddie Fowler scrambled after her, pulling on his jacket as he went.

The rest of the team secretly were glad that it hadn't been up to them.

* * *

Using her copy of the notes DC Wilson had taken when carrying out their initial interviews at The Mutual Cap, DS Cranfield and DC Fowler drove to the address that Sally Pickton had given them. The address of the people that she had had an appointment with on the night Adams had died.

Except that the address didn't exist. Where Number 13 Acacia Grove should have been was Number 15. Some superstitious developer had omitted the number.

Sergeant Cranfield swore.

"Right, let's get round to her home address in Rochleigh and see if that exists. Pronto!"

Fowler flicked the switches and fired up the blues and twos as he tore through the traffic, round the one way system and up the Rochleigh Road, out through the village and into the new development where Sally Pickton had said that she lived.

The house was there. She wasn't. The elderly couple who lived there had never heard of her, and as they didn't have a photograph, they couldn't be sure that the description that Maggie gave of the girl calling herself Sally Pickton was of somebody they might have met at some time.

Back in the car, Maggie pulled out her mobile phone and rang Rochfield Central.

"Alice, it's Maggie. Can you find DCI Sutherland? He should still be in the Incident Room." She waited while Alice connected her.

"Maggie?"

"Yes boss. Bad news I'm afraid. The address she said she was at doesn't exist. It's a missing number. And she doesn't live at the home address she gave. We've been led right up the garden path."

"Get down to The Cap. See if you can get a photograph of her. They must have one in her file. They all carry those identity badges."

"Yes sir." She ended the call. "Eddie, The Cap. Step on it."

He did. Less than five minutes later they were parked on a double yellow line outside The Cap's building. "Wait here with the car, Eddie. I'll take a race up the stairs and see if she's here. Make sure that she doesn't get past you."

Maggie Cranfield took the flights of stairs two at a time passing startled office workers who had heard the commotion of the police siren and come out to see what was going on.

At the top, barely pausing for breath she shoved the door to the reception open, took a quick look round before approaching Wendy Lewis.

"Wendy, is Sally Pickton here this morning?"

"No. I haven't seen her. She didn't report for the Monday sales meeting like she should have."

"Who keeps the personnel files?"

"Mr Harmsbury has them in his office."

"Is he in?"

"Yes, but . . ." But she was talking to Cranfield's retreating back.

Maggie entered Harmsbury's office without knocking.

"What the . . .?" Harmsbury was about to continue, "Sergeant Cranfield. Nice of you to drop in!"

"I need Sally Pickton's file – now!"

"Sally? Is there a problem?"

"Just get the file, sir, and we'll see."

Harmsbury went to the filing cabinet, opened the drawer marked Associates and fingered his way down the alphabet to 'P' and extracted a Manila file. Clipped just inside was a passport sized colour photograph of the girl calling herself Sally Pickton.

Maggie seized the folder from Harmsbury and spread it on his desk.

"She wasn't at the meeting this morning," Harmsbury said.

"I know, sir. And she probably isn't Sally Pickton. I'm going to need this file, the photograph anyway, and her address and reference details. It would be easiest if I took all of it. You can have it back as soon as we've finished with it."

"Right! Go ahead, Sergeant. What's she done? I mean surely she didn't kill Tommy Adams?"

"We'll find out when we find her, sir. I can't say any more at this stage."

Maggie hurried back down the corridor past reception and down the stairs.

"Did she come out?" Maggie said as she pulled her phone out.

"No Sarge. A few curious onlookers, nothing more."

"Alice, get me DCI Sutherland again, please."

"What have you got for us Maggie?"

"Her ID photo and the address she used for her application. Her references and, would you believe, a CRO check that came up clean."

"At the moment I'd believe anything, but does it get us any closer to finding her?"

"We're heading over to this address now, sir."

"Keep me posted. If you don't find her, get back here with that photograph and let our people see if they can enlarge it sufficiently."

* * *

In the Incident Room at Rochfield Central, Andrew Sutherland sat with his head in his hands.

"Bad as that, sir?" Simpson asked.

Sutherland looked up. "Maybe worse, I don't know." He straightened up, "Okay, what have we got? A heavily built man calling himself Mark Spencer, whose picture we have. A girl calling herself Sally Pickton, whose picture we have.

How are they linked?"

"She's his mole in The Cap," Simpson pointed out.

"Why does he need a mole?"

"He's spying on them."

"For himself? For a rival company? What did Adams find out that got him killed?" Sutherland wondered aloud.

"Must have been something that Spencer didn't expect him to find. Something that would have exposed Spencer. The waitress in the Lion said that they seemed to know each other quite well."

"Give Wilson a call; see if it's the same man."

Simpson pulled out his mobile and rang Wilson's number. After a brief conversation Simpson was able to confirm that the phone buyer and the diner were the same person.

"Looks like your theory is panning out, sir."

"Small comfort, laddie! We're back to catching Scottish mist," Sutherland said, "Get me the file with Adams's phone records in it. I want to have a quick look at it."

Sutherland took the file and read through the list of numbers and the notes that his team had written beside each number.

There were calls to and from the City Secretarial and Book-Keeping Agency. A call to a garage that did car servicing for his make of car. Two calls to the municipal leisure centre and one call from a pay phone in the lobby of the Lion Hotel made on the evening of their meal, and the call to the unlisted mobile phone number. Four calls from a double glazing company and three from different life insurance companies. One call to his solicitor at the beginning of the list.

Not much to show for the last four weeks of a man's life.

Sutherland handed the file back to Simpson, "Did anybody speak to his solicitor, Dean?"

"I did, sir. It was after you asked Richardson if they had found any paperwork relating to his solicitor. I phoned round the local solicitors until I got a hit. He called to see about making a will, but never got round to it. I asked his solicitor if he had any family, but it doesn't seem that he had, at least not that the solicitor was aware of. Maybe if he'd kept the appointment we'd know more about that."

"I wonder who'll get his estate now." Sutherland shook his head, "Nobody has come forward to claim the body, have they?"

"Do you want me to find out?"

"Yes, Dean. If only to satisfy me that we haven't missed something else in this investigation."

"Not like Maggie not to follow up on a thing like that," Simpson said.

"Aye, well there was a lot going on. Never mind. Lessons to be learned and all that. I'm going up to my office. Let me know when she gets back," Sutherland headed to the door, "And find out what sort of a car Sally Pickton drives. We need to find it."

"Yes sir."

Chapter 18

On the outskirts of Rochfield, Sally Pickton sat in her car in a lay-by waiting for Mark Parfitt, and wondering, not for the first time, what she had got herself mixed up in.

This was supposed to have been a simple snooping job. Take on the role of a trainee sales agent, go through the training course, maybe even make a few sales, watch her fellow sales agents, gauge how active the company seemed to be, report back.

The arrival at the offices of The Mutual Capital Life Assurance Company of Rochfield of Tommy Adams, a man known to Parfitt, had changed everything.

When she reported his arrival to Parfitt over a cup of coffee in a café in the shopping centre, she thought he was going to have a fit. He choked on his coffee, spluttered and coughed for a full minute, turning an ominous shade of red before calming down. Others at adjoining tables became quite concerned.

Holding a handkerchief to his nose and mouth he had got up and made for the door followed by Sally.

A DEADLY ACCOUNT

Once in the fresh air he motioned for her to follow him back towards the multi-storey carpark.

"What the hell's wrong?" she asked urgently as they approached his car.

"I trained Adams. Years ago, but he was very bright. Had a nose for dodgy book keeping. Could have gone right to the top but threw it all away to come back here and run a furniture shop or something. Never understood it."

"But surely that's what you need, Mark. Somebody right on the inside who can give you all the proper information. The facts, Mark, not just impressions."

"You're right, of course," he had said hurriedly, "I'll have to get in touch with him and sound him out. I'll need you to get his phone number and address. Can you do that?"

"Shouldn't be too difficult. I'll let you know as soon as I have it."

They had parted there. Sally had returned to the offices of The Cap and got into conversation with the receptionist, Wendy, who had a great line in gossip and chat, especially with Sally who was about her own age. Sally had found out the name of the agency in Leeds that had supplied the replacement book-keeper and spun them a plausible yarn about Adams having been asked to report to their London head office, and that she hadn't collected all his details for their records, and her boss was having a fit.

A bored secretary at the agency had divulged the information from their records and been thanked profusely.

Sally phoned it through to Parfitt, little knowing where it would lead.

Adjusting the rear-view mirror, she removed the blond wig and replaced it with a dark brown wig, brushed it out and added plain lens dark rimmed glasses, her Nana Mouskouri look. Taking the glasses off again, she darkened her make-up slightly, added some black mascara and replaced the glasses.

Just as she finished, Parfitt's car pulled across the road from the opposite direction and parked up behind her. She watched in the mirror as he got out and approached her car, wondering what he had in mind.

She wound down the window.

"Are you ready to go?" he asked, wanting to put as much distance between himself and Rochfield as rapidly as possible.

"Where are we going?" Sally asked.

"North. Get as far away as possible and then head back south by the west coast," Parfitt told her. "I'm pretty certain the police don't have any details of my car to work on. There's more chance that they know about yours."

"Shall we ditch it somewhere?" She would be quite happy not to have to drive the clapped out Escort any further. They had picked it up at a car auction with six month's tax and MoT, and insured it under a false name that Parfitt had arranged.

"Might as well leave it here with the keys in it and hope somebody steals it. You have cleaned it out?" Parfitt asked.

A DEADLY ACCOUNT

"Completely. Even put it through a car wash and vacuumed the inside," she said.

"Good girl. Right. Let's go," he said.

She climbed out, and, carrying her shoulder bag went round to the back of the car to get her suitcase.

She thought nothing of Parfitt following her, assuming that he would help her with the heavy suitcase.

She didn't see the blow to the back of the neck.

"Sorry, girl, but you were going to become a liability," he said softly as he eased her body to the ground between the car and the hedge. He returned to his car and reversed it closer to the open boot of her Escort.

Getting out again he crouched at the back of his car, waited until a couple of vehicles had sped past going downhill towards Rochfield and the road had gone silent again before opening his boot, removing her case and swinging it across into the boot of his car. Hearing another vehicle coming up the hill he quickly slammed his boot shut and ducked out of site.

The lorry crawled past and continued into the distance.

Silence again.

Parfitt lifted the girl's inert body with ease and squeezed it into the empty boot of the Escort. He put her shoulder bag behind the driver's seat of his own car before getting the Escort's keys, locking the boot and throwing the keys over the hedge into the adjacent field.

Sweating in spite of the chill November air, he

climbed back into his car started the engine, checked that the road was clear before swinging it round and heading back up the road away from Rochfield and the disastrous events.

How long would it take for Rochfield police to work out who he was and what he had been trying to achieve before the untimely appearance of Tommy Adams?

If Miss Hackett hadn't been taken ill and Tommy Adams hadn't been the one person out of all the book-keepers working freelance in the north of England to be sent to take her place, maybe he would have got away with it and become a very rich man.

It wasn't to be, and now he was on the run.

He had his passport and plenty of cash to get out of the country, but it wouldn't last forever. He would need to empty his bank account, but that could prove difficult at short notice.

* * *

At Rochfield Police Headquarters DI Simpson lifted the phone and dialled the offices of The Cap.

"DI Simpson, Wendy, I need to speak to Mike Blandford urgently. Is he in the building?"

"No, Inspector, but I can give you his mobile number if that would help."

"Go ahead," Simpson said, pulling a pad towards him. He took the down the number and read it back to her to check that he had got it right. "Thanks."

A DEADLY ACCOUNT

He dialled the mobile number that she had given him, praying that it wouldn't be diverted to voice-mail.

"Mike Blandford, how can I help you?"

"It's DI Simpson. I need to know everything you can tell me about Sally Pickton's car."

"It's a metallic blue Mark 2 Escort. Three door hatch, why?"

"She wasn't at the meeting this morning, was she?"

"No, no she wasn't."

"The details she gave us about her place of residence were false, so were the details of the appointment she was supposed to have had on the night you helped her get her car started. We need to find that car and her, as soon as possible. Do you happen to know the reg number?"

"Just that it was a B reg. Not from round here. Something HP, if that's any use. Sorry I can't be more help."

"No matter, sir," Dean said, "We'll go with what we've got. If you remember any more, get back to us as soon as possible."

"Is she in some sort of trouble, Inspector?"

"Afraid so. Big trouble. Let's just hope that we get to her first." Simpson hung up and phoned the control room. He asked that an APB be put out for the car and gave them what details he could.

Then he went upstairs to speak to Sutherland.

Having listened to all that Simpson had put into motion, Sutherland paused before speaking.

"What's your feeling about this?"

"Bad." Dean answered.

"That makes two of us. I think Spencer may decide to cut his losses and that might include tidying up loose ends. Pity we have no knowledge of where he's from, or what he drives. We might know where he plans on running to."

"Back to London?" Dean suggested.

"It may have gone beyond that, Dean. If he's our man for Adams's murder, and he decided to dispose of his accomplice as well, he may decide to go further afield."

"We're no nearer knowing why he killed Adams, are we?" Dean asked.

"I'm thinking the motive was greed, pure and simple. I think Spencer was running some sort of a share scam, but I've no idea how it was supposed to work."

"Could your friend at the Met help there?" Dean suggested.

"That's a thought. If not the exact details, she might know ways of doing it that might point us in the right direction. Look, while I'm talking to her, I want you to make sure that every available patrol car, motorcyclist, traffic car, the works, are checking out every road out of Rochfield."

"How far out?"

"As far as it takes, Dean. Rope in neighbouring forces. We need to find that car. As it is, we may be too late."

Simpson returned to the Incident Room and from there contacted every branch of Rochfield's mobile resources. He contacted each of the neighbouring divisions and asked for their assistance, giving them the scant information that he had regarding the vehicle.

He put out a radio call to all drivers of unmarked cars, including the members of the investigation team and ordered them to be on the look out.

Cranfield and Fowler heard the call. They were a few miles outside Rochfield on their way back from another wasted trip to a misleading address.

"Let's swing over towards Ilkley and come back into Rochfield that way."

"Any reason?" Fowler asked as he took a right turn on to a B road that would take them over the hills towards Ilkley.

"A lot of empty space, not many roads. If I was trying to get out of Rochfield unnoticed, that's the way I'd go," Maggie said.

They were coming down the long hill that led to Rochfield through Rochleigh. In the distance Maggie could see the lay-by.

"Slow down a bit Eddie while I check out the lay-by.

As it was set back from the road, separated by a wide grass verge, it would be easy to fly past it and not see a car parked at the top end of it until, if you were lucky you spotted it in your rear-view mirror.

"Swing round, Eddie. I think we've found it," she said in a rush.

Fowler swung the car round with a squeal of tyres and came up into the lay-by from the bottom end.

Maggie was almost out of the car before it stopped. She ran over to the Escort and looked in.

It was empty.

"Looks like we're too late," Eddie said, coming up behind her.

"Try the boot."

Fowler did, "Locked."

"Do you carry a crow-bar in the back of your car?"

"Yes, Sarge."

"Grab it. See if you can force the boot open."

"But why, Sarge? They're long gone by now."

"Just do it Eddie. And if that doesn't work, smash the side window and we'll try and get at it over the back seat."

Eddie collected the crow-bar from the boot of his car and tried to force the tailgate of the Escort open.

"Here, give it to me. I've always wanted to do this!"

Sergeant Cranfield gave the driver's side window a sharp tap with the curved end of the crow-bar. The little chips of toughened glass sprayed everywhere,

She reached in and sprung the lock, opened the door and folded the driver's seat forward.

"Call for an ambulance, Eddie! I think she's still alive," she shouted over her shoulder. Fowler pulled out his mobile, saw there was no signal so used the car radio.

"Delta Charlie five-eight to control," Fowler said.

"Come in five-eight."

Fowler gave his location and requested an ambulance and a Fire Service rescue vehicle priority one, "Seriously injured suspect. Let Big-Top One know. And call out SOCO while you're at it. We may need them, and cancel that APB."

He returned to the escort.

Maggie was talking softly and calmly to the girl who was curled up in the boot space of the car.

Maggie didn't immediately recognise the girl with the very short mousey hair. A brunette wig lay beside the head. A pair of glasses with a broken lens struggled to stay on the girl's nose. Maggie gently removed them.

"Sally? Sally Pickton?"

The girl moaned but did not answer.

"Don't worry Sally. You're going to be alright. An ambulance is on its way." Maggie reached down and felt the girl's neck. Her pulse was weak. Her breathing was shallow. Maggie continued to talk to her, to try and elicit some form of response.

Faintly in the distance, Maggie could hear the sirens.

"Won't be long now, pet. You just hang in there."

Another moan, weaker than the last.

The blue flashing lights, the screaming sirens, and running feet, the fire crew went to work with their equipment and forced the tailgate open. The ambulance paramedics took over as a well drilled team, assessing the girl's life signs, giving oxygen and a stimulant, checking pulse and blood pressure.

Maggie stood back and watched, quietly

praying that Sally Pickton would survive her ordeal and be able to reveal who Mark Spencer really was and also the make and colour of his car so that they could track him down.

It seemed to take an eternity before the ambulance crew determined that it would be safe to remove Sally Pickton from the car and stretcher her to the waiting ambulance.

Maggie watched intently and was oblivious to the figure approaching.

"Sergeant, you look rooted to the spot!" Sutherland said quietly.

Maggie gave a start. "Yes sir."

"She's going to live?"

"I hope so, sir. Look, I'm sorry I messed up. . ."

"We've all done it at some time or another. Don't let it get to you. Now you get Fowler to follow that ambulance and you stick as close to that girl as the medics will allow. Impress upon them the need to be with her when she is able to talk."

"Yes sir." Maggie sought out Eddie Fowler and they got back into his car ready to follow the ambulance. Sutherland came over. Maggie lowered her window. "Sir?"

"I'm thinking that a wee bit of deception is called for. We're going to let it be known that the body of a woman was recovered from a car at this location. We're going to make it appear that she was dead. I don't want Spencer to know that's she has survived."

"You think he'll come back and try to finish her off?"

A DEADLY ACCOUNT

"I'd rather he thought she was dead and couldn't finger him. It might slow him down a bit, especially as we don't know what he has in mind."

"Got you sir. As far as the public are concerned she was dead when we got to her. I'll brief the ambulance crew and the hospital staff."

"Good. They may not be too happy about it, but stress that you think he'll come back and try again, and it's for her safety. You know the sort of thing."

Maggie nodded, "Can you talk to the Fire Service, sir?" The ambulance was pulling away. Fowler put the car in gear and followed. He put his flashing blue lights on but let the ambulance make all the noise.

"Do you think she'll make it, Sarge?" Fowler asked.

"I bloody hope so, Eddie. She's the only chance we have of catching Spencer."

They followed close behind the ambulance as it weaved its way through the traffic to the emergency entrance of Rochfield Infirmary where, already alerted a team of trauma specialists stood ready to receive their latest patient.

Leaving Fowler to return to the factory with instructions to send somebody from uniform to standby ready to drive her, Cranfield hurried into the A&E department behind the paramedics who were pushing the gurney with Sally on board, working at her all the time.

No stranger to the routine or to Rochfield Infirmary, she held her warrant card at the ready, flashing it at whoever stood in her way until they reached the cubicle. The senior trauma surgeon blocked her way.

"Sorry sergeant. It's up to us now. I'll keep you posted as much as I can."

"Remember, she's a crime scene. And I need to talk to her as soon as possible. We've a murderer to catch, and she's the only one who knows who he is."

"We'll do our best, sergeant." And with that he disappeared behind the screen.

Maggie was able to grab one of the plastic chairs and sit guarding the approach to the cubicle.

He returned after five minutes.

Maggie looked up.

"She was very lucky that you got to her when you did."

Small comfort to Maggie, who felt that had she done her job properly in the first place, Sally wouldn't have been in A&E in the first place.

"Yeah." Was all she could think of to say, "And?"

"We're taking her to X-ray and then theatre. There's some damage to her neck. It may be broken. There's a serious gash to her forehead and she's showing signs of concussion. That will have to be monitored closely for the next twenty-four hours. I'm sorry but she won't be in any position to talk for some time. We're keeping her in an induced coma."

"Doc, I need you to do me a huge favour. Like I said, she's the only person who can tell us who this man really is. If anybody comes snooping around, she died, okay. Couldn't be saved. Anything you like until we catch this man. We're not even sure that Sally Pickton is her real name"

"Well, here's hoping she's not suffering from amnesia on top of all this!" the surgeon said giving Maggie a weak smile. "Look, there's nothing more that you can do here. She's going to be in theatre for some time while we immobilise her head, neck and upper body. Until we've done that she still could die. One wrong move . . ."

Maggie didn't need it spelt out. She nodded and stood up.

"I know you're going to be busy, but if you can, please keep me informed." Maggie tried to hand the surgeon one of her cards.

"Give it to Staff Nurse Porter on the desk. Jane will know what to do, and tell her what you've told me. She's the person through whom most of the information will flow anyway."

"Thanks. And good luck, doc."

Maggie watched as the gurney was wheeled back out of the cubicle and carefully down the corridor away from her towards the X-ray suite.

She went across to the nursing station and checking to see whose name tag said Jane Porter, handed over her card and gave the same instructions to the nurse.

"What happens if it's one of the family?" the nurse asked.

"She's not from round here, Jane. Just give them my number; I'll talk to them, any time, night or day. Sally Pickton probably isn't her real name, so the chances are if anybody, especially a man, asks for her by that name, it's the man who tried to kill her."

"Kill her!" Jane Porter exclaimed, "I have her listed as a traffic casualty!"

"Good. Stick to that story. We'll not contradict it."

Maggie walked slowly back through the A&E waiting area past the admission desk and stopped, retraced her steps and leant to the grille, showing her warrant card, "If anybody comes asking about the girl who was wheeled in. Inform them that she died without regaining consciousness, Speak to Staff Nurse Porter and her surgeon. They will be able to fill you in on the details. Staff Nurse Porter has my card. I'd like to be informed if anybody asks about her, is that understood?"

The two receptionists nodded.

"And can you make sure that anybody on your staff that accesses the records of Sally Pickton has the same information. Jane will explain."

The receptionists nodded again curious as to what was going on.

When Maggie continued towards the exit one of them went through to the nursing station and had a hurried conversation with Jane Porter.

Outside in the fresh air Maggie looked around for her driver. Tom Jones waved her over to an unmarked Volvo.

A constable that she hadn't met before got out of the passenger seat. He was out of uniform. "Mr Sutherland sent me to wait inside in case the girl needs close protection, sergeant."

"Thanks. He told you the background and why

she's going to be reported as dead?"

"Yes Sarge."

"Good. Show the reception your warrant card. Tell them I sent you."

She watched him head through the automatic doors and turned to Tom Jones.

"Not in your jam sandwich today, Tom?"

"No Sarge. Got unmarked duty. How's the girl?"

"As far as anyone knows, she died without regaining consciousness. In reality, her condition isn't much better than that. God knows when we'll be able to speak to her," Maggie said.

"What happened to her? I take it she wasn't in a car crash?"

"She was hit from behind across the back of the neck. Personally I think the killer used the edge of his hand."

"Like that karate stuff?" Tom Jones said.

"Something like that, yes. But she hit her head on the tailgate. That's given her a nasty cut but probably saved her life. She has concussion and a possible broken neck, but she's alive. They're operating on her now."

"Shit!" He held the door for Maggie and closed it after her. Back in the driving seat he started the engine, "She isn't out of the woods yet, then."

"No. She might not make it even now. We'll just have to hold our breath and pray," Maggie said.

"Where to, Sarge?"

"Back to Central. I'll need to speak to Mr Sutherland."

Chapter 19

Parfitt kept driving. He had the radio on to catch every news broadcast. The longer the day went on without a report of the girl's body having been found, the more miles he could put between him and Rochfield.

He had to work out a plan, and quickly. He knew that his false name of Spencer couldn't stand up to scrutiny and as soon as his real name became known to the police they would lock his assets up so tight he wouldn't be able to survive.

Unsure of how secure off shore accounts were, it was a risk he would have to take.

He needed to find a working phone box and call his bank.

Having found an off street carpark, he walked into the centre of Ripon and found a public telephone close to the cathedral. Using his phone card he rang his bank in Holborn and asked to speak to the manager, with whom he had had many dealings over the years.

"Elliott, it's Mark. Look, I've been offered a nice property in Barbados for the right money. How long will it take for you to transfer the funds to my Cayman Island account?"

"A couple of days at most. Should be cleared funds by midday local time tomorrow, Tuesday. I'll need you to sign some papers though."

Mark hadn't expected that, but sounding cheerful asked if that was really necessary. He was at the airport and his flight was just about to be called.

"When will you be back?" Elliott Tanner, his bank manager enquired.

"Oh, Thursday morning. I'm just flying out to look the place over and pay the deposit, but I need the funds to be in place before that to show good faith. You know what these people can be like."

"Wish I did old son. Bit out of my league. Look, it's bending the rules a bit, but just make sure you pop in on Thursday and sign everything. I'll let customer services know to expect you."

"Oh thanks, Elliott, I owe you one."

"I'll hold you to it, Mark. Enjoy your trip. See you on Thursday."

Heaving a massive sigh of relief, and hoping that he had got away with it, Parfitt crossed the road to a coffee house to have a late breakfast and plan his next move.

At least he now had funds in place; enough money to live comfortably off for a few years if he was careful. And, maybe he would get lucky and find a new scam to refill the coffers.

He pulled out his Filofax and turned to the maps section in the back and found Ripon. For a speedy getaway the motorway network was the obvious choice. It had one major drawback – too many cameras. The same was probably true for the major roads network.

He traced a route north and west that would take him around the top of the Yorkshire Dales National Park from where he could begin his journey southwards.

At some point he would have to get rid of the car. A market town with lots of parking space and a mainline railway station would be ideal. Ditch the car; take a train south, then maybe a bus back to London Victoria bus station. It would be a pity to have to give up the Carlton, but as a car it wasn't so rare as to attract attention.

At the Victoria Coach Station he could retrieve his emergency suitcase from the left luggage department. He would phone ahead and book a hotel room near the station for the Monday night.

Looking up his list of world time zones he deduced that if he phoned his Cayman Island bank at six in the evening UK time it would be round midday, one o'clock in George Town. He would be able to confirm that the funds were in his account by Tuesday evening.

He could then catch a train to Dover.

He had enough money to get out of the country without any difficulty and to buy a ticket in Paris to just about anywhere in the world. Air France flew just about everywhere, including a lot of countries with no extradition treaties with the United Kingdom.

His mind made up, he bought another coffee, drank it and returned to his car.

The news was just coming on the radio.

No mention of bodies in cars.

A DEADLY ACCOUNT

After filling the Carlton at the next petrol station, Parfitt followed the road signs to put him on the A684 which he followed to the point where he joined the A683 heading south.

Although it was almost winter, the late autumn sun followed him on his journey, making it a more than pleasant run in the country. The executive car swallowed up the miles of country roads. He was almost alone for most of the time so little traffic at that time of year. In the height of the summer holiday season he imagined that these winding back roads could be clogged with traffic.

In Preston he found a suitable carpark, locked the car, pocketed the keys and headed to the train station from where he bought a single ticket to Bristol, boarded the train and settled back to enjoy the trip down England. While waiting he had bought a book to read, which he did on and off for the journey.

He had finished it by the time the train pulled in to Bristol Temple Meads.

Leaving the station he had only a short walk to the Bristol Bus Station where the National Express service would carry him in total anonymity to London Victoria. He bought another book and a pocket radio to have something to read, and to have some means of getting the latest news.

* * *

Sitting in the Volvo, DS Cranfield's mind went back half a year to the last time she had attended

Rochfield Infirmary's A&E department on police business.

On that occasion the outcome for the patient had led to the arrest of Michael Hydinge on multiple counts of rape and murder.

This time she hoped fervently that the outcome would be more favourable and that the police would be searching for a man who had only committed one murder, that of Tommy Adams.

Constable Jones, knowing some of what the sergeant was going through kept silent.

He only spoke as she was getting out of the car, "It'll be okay, Sarge, you'll see."

Maggie nodded by way of reply, not trusting herself to speak.

"Reg, any idea where Mr Sutherland is?" she asked as she reached the front desk.

"Incident Room, Maggie. Said to tell you as soon as you came in."

He pressed the door release button to save her time.

She hurried down the corridor.

Apart from Young Eric and Vikki Gibson working at their computers, Sutherland and Simpson were the only ones in the Incident room when Maggie pushed the door open.

"How's the girl, Maggie?" Sutherland asked.

"They've taken her into theatre. The trauma surgeon said that they were going to keep her in an induced coma to reduce the risk of movement of her head. She may have a broken neck."

"Does the surgeon think she'll come through it?" Simpson asked.

"He's not committing himself at this stage. They are going to have to immobilise her head, neck and upper body probably."

"How long before we can talk to her?" Sutherland asked.

"He wouldn't say, but I got the impression that it could be days rather than hours."

"That could be too late," Sutherland said.

"I know sir, I'm sorry. I messed up."

"Take a seat, Maggie. You look exhausted." He pointed to a chair close to where he and Simpson were seated.

Maggie sat, not looking at either of them. Was this the point where Sutherland asked her to leave the team, or worse, Rochfield?

"Maggie, we all make mistakes. All of us. Some are big ones, some are little ones. The size doesn't matter. What is important is this: Never forget your mistakes, but don't dwell on them. Dwelling on mistakes is the road to crippling inertia. Remember them so that you don't repeat them, Maggie. That way you'll be a better detective. If you're going to beat yourself up over every wrong decision or mistake you make, you'll be no use to me or those round you. Do you understand?" He had spoken very quietly.

Maggie nodded, "Yes sir."

"Good. Now, back to the present. I presume you've left instructions for the hospital to call you if anything happens to the girl," Sutherland said.

"Yes sir."

"Well, let's hope the news we get is better than expected, and that we get to talk to Sally Pickton sooner rather than later."

"What if we can't, sir?" Maggie asked.

"Sadly that will probably mean that this bastard escapes the net. Simpson and I were discussing our options. I favour a press release stating that the body of a girl believed to be an employee of The Mutual Cap was recovered from a vehicle on the outskirts of Rochfield this morning. We'll go into details of her car and where it was found and ask if anybody driving along that road spotted anything unusual around the time in question. We'll deliberately avoid any mention of whether the girl is alive or dead, and just give a description of her. Does that sound plausible to you?"

"I can't see what else we can do, sir. I've already spoken to the surgeon, to Staff Nurse Porter on the nursing station in A&E and the receptionists and asked them to let me know if anybody rings up or comes in asking questions. Anybody who does is to be told that she died without regaining consciousness."

"Perfect. Let's hope that it works."

"What advantage will it have, I mean letting it be known that she has died?" Maggie asked. She had followed Sutherland's instructions, but had thought it was to protect the girl in case Spencer tried to have another go. Now she wasn't so sure.

"We're guessing at this stage, that Spencer has left the district, but as we haven't a clue what he drives, any more than we know where he's going or what his plan is, we have little or no chance of catching him. I'm hoping that this bit of misinformation might slow him down."

"Slow him down? I don't understand."

"Well, if he thinks that she's alive and likely to talk, there's a possibility that he'll run faster, if you know what I mean."

DS Cranfield nodded, "And if she's already dead and hasn't talked he remains the invisible man!"

"And can take his time over making his getaway. I've already put out an APB but it's in the name of Spencer, and I'm fairly certain that was a name he made up for the staff of the Lion. His first name may well be Mark, since Adams was heard calling him that, but as far as Fowler can be sure after questioning the staff again, Adams didn't use a surname at any time."

* * *

Seated on the National Express coach as it headed eastwards into the darkening afternoon, Parfitt sat reading his novel and listening to the radio through an earphone.

He heard the news bulletin clearly, and exhaled a sigh of satisfaction. There was no mention of the Rochfield police having any specific suspect. They were just asking for witnesses to come forward, but he didn't expect there to be too many of those. The vehicles going downhill were going too fast, and there had really only been one lorry going up hill, and he had been crouched beside his car while it passed. He doubted that the driver would have seen more than a blue Escort and a black Carlton, if the driver had even been capable of registering what make of vehicles had been in the lay-by. There was no way they could have caught sight of him or his car's number plate.

He relaxed and slept for most of the remaining journey, only waking as the coach started its crawl through the evening traffic into London.

Once at Victoria Coach Station he made his way to the left luggage department and redeemed his case, paying the outstanding storage charge without question.

From there he took a cab to his hotel and checked in, was shown to his room and locked the door behind him.

After a long bath he dressed in some of the casual clothes from his retrieved suitcase and, with cash in his wallet, and the rest of his funds safely hidden, he left the hotel to go in search of a good evening meal.

* * *

In Rochfield the evening was drawing in, electric lighting was taking over from daylight. Curtains and blinds were being drawn.

The investigation team assembled in the Incident Room to go over the day's events and the latest information.

Sutherland did a quick overview and then threw the meeting open.

Fowler spoke up. "Gov, we got a call from the driver of a lorry that passed the lay-by at about that time. Says he saw a blue car, possibly an Escort parked in the lay-by with a bigger, black car parked up behind it, facing the other way. Says that the boot of the blue car was open but couldn't see anybody. Thought somebody might have been changing a wheel."

"So we're looking for a black car, probably some form of executive saloon," Sutherland said and wrote it up. "Anything else?"

One of the phones rang. Maggie picked it up.

"Sergeant Cranfield . . . Right, I'll get over there straight away. Thanks."

She hung up. "That was the hospital, sir. It seems that Sally Pickton has been very lucky. The surgical team were not needed. No sign of damage to the neck vertebrae or spinal column. It appears that she must have been bending forward as he struck.

"From the look of the blow it was almost certainly from the edge of a hand. The blow simply helped her head on its way to impact the tailgate. Because she was knocked out, Spencer must have thought she was dead. He was in such a hurry that he didn't bother to check. Just dumped her in the boot of the Escort and drove off."

"Can she talk?" Sutherland asked.

"She's regained consciousness and is in a secure side ward. The constable you sent is keeping watch over her."

"Get over there right away, Maggie. Find out as much as ye can," Sutherland said, feeling more cheerful than he had in days.

The rest of the room watched her go. They had seen the look of relief both on Cranfield's face and that of their boss.

"Until we find out what she can tell us, there's not much point in continuing this session. I want you all to stick around until they get back. Go and get something in the canteen. This could be a busy evening."

Chapter 20

DS Cranfield drove to Rochfield Infirmary in her own car and parked in one of the public parking spaces. She walked up to the A&E reception and asked for the surgeon she had spoken to earlier.

"You'll need to speak to Staff Nurse Porter at the nursing station; she might be able to help you."

Maggie thanked the receptionist and went through the waiting and triage area to the nursing station.

Staff Nurse Porter looked up, "Sergeant Cranfield. Good news!" she said quietly and scribbled on a piece of scrap paper. "You'll find her here. Your constable is with her." She passed the piece of paper over.

"Thanks," Maggie took the paper and read the ward details.

"Down the corridor turn left, up two floors," Jane Porter murmured.

Maggie followed the instructions and rode the lift up to the floor. Finding the ward was no difficulty and she could see the constable's head through the glass of the side ward.

She tapped gently on the door before going in.

"How's she doing?" Maggie asked.

The girl in the bed looked to be asleep.

"According to the medics, she's doing well Sarge. She hasn't spoken yet, though," the constable said quietly.

Maggie changed places with the constable, "Sorry, I don't know your name, constable."

"Collins, Sarge. David Collins."

"Here, head down to the coffee shop and see if you can round up a coffee, white, no sugar. Get something for yourself while you're there." Maggie handed over a ten pound note, "Don't get carried away! I'll need the change for the carpark!"

The constable took the note and left the side ward.

Maggie turned to the figure in the bed. Sally Pickton's head was bandaged where they had sutured the gash.

"You've had a narrow escape, Sally. Like to tell me about it?" Maggie said, not sure if it would elicit any response.

The girl's eyes fluttered and opened.

"Are you the one who found me?" All trace of her Yorkshire accent had gone, replaced by an unexpectedly educated voice.

"Yes. My name is Detective Sergeant Cranfield. Call me Maggie. Sally, I need you to tell me who did this. We've got to catch him in case he tries to make his work permanent." Maggie was quite sure that Spencer was long gone, but it was the only leverage she had. Sally Pickton was an accessory to murder. That much couldn't be changed.

"His name is Mark Parfitt. He's from London."

"Do you know where we can find him?"

"He'll not have gone back home. He'll be holed up somewhere."

"Any idea where?" Maggie asked.

"Some hotel probably. Not a plush one, something comfortable but anonymous. That's his style."

"Sally, are you related to him in some way?"

That brought a weak laugh.

"No. I just sort of work for him, the bastard. He promised to take me with him if I helped him out," the girl said.

"What can you tell me about his car?"

"Black Vauxhall Carlton. He'll have ditched it by now probably."

"And he didn't say where the two of you would be going?" Maggie asked.

"Just abroad, that's all. Christ my head hurts!" The pain medication was wearing off.

"If you hadn't hit your head on the tailgate, he'd have broken your neck and you'd be dead. The same as the man you helped him throw in the river."

"I didn't want to do it. Honestly. He made me," she said anxiously.

Maggie nodded.

"What will happen to me, Sergeant?"

"That will depend on how much help you can give us, Sally. I can't make any promises or any deals, but it will all be taken into consideration."

"Does that mean I'm under arrest?"

"Yes, technically it does. You have the right to remain silent, but anything that you fail to mention when questioned and later rely on in court may not be admissible in evidence. Anything that you do say will be recorded and may be used in evidence against you. Do you understand the caution?"

"Yes, yes I do."

"Is Sally Pickton your real name?" Ds Cranfield asked.

"No. It's Louise Baker."

"Louise Baker I'm arresting you as an accomplice in the murder of Thomas Adams on or around the evening of Tuesday 20th October this year. Louise, we need to find Parfitt. We need to know everything that you know about him. Down to the last detail, no matter how insignificant it may seem. Now, because you are under arrest you are entitled to a solicitor, but all that can take time. If he's planning to come back here, and he might if he finds out that you are still alive, or to skip the country, he'll get away with it and you'll be left holding the baby, so to speak."

Constable Collins arrived back with the coffee for Maggie, and was carrying one for himself. He handed over her change.

"Thanks Constable. Stay with her for a few minutes while I phone DCI Sutherland."

Maggie went to the ward desk and asked to use their phone. She reported the scant information that she had gleaned from Louise Baker and informed Sutherland that she had placed Baker under arrest.

"Any way we can get a solicitor up here, boss?" she asked.

"See if you can get her to talk without one. If she won't, she won't. I'll see what I can do. Meantime I'll put out an APB on the black Carlton and see if that gives us any leads. I'll be in my office when you get back to me."

Maggie returned to the side ward.

"Right, Louise. We're going to try and get you a solicitor as soon as possible, but at the moment I'm not interested in your part in all this. All I'm concerned with is anything you can tell me about Parfitt. Like I said, the more you tell me, the better chance we have of catching him, and the more we can tell the court about how much you helped us. I'll not ask you any questions about what you've been doing, do you understand?"

"Yes. What do you want me to tell you?" The girl called Louise asked.

"What do you know about Parfitt? How well did he know Adams for example?" Maggie began.

"Oh, that came as right shock when I told him who had taken over from old Miss Hackett. Seems they used to work together years ago. He threw a right wobbly when I told him!" Louise said.

"Do you know where that was? Where they worked?"

"He did mention it once," she gave Maggie the name of the accountancy giant where the two men had worked, where Parfitt had trained Adams.

"I take it he's not working for them now?"

"Do me a favour!" Louise tried to laugh but it hurt. "He sort of went out on his own. Found he could make more money running scams. That's how I met him."

"We'll wait until your solicitor gets here before going into that, Louise. Back to Parfitt's car. You don't happen to remember the registration number, do you?"

"Just that it was new last year. He was really proud of it."

"Do you happen to know what bank he used?"

"Used cash mostly, why?"

"If we knew that we might be able to find out what he's planning to live on while he's on the run."

Louise thought for a few moments, "There was one occasion where he had to give me a cheque. Let me think now . . ." she closed her eyes in thought.

Maggie waited.

"It was in Holborn!" Louise named the bank. Maggie returned to the nurses' desk and relayed this information and the fact that the Carlton had a 1991 registration.

Back at Rochfield Central Sutherland wasted no time in contacting the Met and asking them to try and find out what they could.

Half an hour later his phone rang.

"Sutherland."

"DI Craig, Chief Inspector. I think we may have got lucky. I just managed to get hold of his bank manager before he went home. He got a call from Parfitt this morning asking for a load of money to be transferred to an account in the Caymans. Parfitt is supposed to be flying out to

Barbados for some property deal today but the manager wasn't a hundred percent convinced that Parfitt was phoning from the airport like he said he was. Parfitt has arranged to come in on Thursday to sign the papers. I laid it on thick and got him to stop the transfer," Craig said.

"Good thinking Inspector. With any luck Parfitt will check with his bank in the Caymans before making the next move. I take it the bank manager is clued up enough to explain that his bosses refused to sanction the transfer without the client's signature, or something?"

"Exactly that sir; what do you think Parfitt will do?" Craig asked.

"All we can do is hope that having let it be known that the girl he was working with is dead, that he'll fall for it and go round to the bank and sign the papers. Can you lift him and hold him for us?" Sutherland asked.

"I'd be delighted to, sir. I made a few enquiries with our fraud people. It would seem, in the words of the Pythons, 'He's been a very naughty boy!" When you've finished with him, they'd like to ask him a few questions."

"By 'they' do you mean Janet Black?"

"Yes. When I mentioned your name I could almost hear her rubbing her hands with glee. Seems you know each other"

"Aye, we've met. I gave her a call about this case a few days ago. At the time I was more concerned with the company that the victim was working for. I thought that might have been the motive for the murder."

"Well, I'll give you a shout as soon as I hear from Parfitt's bank manager. I was thinking, Chief Inspector, if, as the bank manager suspects, he wasn't flying out this morning, but may hang around somewhere in London before phoning his offshore bank, it will be tomorrow evening our time, sometime after six. He won't be able to contact the Holborn bank until after ten on Wednesday morning."

"Which means he'll be hanging around somewhere for thirty-six hours or more. That would be enough to make him very jumpy. What do you suggest we do, Inspector?"

"Tricky. Doing nothing is probably the best option. The problem may be with the media. If it's a slow news day they might make an issue of it. Do they have a picture of him?"

"We haven't release it yet. Thanks for your advice, Inspector. What the media don't know can't do us any harm!" Sutherland said.

"Exactly. Look, I'll keep you posted. As soon as I hear from his bank manager, I'll be in touch," Craig said.

"I look forward to it. Good luck, Inspector."

Sutherland replaced the phone and sat back in his chair.

Simpson knocked and entered, "Any news, Andrew?"

Sutherland brought Dean up to date.

"Hey, that's good. Looking like a result," Dean said.

"Only if Parfitt acts as predicted," Sutherland cautioned.

"Well, he'll be in for one hell of a shock if he flees the country only to find that he's got no money to live on!" Dean laughed.

"Serve him bloody well right if he did, Dean, but it wouldnae help us catch him."

"We were lucky that everybody hadn't gone home for the day!" Dean said ruefully.

"Sometimes the breaks go with you," Sutherland stood up. "I'm heading over to the hospital to have a chat wi' Maggie and this girl. I haven't been able to get hold of a solicitor yet. I'm going to see if Louise Baker, a.k.a Sally Pickton, minds if she doesn't get representation until the morning, or even when she gets discharged from the hospital. We'll have to arrange for a round the clock watch to be kept on her. Can you sort that out, Dean?"

"Leave it with me, Andrew, I'll speak to the custody sergeant and see who he can spare from the evening and night shifts."

* * *

Armed with directions from Sergeant Cranfield, Sutherland used the main entrance to the hospital. He had collected a bunch of flowers from the twenty-four hour garage near the hospital and joined the throng of people going to visit relatives.

"Nice touch, sir," Cranfield said when she saw him coming through the ward reception area.

"Call it disguise, Maggie. Introduce me to the patient."

"Louise, this is my boss, Detective Chief

Inspector Sutherland. Sir, meet Louise Baker."

Sutherland nodded at Louise.

"Have you got him?" she asked.

"We're closing in. At least that's if everything goes to plan and Mr Parfitt hasn't already left the country. How well do you know him?" Sutherland asked.

"So so. I've worked for him a couple of times, but I can't say that I really know him."

"Aye, that I can believe. Otherwise you wouldn't be in this mess Miss Baker. I haven't been able to secure the services of a panel solicitor yet, but we hope to have one here first thing in the morning."

"Thank you."

"We probably won't try and interview you properly until you have been discharged from this hospital. Is that alright with you?"

"Yes Chief Inspector."

"You won't mind if I ask you one question, and it has nothing to do with the situation you find yourself in today."

"Ask away. I don't mind."

"How did you happen to meet up with this man Parfitt?"

"It was a few years ago. I was trying to earn money to put myself through uni . . ."

"Doing what?" Sutherland cut in.

"Waitressing at a club in the West End. He was a member in those days. We got talking late one night. He was a bit drunk having made a pile of money at the tables. I think he was a bit lonely though. He was on his own, no one to share the fun with so we chatted and one thing led to another. I remember telling him about the conversations I used to overhear in the club. You'd be amazed how indiscreet people are round the invisible staff! He was fascinated. That's how it started. I'd pass information to him and he'd give me a back hander if it turned into money. Then he had me doing jobs like the one here. Scoping a place out and feeding him information."

"What did he do with the information?" Sutherland asked.

"I think it was some share dealing scam. What do you call it? Insider trading or something. I think he made a shit-load of money at it sometimes."

"And you? Did you do well out of it?"

"Crumbs from the rich man's table, I think. But sometimes they were big crumbs, if you get my meaning."

Sutherland nodded and turned to Maggie, "You've charged Miss Baker, I presume?"

"Yes sir."

He turned back to the young woman in the bed, "We'll leave you to get some sleep. Remember, you've had a serious concussion. The medical staff will be looking in at very regular intervals. Please don't try to leave, Miss Baker. No matter what you may think, until we've caught Parfitt there's always a chance he'll try again, and a hospital is still a secure environment for you. Okay?"

"Yes Chief Inspector. Thank you for the flowers, by the way," Louise said.

"Aye well, they brighten the place up a bit," he turned back to Maggie, "We might as well get on home. There's nothing more to be done here today."

Maggie gathered up her bag, they both said goodbye to Louise Baker and nodded to the constable sitting in the corner.

"Your relief will be here soon, constable."

"Thank you sir."

Sutherland and Cranfield made their way out of the hospital together.

"Got any change, Maggie? I only have a tenner here."

Maggie paid their parking charges and handed Sutherland his ticket before walking across the carpark together, reaching Sutherland's car first.

"I'll see you in the morning, Maggie. Promised Mrs Sutherland I'd be home on time tonight, he said.

"See you in the morning, sir." Maggie watched him drive away as she walked the short distance to her car and followed him out of the carpark. She still felt bad about not checking the girl's details properly. It might have prevented Louise Baker almost getting killed and helped catch Parfitt before he disappeared.

More than anybody, she hoped that they would catch him soon.

Chapter 21

In London the evening had turned wet. After enjoying a good meal in a restaurant about a mile from his hotel, he didn't feel like walking in the rain. Parfitt hailed a taxi and scrambled into the back.

"Where to Gov?"

Parfitt named his hotel and relaxed back in the seat as the cab sped him efficiently to his destination. He paid the driver, added an appropriate but not excessive tip and hurried into the lobby of the hotel.

He had over a day and a half to kill before he could make his phone call to check that the funds were in place. As soon as that was done he would catch the boat train to Dover and the next ferry to France.

With that reassuring thought in mind he went up to his room, locked the door behind him and settled down for a good night's sleep.

The London skies had cleared by morning.

Parfitt, not knowing when he might enjoy one again, took advantage of the inclusive full English breakfast and stoked up on a fry, a full pot of coffee, toast and jam.

The breakfast made him feel slightly nostalgic. It took care of an hour of waiting time, and it stopped him from clock watching.

Having finished, he returned to his room, checked that he hadn't forgotten anything, closed and locked his case and then returned to reception to check out.

Once outside on the pavement he looked up and down the road. Nobody appeared to be taking any notice of him. Seeing a London Taxi pulling up outside the hotel to disgorge an elderly couple and their cases, he raised his hand to the driver.

"Victoria coach station, driver."

"Hop in mate," the cabby said. Parfitt watched as he took his fare from the tourists, thanked them and climbed into the driver's seat. After resetting the meter he pulled a tight U-turn and headed back up the road in the direction of the station.

Parfitt paid and got out with his case which he wheeled after him into the concourse and back to the Left Luggage department.

Looking at the coach station clock he could see that he had probably seven hours to wait before he could make the international phone call to his Cayman Island bank.

He toyed with the idea of phoning his bank in Holborn, or going over there and getting the papers signed in case Tanner had had second thoughts, but dismissed the idea.

He wanted to get the confirmation from his offshore bank and get out of the country as fast as possible. He put great faith in the channel port as being an easier exit route than an airport. Airport security, both in and out was getting tighter all the time.

He decided to wander down Belgrave Road towards the river and along Millbank to the Tate Gallery and spend a couple of hours gazing at the Turners, before making his way back to Victoria Station to get the Circle Line to South Kensington. He used up some more time visiting each of the local museums, The V&A, the National History Museum and the Science Museum, concluding that of all of them he liked the Natural History the best.

* * *

Parfitt wasn't the only person waiting for time to pass. In Rochfield the Major Incident team had been stood down and the Incident Room returned to its less glamorous role of a conference room. All of the equipment that had been installed for the duration of the investigation had been returned to storage, except the Murder Boards and Young Eric's computer equipment.

The boards and Eric's computer had been moved back to CID.

He and Vikki Gibson went back to the task of putting police records onto the system and hoping for another little pixelated man to wander across the screen.

Upstairs in his office Andrew Sutherland spent the time doing paperwork, a job that had the impression of making the hours go slower rather than faster.

DI Simpson and DS Cranfield were out of the building investigating a robbery with violence at a jewellers shop down one of Rochfield's side streets. The shop dealt in top of the range watches, rings and other jewellery, including bespoke custom made items that the present owner, a fourth generation craftsman in precious metals produced to order.

It turned out that the victim had been more frightened than injured, though the perpetrator had threatened him with a small hand axe and punched him in the face.

The punch had resulted in a nose bleed, but not a broken nose. The ambulance crew were just packing their equipment away when Simpson and Cranfield arrived.

As the interior of the shop was small to the point of bijou they waited until the last paramedic had left before entering.

"Mr King, I'm DI Simpson, my colleague is DS Cranfield. Are you okay to talk to us?"

"Yes. Bit lucky really. It could have been worse."

"Can you describe the man?" Simpson asked.

"Stocky, heavily built. He charged in just as my last customer was leaving."

"How was he dressed?" Cranfield asked, pen poised over her notebook.

"Jeans and a leather bomber jacket. He was pulling a mask over his head as I looked up so I didn't get a good look at him."

"We have to ask this, was he white?"

"Yes. Not black or Asian. I caught a glimpse of

his neck just before he pulled the mask the whole way down."

"You say a mask. Could you describe it?" Simpson asked.

"One of those stupid latex Halloween masks that seem to be all the rage this year. One with straggly black hair and boils all over it."

The two detectives had seen a number of them being worn around the town and in the park on Saturday night.

"Was he local? Did he say anything?" Cranfield asked.

"Sounded local, but it was a bit muffled behind the mask. He seemed more intend on smashing the display glass and scooping whatever came to hand into his pockets."

"How come he punched you?" Simpson wanted to know.

"It seems that I got in his way! It was all very quick. And then he left."

"On foot?" Simpson asked.

"I heard a motorbike revving up and then a squeal of tyres. I think he must have had an accomplice waiting outside."

"Did it sound like a big powerful bike?"

"No. Not deep and throaty, more a high pitched whine like it was struggling to carry two people. By the time I got from behind the counter and through the door it had disappeared round the corner."

"Back onto the one way system or the other way?" Cranfield asked.

"The other way. I could still hear it, but I'm not

sure whether the sound was coming from the right or the left."

"Mr King, was he wearing gloves?" she asked.

"Yes. Black leather. Not biker gloves, thinner than that."

Maggie looked back over her notes, "About how tall was he?"

King paused for a moment and then went to the door. He pointed to the position where the top bolt was secured, "A couple of inches shorter than this. Not as tall as either of you."

Simpson looked round the shop, noting the smashed glass and overturned displays, "Have you any idea what has been taken?"

"It'll take a few minutes to see what he hasn't taken. From that and my stock sheets I can tell you what's missing."

"Mr King, can you get on with that? I will need to call our forensic team to get them to go through the shop area and see if they can find anything, though I'm not holding my breath. Looks like this man was intent on getting in and out fast and leaving nothing behind, but we have to check anyway. I'm also going to get a constable down here to stay on the premises while you take stock."

"Thank you."

"You'll need a case number for your insurance company and if you want to add anything to what you've already given us. We'll be back in a couple of hours to take a formal statement and get the list of what's missing."

DS Cranfield supplied the case number written

on one of her business cards, "Ask for me if you phone."

"Thank you again. I'll see you later."

Simpson used his mobile phone to call SOCO, and then Rochfield Central and get a car to bring a beat officer to the scene before he and Cranfield drove back to the factory.

"What do you make of that?" Maggie asked.

"Probably got the idea from some bad TV programme. Latex masks are a bit of a novelty for our local thugs."

"Novelty! I like that! Any ideas who it is likely to be?"

"The getaway transport is interesting though. I'm going to run it past Young Eric. See if anything like that has been reported before. Sounds like it might have been a moped, or at best a scooter. Don't get too many of those with a passenger seat."

They took the stairs up to CID and went to see if Eric could help.

"Give me what you've got and we'll see."

Maggie read out her notes.

Eric typed furiously.

The computer did its thing.

The little pixelated policeman walked back and forth before stopping, his beacon flashing on and off.

"Got something!" Eric said and typed some more. The little policeman did a few more traverses of the screen; flashed some more and then the printer started chattering.

Eric tore the sheet off and handed it to

Inspector Simpson.

"Just like that, eh!" Simpson started to read.

"The future of policing," Maggie said.

"Won't work without the boots on the ground, Sarge," Eric said. "The computer can't ask the questions or chase across fields to catch a crook, if you know what I mean."

"Very comforting to know, Eric." Maggie turned to Simpson, "What have we got?"

Simpson broke into laughter, "We call him Fat Larry! He's a small time villain from the Oakridge. Fancies himself as a rival to the Talbots. As if! Never graduated beyond a provisional motorcycle license. Limited to 125cc. A very noisy, usually not very fast means of transport. Even slower with two people on board."

"Is this his sort of crime?" Sergeant Cranfield asked.

"Must be getting desperate. Too many alarms in private houses these days. His usual style is breaking and entering. Usually cases the property for a few weeks in advance. Makes sure it's empty before going in. He's been in and out of prison most of his life, from juvenile to adult."

"Not the world's most successful villain then."

"He's been clean for a year or so now. Doing odd jobs round the place. Quite handy with his hands, so I've heard." Simpson handed the report back to Eric. "Thanks Eric." He turned back to Maggie, "Rather than waste time going over to the Oakridge ourselves, we'll send uniform to pick him up. They can turn his place over while they're there."

"Okay. What's next?"

Simpson went over to the filing tray and pulled out the next reported crime sheet.

"Has the boss seen this?" he asked aloud.

"What is it sir?" DC Fowler asked.

"A report from Preston CID. They think they've found Parfitt's car."

"How did that get in there?" Maggie asked.

"It may have come up from the Incident Room, Sarge. We tidied up in a bit of a hurry. Sorry," Fowler said.

"Maggie, you handle this. Phone them up and see if it's on the level. I'm going up to see Mr Sutherland."

DS Cranfield took the sheet, went to her desk and phoned Preston CID.

Reading from the report she asked to speak to DC Grant.

"It's DS Cranfield, Rochfield CID. Just got your report about our missing black car. What can you tell me?"

"One of the parking attendants noticed that it had been there since the previous morning and that there was no pay and display ticket on it. He'd heard your news item about looking for a black executive car and asked us to check on it. Registered to a man named Parfitt from London. We got the details from Swansea and my Gov'nor asked me to contact you. But that was a couple of hours ago."

"Yes, I know. We've just closed down our Incident Room earlier today, and it got caught up in the move. Where is the car now?"

"We've had it brought in to our vehicle pound on a trailer."

"Any chance of getting into it?" Maggie asked.

"There's no keys with it, if that's what you mean, Sergeant."

"Any possibility of getting a locksmith out, rather than smashing a window?"

"I'll ask my boss and call you back."

"Don't worry, constable, we'll foot the bill!" she told him.

"I'll get on to it right away." DC Grant hung up.

"And I thought Yorkshire folk were supposed to be tight wi' money," she muttered as she replaced the receiver.

She followed in Simpson's footsteps up to Sutherland's office.

"Come on in Maggie," Sutherland said as she put her head round the door, "Is it his car?"

"According to Swansea, yes. I've had to tell Preston that we'll pay for a locksmith."

"Huh! Remind me not to do any favours for them the next time they ask. I've never heard the like!" Sutherland was not amused. "Let me know as soon as they get back to you, Maggie."

"Yes sir."

"Dean tells me you're about to make the acquaintance of Lawrence Edward Dodds."

"Fat Larry! Yes, so I believe."

"And I thought the useless so-and-so had decided to go straight," Sutherland said, shaking his head sadly. He looked at both of them, "Enjoy your afternoon, folks."

A DEADLY ACCOUNT

Dean and Maggie returned to CID to wait for uniform to tell them that Dodds was downstairs ready to be interviewed.

Fat Larry was no master criminal. Not only had the police lifted him, they had his Yamaha bike, his accomplice – his sister – and the proceeds of the robbery.

The sister had ridden the bike and was in Interview Room One.

Larry and the loot were in Interview Room Two.

Dean and Maggie started there.

"A bit of a departure from your usual routine, Larry!"

"Morning Mr Simpson. Who's this?" He looked up at Sergeant Cranfield.

Simpson made the introductions.

They sat down opposite the hapless Mr Dodds.

"How can you be so stupid, Larry? What is it? Nearly two years since you came out. And why a job like this?"

"Dunno, Mr Simpson. Seemed like easy money. No cameras, no panic buttons, nothing. He was asking for it."

"Oh come off it! Nobody is 'asking for it' as you put it. He's just a craftsman trying to make an honest living. Something we thought you were learning. And to drag your sister into this. What was that all about?"

"She's got the bike license."

Simpson burst out laughing, "And that makes it alright? Getting nicked for riding the bike should be the least of your worries. Now she's going down as an accessory."

"First offence Mr Simpson. They won't give her time."

"Maybe not, but now she'll have a criminal record. Hope she wasn't planning on taking any holidays in the States, or a whole list of other countries around the world that don't take kindly to people with criminal records. And it's buggered up any job prospects she might have had."

"Job prospects, Mr Simpson. Don't make me laugh! Why d'you think we done this? There are no bloody jobs! Not for her. Not for me. Honestly Mr Simpson, I've tried. I have, really." He was on the verge of crying. "You ask my parole officer. Nobody's hiring anybody. Least of all the likes of me. We was desperate, Mr Simpson."

"But why the violence?"

"I didn't mean to hit him, Mr Simpson, but he tried to grab my mask. I mean, he'd have seen it was me, wouldn't he." Larry stopped talking. "Anyway, how come you got onto me so fast? Nobody saw us."

"You shouldn't have used the bike, Larry," Sergeant Cranfield said.

"What's she on about?"

"We have a very clever lad working for us these days Larry. A very clever lad with a very clever machine," Simpson said. "It's called a computer. He puts all the information from every arrest, every police report and every witness statement. The machine thinks for a few seconds and then prints out a report based on all of that information. The report gives us the computer's best guess as to who the likely suspect is. This time it was you."

"Fucking hell!" He turned to Sergeant Cranfield, "Sorry ma'am that sort of slipped out," he apologised. "I've been nicked by a bloody machine! Hey, Mr Simpson, that's not fair is it? I mean bloody computers. They're going to put us all out of a job at this rate, you included."

"I take it that you're not going to try anything stupid and time wasting by denying any of this?" Simpson asked.

"What's the point?"

"Exactly. Sergeant Cranfield will take your statement while I go and have a chat with your sister."

"Is there anything you can do for her, Mr Simpson?" Fat Larry was pleading.

"I'll see. Just give Sergeant Cranfield **your** statement." He laid heavy emphasis on the word 'your', it wasn't lost on Larry Dodds.

"Oh yeah! My statement, Mr Simpson, yeah, my statement."

Simpson nodded and left the room. The constable returned and watched while Sergeant Cranfield wrote down Dodds's statement. About how he had done the job all on his own including being the person riding the bike on his own.

Simpson went next door to talk to Yvette Dodds. He asked the constable to leave the room.

"I'm not saying nothing, Mr Simpson," she began before he could speak.

"No need, Yvette. According to your brother you were nowhere near the jeweller's shop, had no part in anything, and certainly weren't riding the Yamaha to help him get away. I'm sorry that you've been inconvenienced. We'll be releasing your brother on police bail as soon as he's finished his statement, then you'll both be free to go. Try and keep him out of trouble until his day in court."

"Yes Mr Simpson. Sorry Mr Simpson." She looked down at the table, picked up her cigarette, took a last drag on it and stubbed it out.

"Yvette, how bad is it?"

"I lost my job, Mr Simpson."

"Where were you working?"

"Miller's."

Miller and Co had been a small stitching company making school blazers that had recently closed. Cheap foreign imports had killed their business.

"Good with your hands?"

"Yeah. Loved the stitching, I did."

"Have you tried the Mill?"

"What, Croziers?" Yvette Dodds looked on a job in Croziers as being a sentence to hard labour such was its unwarranted reputation.

"I was thinking of Featherstones. If you can learn stitching, you can learn a mill job, lass. Don't throw your life away. Larry isn't worth it, no matter how much you value family loyalty."

Inspector Simpson scribbled a name on the back of one of his business cards. "Go and speak to her. She's their personnel lady. Tell her that I sent you. I can't promise anything, but it's worth a try."

"Thank you Mr Simpson." She took the card and put it in her pocket.

"Wait here until your brother is released, Yvette. Don't let me see you back here again."

"No Mr Simpson."

Sergeant Cranfield was finishing taking Lawrence Dodds's statement when Simpson entered. He waited until she was ready for Dodds to sign it before asking to read it.

Taking the closely written pages from her he read rapidly, glad to see that Fat Larry had taken the hint before handing it and the ball point to him.

"You can sign it, Larry. Your sister is waiting in the next room. She'll be glad to know that we are not convinced that she had any part in this and you will be bailed to appear before Rochfield Magistrates' Court in the morning. Make sure you're there. Do I make myself clear?"

"Oh yes, very clear Mr Simpson. I'll be there."

Simpson instructed Sergeant Cranfield to deal with the bail conditions and returned to the CID room.

Cranfield joined him there after seeing Lawrence and Yvette Dodds off the premises.

"What was all that about?" she whispered.

"Yvette lost her job when the clothing factory closed. She got the minimum redundancy paid by the state because the place was bankrupt. Fat Larry's not been getting much work either. It was easier to get him to cop the lot and let her go. I've told her to go and speak to the personnel lady at Featherstones. I've a feeling she'll do really well there."

"And as nobody has been asked to come forward to tell us what they saw, and Mr King only heard the motorbike, he didn't actually see anything, we have no way of proving otherwise."

"Exactly."

Maggie's desk phone rang.

"DS Cranfield," she listened. "Hang on a sec while I speak to my boss." She turned to Simpson, "It's Preston. There's a suitcase in the boot and a lady's shoulder bag under the passenger's seat. Should we get Ed's people to recover the vehicle to their labs?"

"Yes. I'll arrange it. You tell Preston to leave it all intact. We'll take it from here."

* * *

With the Carlton brought back to Rochfield's crime scene unit's facility under wraps, there would be fewer problems with the chain of evidence. Richardson's people would examine it minutely for trace evidence.

Evidence of who had been where inside the vehicle.

Was this the vehicle used to transport Adams's body?

Had Louise Baker been in it?

Was anybody else in the vehicle at any time? And if so, could they be identified, and did they have anything to do with Adams's murder?

The day wore on. Thick cloud rolled in from the south east bringing rain. Lights came on early.

A DEADLY ACCOUNT

* * *

In London, the rain had already arrived.

Mark Parfitt tried to make up his mind whether to get a meal first and then make the phone call, or to wait until he had the information and grab a quick meal before boarding the train to the coast.

He settled on the latter, left the shelter of the Science Museum and hurried through the streets back to South Kensington tube station, joining the massing throng of damp commuters on the platform jostling for the next east bound train.

It was standing room only as the District line took him the two stops to Victoria. He was swept out of the carriage by a tide of fellow travellers all heading for the same mainline station to get trains to the suburbs and further afield.

Parfitt walked in the same direction until he was in the main station concourse. He spied the banks of public phone boxes and waited until one came free before entering and pulling the door tight behind him, shutting out the never ceasing roar of noise that was the background music of a busy station.

Pulling his phone card out, he went through the identification routine before punching in the international code and number of his bank in the Cayman Islands.

After a few moments he could hear the unfamiliar ring tone of that country and then his call was answered.

After explaining that he was telephoning from

London, England and giving his six figure identification number and three letters from his memorable word, he was allowed to proceed with his question.

"Can you confirm that you have received the funds from my UK bank?" He gave the details of the transaction.

There was a considerable pause while the person at the other end of the long distance call used that information to access his account.

"No sir, Mister Parfitt, we have no such transaction in your account at this time. I am suggesting that you contact your own bank in the United Kingdom and ask for confirmation that the transaction has indeed been processed. They should be able to give you the full transaction identification number. With that, you should be able to find out exactly where in the system the transaction is. These things can take a bit longer sometimes."

Parfitt knew that it would be pointless arguing, or venting his frustration on the unseen bank teller in the Caymans. Elliott Tanner had said that these transfers could take longer.

He thanked the Cayman Island teller for his help and hung up.

Now he would have to decide whether to continue out of the country and phone again from Paris, or wait until morning and contact his own bank.

Either way, he would have to retrieve his suitcase. He set off on the short walk to Victoria Coach Station.

A DEADLY ACCOUNT

He was alright for cash to get a bed for the night.

Once he had collected the case, he pulled out his Filofax and looked up the number of another hotel that was not too far away from Victoria. They had a last minute cancellation. He took it, "I'll be there in twenty minutes, be sure of it."

With his case, he went out onto the Buckingham Palace Road and hailed a cab.

At the hotel he filled in his details and paid for the night in cash. He decided to change into some dry clothes, leaving the damp outer garments hanging over the radiator to dry.

He pulled out a lightweight raincoat from the bottom of the suitcase, left everything else in the room and headed out to find a restaurant.

Chapter 22

Ed Richardson and his technicians returned to the Carlton at eight o'clock the next morning to continue isolating and identifying the trace evidence from inside the vehicle.

They collected fingerprint evidence linking five individuals to the vehicle.

From the suitcase and shoulder bag they were able to lift prints that matched two of the sets already catalogued. One set belonged to the owner, Parfitt, whose prints were most numerous on the vehicle inside it and out. The other set were most likely to be those of Louise Baker as they were found on items in both the case and the bag.

They found fingerprints in the car that matched those of Tommy Adams, the victim. These fingerprints were exclusively round the front passenger door and side window.

In the boot they found fibres similar to those of Adams's track suit top. Because of his swim down the river, there were no boot fibres to be found on Adams's clothing to seal the case.

There were traces of mud in the foot-wells on both the driver's and the front passenger's side that would probably prove a match for mud along the riverside path.

Richardson sent one of his people back to the scene where the two sets of footprints had been found to collect some random samples, and to gather other samples further up the path.

He then set his technicians the task of comparing all of these samples.

He hoped by the end of the day to prove who had been where.

* * *

Fortified with another full English breakfast, Parfitt returned to his room and at ten thirty phoned his bank.

"Can I speak to Mr Tanner please? It's Mark Parfitt."

He waited for a few moments before Tanner came on the line.

"Mark, I'm so sorry. I did try phoning your house just in case you had decided not to fly out, but got no answer. Are you in Barbados?"

"What the hell's going on, Elliott? Where's my money?"

"Still here I'm afraid," Tanner replied smoothly. "That's what I tried to call you about. The directors have been in. They've expressly forbidden me to make the transfer without your signature. I mean, it's such a large sum of money. There was nothing I could do. I hope this hasn't ruined your chances with the property deal."

"I missed my flight and can't get another 'til this evening. I'll get a taxi over and sign all the paper work. Should be with you in about half an hour."

"I'll have everything ready for you, Mark. Don't worry; we'll soon get this sorted out. I can even authorise an express transfer just as soon as we have your signature. The money will be waiting for you when you land in Barbados."

"Well, that's some consolation. I'll see you shortly."

Parfitt hung up. He took his suitcase down to reception, "Can you look after this for me for an hour or two? I've got to go and sign some papers urgently before I leave for the airport and I don't want to be lugging it round after me."

"Not a problem, sir. It will be waiting in the cloakroom for you. Just ask at the desk."

Parfitt went out of the hotel and started walking in the direction of Hyde Park Corner where he entered the underground and took the Piccadilly line to Holborn. The tube took him rapidly under the West End towards Holborn. He cursed banks and bureaucracy in general under his breath.

Once out of Holborn tube station he crossed Kingsway at the traffic lights and walked down High Holborn towards his bank totally unaware that Inspector Craig was being kept informed of his every move by the plain clothes units on the ground that had picked him up as he exited the station.

Other officers had been watching every cab and private hire taxi that stopped in the area to let passengers off.

A DEADLY ACCOUNT

Craig stood just inside the door of the bank with one of his sergeants, a lady much the same age as Craig who could pass as his wife on such occasions.

The voice crackled in his ear, "Suspect just entering the bank."

Craig nodded to Tanner who stepped out from the customer service room where he had been waiting as if going to speak to a cashier.

Tanner acted the part to perfection.

"Mark, that didn't take you long! I have all the papers ready for you. Just give me a minute, will you?"

Mark Parfitt was so intent on watching Tanner that he didn't see the man and woman close in on either side.

"Mark Parfitt, a.k.a. Mark Spencer," he said quietly, "I am Detective Inspector Craig, London Metropolitan Police, and this is Detective Sergeant Collis. We have a warrant for your arrest issued by Rochfield CID in the county of Yorkshire for the murder of Thomas Adams." He then proceeded to caution Parfitt. "If you come quietly and don't make a fuss, I'll not have to handcuff you. If you try to escape before we get you into our vehicle, I must warn you that there are ten very fit young constables outside that would be delighted to prevent you. What's it to be?"

Parfitt raised his hands slightly, shrugged and said, "What is they say? It's a fair cop! Oh bugger!"

He went quietly and was seated between two

plain clothes officers in the back of the police car with Inspector Craig in the front. Sergeant Collis drove them to Holborn police station.

* * *

The phone in Sutherland's office rang, he picked it up. Simpson was across the desk from him.

"Sutherland here."

"DI Craig Chief Inspector. We've got your man."

Sutherland gave Simpson the thumbs-up.

THE END

ABOUT THE AUTHOR

Ric Thompson was born in Belfast in 1946 of an English mother from Lancashire and the eldest son of a wealthy land owning Ulster Scots family. Both of his parents had been in the Royal Navy, but he never felt inclined to a life in uniform.

After leaving one of England's prestigious private schools, known as a Public School for some perverse reason he joined a large Irish Linen company and from trainee manager worked his way up to the position of Factory Manager, at which point he realized that he was never going to become a director and make the real money.

He worked at several interesting and varied forms of self-employment and for relaxation started writing, something that he had been doing from schooldays, but not seriously.

The creation of Rochfield and the police team emerged from the first book in the series – Killing The Witch. Pleased with his creations he has continued to add to the series over the last ten years and hopes that you enjoy them too.

If you like the books tell your friends. Posting reviews also helps. If you don't, or have suggestions for improvements, plots, characters – even yourself! – tell me. Email: ric.thompson@tms-email.co.uk.
Also on Facebook, and Twitter #RicsFiction.

Printed in Great Britain
by Amazon